"MACY BECKE[TT
BL[ ]**

"Witty a[ ]
tug you[ ]
—N[ ]

"Hilarious, heartwarming, sexy, and real—you'll fall in love, guaranteed!"
    —*New York Times* bestselling author Lori Foster

"Fun and flirty with characters you'll love page after page."
    —*New York Times* bestselling author Christie Craig

"Written with a sassy wit . . . charming."
                            —*Chicago Tribune*

"Delightful . . . a sweet mix of lighthearted romance and down-home charm."   —*Publishers Weekly*

"Heaping doses of heart, passion, and laughter."
                            —*RT Book Reviews*

"Sweet, fun, and entertaining."
                            —Nocturne Romance Reads

continued . . .

Also by Macy Beckett

Make You Blush
(a novella)

MAKE YOU MINE

THE DUMONT BACHELORS

Macy Beckett

A SIGNET ECLIPSE BOOK

SIGNET ECLIPSE
Published by the Penguin Group
Penguin Group (USA) LLC, 375 Hudson Street,
New York, New York 10014

USA | Canada | UK | Ireland | Australia | New Zealand | India | South Africa | China
penguin.com
A Penguin Random House Company

First published by Signet Eclipse, an imprint of New American Library,
a division of Penguin Group (USA) LLC

First Printing, May 2014

ISBN 978-0-451-46533-7

Printed in the United States of America
10 9 8 7 6 5 4 3 2 1

PUBLISHER'S NOTE

This is a work of fiction. Names, characters, places, and incidents either are the product
of the author's imagination or are used fictitiously, and any resemblance to actual per-
sons, living or dead, business establishments, events, or locales is entirely coincidental.

To my street team, Macy's Mavens. Thank you for spreading the word about my books. You ladies are the best!

Chapter 1

Allie Mauvais noticed her customer's gaze darting, once again, to the legal disclaimer mounted on the wall above the list of two-for-one bakery specials. Something in the stiff set of the woman's shoulders told Allie she'd come to the Sweet Spot looking for more than a chocolate-chip muffin.

Most people did.

"That's state-mandated—just ignore it." Allie reached over the counter to squeeze the young blonde's hand. No wedding ring. She probably wanted a love charm. "Unless you're checking out the scones, in which case, go with the brown sugar pecan. It's better than sex."

The woman released a shaky laugh and nodded at

the trays of crullers displayed behind glass doors. She looked vaguely familiar, but Allie couldn't place her. "Smells like heaven in here. I can already feel my waist expanding."

"Calories don't count in my shop, baby," Allie said with a wink. "Voodoo priestess, remember? Isn't that why you're here?"

The girl chewed her bottom lip and squeezed her leather clutch hard enough to choke the little Dooney & Bourke duck. "Um . . . kind of. I drove up from Cedar Bayou."

"Hey, I'm from Cedar Bayou!"

"I know. We went to school together. You were a few years ahead of me, though." She peeked up through her lashes and added, "Shannon Tucker? You probably don't remem—"

"Oh," Allie interrupted as the pieces clicked. "Jimmy's little sister, right? You ran the school paper."

"Yeah." Shannon grinned, losing an inch of height as her posture relaxed. "I can't believe you recognize me. I never had the guts to talk to you."

Not surprising. The upside of being a direct descendant of New Orleans's most infamous voodoo queen was that people didn't screw with Allie, not even when the Saints lost the Super Bowl. Sure, the whole parish had blamed her, just as they had the time Sheriff Benson broke out in shingles, but they'd done it quietly from their living rooms. Even when she'd escaped to the city, the locals had pegged her for Juliette Mauvais's great-great-granddaughter. The eyes gave her away—one amber, one gray, just like Memère's.

But the upside was also the downside.

Allie *wanted* someone to screw with her once in a while. The men from her superstitious parish weren't brave enough to risk the "Mauvais curse" and ask her out, not that she found any of them particularly appealing. Well, except for one, but his tendency to cross to the other side of the street when she walked by put a damper on their would-be love affair.

"You're talking to me now," Allie said. If she couldn't find romance herself, at least she could spread the love for others. "What brings you in?"

Shannon cleared her throat and leaned forward, lowering her voice despite the fact that they had the whole shop to themselves. "I've heard you can *see* things."

Allie nodded. She could see all kinds of things—like facial expressions and body language. The kinds of things anyone could see if they paid attention. She could hear, too—the subtle changes of inflection or tone that often contradicted the spoken word. People didn't need voodoo heritage to understand one another. They just had to turn off their iPhones and take their heads out of their asses every once in a while. Luckily, they had Allie to do it for them. Maybe she didn't have magical powers, but she gave her clients the prodding they needed to find happiness.

"My friends say you can read the bones," Shannon whispered, then immediately straightened and clarified, "not that I believe in all that."

A smile tipped the corners of Allie's mouth. Of course Shannon believed in *all that*. Everyone in Cedar Bayou did, whether they admitted it or not. They claimed such nonsense was beneath them, but they still came, still defaced Memère's tomb with markings and oddball trinkets in exchange for favors from her spirit. Voodoo was rooted deeper than the tupelo gum trees in these swamps. It was tangled up with good Catholic upbringing until no one could separate one from the other. Even Allie attended Mass each Sunday morning, right before returning home to assemble gris-gris bags for her customers' protection and luck.

Around here, everyone believed, even if they didn't.

That said, Allie had more faith in the power of the human psyche than in Memère's curses or Father Durand's holy water. The mind was a powerful thing, and she knew how to direct it. She pulled her mat from beneath the counter and spread it on the Formica surface, then asked, "What do you want me to look for?"

A light flush stained Shannon's cheeks. "I want to know if you see anyone . . . you know"—swallowing hard—"special . . . in my future."

"Ah." A love charm, just as Allie had predicted. "I'll do my best, but you need to understand something first."

"What's that?"

"The spirits only reward the faithful." She traced one pink-polished index finger around the circle inked on to her mat. "You've got to trust them. Can you do that?"

Shannon nodded.

"Because if you can't, we're wasting our time."

"I'll believe."

"Okay." Reaching below the cash register, Allie pulled out a small Tupperware bowl full of bleached chicken bones from the Popeyes three-piece meal she'd scarfed down last week. She had no clue how to perform this ritual—few folks did these days—but nobody needed to know that. She set down the container and reached for Shannon's hands. "First, we'll say a prayer."

Shannon quirked a brow. "To God?"

"Of course. Who else?"

"Oh, okay."

"Don't believe what Hollywood tells you. Voodoo's not evil."

"Sorry. I didn't realize . . ."

Allie was used to it by now. Dark magic, the kind Memère had supposedly used in her curses, was considered by believers to be hazardous to the soul, though the general public didn't know that. Most voodoo doctors and queens used their gifts to benefit others. Though it was psychology, not voodoo, at the heart of what Allie did, she considered herself a healer all the same.

The two linked fingers, bowed their heads, and asked for guidance in finding Shannon's life partner. After "amen," Allie scattered the small bones within the circle. While she hunched over the mat, pretending to study the significance in the patterns, she searched her memory of the parish for anything useful that might lead to a match. She'd spent her childhood on the outside looking in, but she'd always paid attention.

Someone'd had a mad crush on Shannon. . . . Who was it? Allie closed her eyes and considered a moment, trying to summon his image. Finally, the answer came. John Paul Romain, the simple-but-cute alligator farmer who lived on the bayou with his *grandpère*. He'd pined after Shannon like nobody's business—everyone knew he was sweet on her. More importantly, JP was good people, and still single the last time Allie went home to visit. Her instincts told her the pair could make a great fit, but that Shannon needed to work for it before she'd appreciate an unsophisticated good ol' boy like JP.

"See this bone, here?" Allie said, pointing to what remained of her Cajun-fried drumstick. "It's the largest and most important, but it's near the bottom of the circle, like it's been discarded. This tells me you've already found your match, but you turned him away." She glanced at Shannon and asked, "Have you snubbed anyone who genuinely cared for you?"

Slowly, Shannon's eyes widened. "Well . . . yes, but that was—"

"Ooooh." Allie sucked a sharp breath through her teeth. "That's bad. The spirits of our ancestors don't like it when we ignore their help."

"So, he was really the one?"

"What does your heart tell you?" Allie asked. "How does it feel to know you can't have him anymore?" If that didn't hook her, nothing would. No one could resist the allure of the forbidden.

"What do you mean, I can't have him?" Shannon replied in a sharp pitch.

Bingo.

Allie nodded at the bones. "It's all spelled out right here. He's off the market, at least where you're concerned."

"But . . . but . . . JP said he'd wait—"

"Do you love him?"

"I don't know." Shannon tossed her clutch onto the counter. "I wasn't sure before, but now I think maybe I do." Despite Shannon's doubts, the desperation in her eyes when she said, "Is there anything I can do to get him back?" told Allie the woman had it bad.

Allie studied the bones. "Maybe. Won't be easy, though. Even if he's responsive to you, the spirits might interfere. You'll have to do penance." She shook her head. "No guarantees."

"Just tell me what to do, and I'll do it."

Biting back a smile, Allie grabbed an order pad from her apron and ripped free the top sheet. She bent down and wrote a list of chores to perform in atonement. When she added the final task—*Leave an offering of pralines at Juliette Mauvais's tomb*—she made sure to warn, "But don't scratch the triple-x marking into the wall. Memère's spirit doesn't like it."

Shannon nodded and took the slip of paper, then opened her clutch. "Thanks, Miss Mauvais. How much do I owe you?"

Allie flashed her palm. "I can't take money for interceding with the spirits on your behalf. It's bad juju. However"—she gestured at a tray of sticky buns—"I've heard Romain men are fond of these."

Shannon grinned in understanding. "I'll take them all."

After Allie boxed up the order, she taped her business card to the top. "I cater," she said. "Tell your friends."

"Will do."

"Come on, I'll walk you out."

Allie scooped up her chicken bones, folded her mat, and returned the supplies to their rightful place beneath the counter. She couldn't help feeling a needling of jealousy for Shannon and JP. Maybe they needed a push to get them started, but at least the foundation was there. They loved each other.

Allie wanted that for herself. She was tired of mixing love potions and gris-gris for everyone else while remaining the eternal bridesmaid—figuratively speaking, of course. She didn't have any close friends to ask her to stand up beside them in church, and her sister was no closer to holy matrimony than Allie was.

With a sigh, she stepped from behind the counter and strode outside, making sure to prop open the front door so she could hear the phone. After inhaling the sweetness of cinnamon and vanilla all morning, Allie found the humid summer air smelled too sharp, like a mingling of garbage and car exhaust.

And the heat!

Allie's mama and daddy, God rest their souls, used to say South Louisiana in August was hotter than a two-pricked goat in a pepper patch. Allie'd survived twenty-six of these summers, and she'd never gotten used to it. She shut the door, figuring she'd rather miss a phone call than air-condition the whole street on her dime.

She took a moment to fasten her heavy curls into a twist, closing her eyes in relief when a breeze cooled the back of her neck. When she opened her eyes again, she saw a stunning face that had her stomach dipping into her bikini briefs—a face she couldn't seem to banish from her most secret fantasies, no matter how much distance or time hung between them. Unfortunately, she repelled him like they were the same ends of a magnet— for every step she took forward, he took one back.

It wasn't fair.

"Ladies," Marc Dumont said with a cautious tip of his head. His gaze darted to the other side of the street, revealing how badly he wanted to cross it and get away from her. Some things never changed.

Shannon fired a glare at Marc before turning on her heel and stalking away without another word. He'd probably broken her heart, a virtual rite of passage for half the girls back home, Allie included. Junior year, he'd dropped her like a Crisco-coated stone after a single kiss, just a teasing brush of lips that had left her hungry for the next nine years.

So unfair.

Allie couldn't help glancing at his mouth when she said, "It's been a while. You look good."

Too good—tanned and toned in all the right places. He'd grown out his hair so the chestnut waves nearly brushed his shoulders. It gave him a dangerous edge, especially when paired with the few days' growth along his steely jaw. He shoved his hands into the front pockets of his Levi's and grinned, drawing out the cleft in his chin.

"So do you." The low timbre of his voice gave her dirty thoughts. "Real good."

Was it just her eager imagination, or was that a spark of lust in his gaze? Her pulse quickened at the possibility that he'd overcome his aversion to her. Something in the slow, easy way Marc moved told her not even a brown sugar pecan scone could hold a candle to a night in his bed.

Maybe it was time to get serious and find out—to go after what she wanted instead of wishing for other people's happily-ever-afters. It was worth a shot. She didn't have any appointments for the rest of the day, and her apartment was right upstairs.

"Thanks." She hitched a thumb at her shop. "Want to come inside and catch up? It's awfully hot out here."

No shit. It was hot out here all right—in a way that had nothing to do with the brutal Louisiana sun. Marc glanced at the sign hanging above Allie's camelback store. THE SWEET SPOT: SOMETHING TO TEMPT EVERY SAINT IN NEW ORLEANS. He was no saint, but he was sure as hell tempted. A man would have to be gay, castrated, or dead not to sport wood around Allie Mauvais.

She swept the back of her hand across her forehead, then blotted her flushed olive cheeks. One black curl escaped her twist and sprang free, refusing to be tamed . . . just like all Mauvais women. She looked like a wild Gypsy who'd just rolled out of bed with her lover, and when she locked those mismatched eyes on him, Marc's jock twitched.

Damn. He'd like to inch up the hem of that short denim skirt and find *her* sweet spot.

But Marc never would. Not even he was that stupid.

"Maybe another time," he lied.

He had no intention of spending a moment alone with her. He'd learned his lesson back in high school. Against his pawpaw's advice, Marc had asked Allie to junior prom. He'd kissed her that night and had awoken the next morning to boils beneath his boxers. Pawpaw always said sex with a Mauvais woman would rot your pecker, and after that incident, Marc wasn't taking any chances with his manhood.

Why risk it?

"Sure, another time." When she arched to stretch her lower back, her breasts strained against the front of her thin white T-shirt, revealing the lacy pattern of her bra. Lord have mercy. "How's your family?" she asked, lips twitching in a smile as she caught him staring. "I heard you're going to be a big brother again."

"Yep, in December."

"How many kids does this make for your daddy?"

"Six." With five different women, but he didn't need to tell Allie that. She probably knew better than anyone.

According to legend, it was her great-great-grandma who'd cursed his family, vowing the Dumont men would never be lucky in love. It must've skipped a generation, though, because Marc was real good at getting lucky. Some might say an expert. He had women all over the parish—willing women who didn't ask for more than a night of sweaty, tangled flesh and a quick good-bye. And unlike his dad, Marc had enough good sense to keep it wrapped. So what if a Dumont man hadn't made it to the altar in almost a hundred years? If you asked him, that was a blessing, not a curse.

Allie took a step closer and fanned the back of her neck, filling his senses with the candied scent that clung to her body. It made him want to lick her throat to see what she tasted like.

"Been behaving yourself?" she asked.

"Only by default." Marc retreated a pace. "I'm taking over the *Belle*. She keeps me pretty busy."

That seemed to surprise her. "Your daddy's retiring?"

Marc shrugged. "Had to happen sooner or later."

But truth be told, the news had surprised him, too. In all the years Marc had spent working aboard his family's riverboat, his old man had never found a nice word for him, never clapped him on the back for a job well done or given any indication that he'd trust Marc with the Dumont legacy. When he'd deeded over the *Belle*, he'd left Marc with seven words: *She's yours now. Don't muck it up*.

The old man neglected to disclose how much work the *Belle* needed or how much it would cost. Or, more importantly, that he owed the waitstaff and cleaning crew two months' back wages. But if everything went according to plan, the two-week Mississippi cruise he'd booked should draw enough income to pay off the bank.

Which reminded him . . .

"I should run." He nodded toward the French Market Place. "There's a lot to do before the next trip."

"Good luck. Don't be a stranger, baby." She winked an eye—the one the color of aged bourbon—and pulled open the door to her shop. A blast of cool, delicious air rushed onto the sidewalk as she stepped inside, and Marc pulled it deep into his lungs while his mouth watered.

Damn, he wished he could stay, and not for a bear claw, either.

He peeked through the glass and watched the gentle sway of Allie's hips, then exhaled in a low whistle. If only she weren't a Mauvais.

Marc shook his head and strolled onward. For no real reason, he crossed to the other side of the street before continuing to the river.

Chapter 2

Marc shielded his eyes and gazed at the love of his life. She was seventy-five years old, high maintenance, and she'd been ridden hard by thousands of men, but he'd never beheld a more glorious sight than the *Belle of the Bayou*.

Sunlight glinted off the solid brass roof bell, polished to a gleam by Marc's own loving hand. You couldn't see it from here, but his family crest was engraved deep into the metal, a testament to four generations of Dumonts who'd broken their backs to keep *Belle* riverworthy. The steam whistle perched nearby like an open-beaked eagle, ready to call travelers aboard for relaxation and adventure.

Marc took in all four white-railed decks, lined with arched windows and doorways, and pictured them teeming with guests, imagined the inimitable noise of conversation and laughter reverberating off the water. From there, his eyes moved upward to the twin black smokestacks and the pilothouse beyond, where he would soon stand at the helm for the very first time as captain.

Lord, he couldn't wait.

Even though *Belle* threatened to drown him in a tidal wave of debt, he couldn't deny the surge of pride beneath his rib cage every time he looked at her.

But there was work to be done. A rhythmic percussion of clunks pierced the air as workmen hammered at the oak paddle wheel, repairing damage from last season's collision with a bridge. John Lutz had parked his familiar windowless van near the dock, which meant the mechanics were already in the boiler room. Now Marc needed to schedule the last round of interviews and meet with his managerial staff—his brothers and Pawpaw.

Time to quit standing around.

He jogged up the bow ramp onto the main deck, then took the stairs to the second-floor dining room, where they'd always held their staff meetings. It was no coincidence that the executive bar—and all the top-shelf liquor on board—was located in that room. A couple fingers of Crown Royal Reserve made working with family a whole lot easier.

Marc tugged open the door, relieved to find the air conditioner running again. Nothing put a damper on a cruise like the reek of three hundred sweaty vacationers. He noticed the ancient red-and-gold-patterned carpeting had been steam cleaned. He hated that carpet. It had always reminded him of the creepy-ass hotel in *The Shining*. Maybe next season he'd have the cash to replace it.

All the tables were bare, chairs were stacked along the wall, and clear plastic bags of white linens from the dry cleaner had been tossed in the corner. Marc crossed to the far end of the room, where three heads were huddled in conversation—two blond, one gray. At the sound of his footsteps, Nick and Alex glanced over their shoulders and gave him a wave.

"Cap'n," Nick said with a mock salute, then took a deep pull from his Heineken.

"Cap," Alex parroted.

Most folks would never believe Marc was related to the towheads. He had Pawpaw's tawny complexion, while Alex and Nick had inherited their mama's Swedish coloring: blue eyes, fair hair, and skin that had to burn a few times before it tanned. Of Daddy's brood, these two were the only ones who shared the same mother, but that's because they were twins. Identical—right down to the matching cowlicks that swirled the hair above their left brows.

Marc had resented his baby brothers when Daddy had left his mama for theirs, until the same thing had happened to them a few years later. It was then, at the tender age of seven, that he'd learned to quit blaming his siblings for the sins of their father.

"Papa was a rolling stone," all right. But no matter which woman he shacked up with, he'd always made time for all five of his sons . . . if working them to death aboard the *Belle* counted as quality time.

Marc took a seat at the head of the table, and Pawpaw pushed a tumbler of amber-colored liquid toward him. Breaking out the hard stuff already? That wasn't a good sign.

"Drink up, boy," Pawpaw said. "You're gonna need it."

Marc ground his teeth and glared at his brothers.

The last time Pawpaw said those words, Nick had seduced the state inspector's daughter and nearly cost the *Belle* her license.

"What'd you do?" he asked them. "Or should I say *who*?"

The two shared a quick glance before simultaneously admitting, "The jazz singer."

"Both of you?"

Alex held his palms forward. "She came on to me in the ballroom and practically ripped my pants off. How was I supposed to know she thought I was Nicky?" He elbowed his twin. "He didn't tell me he was seeing her."

"Well, 'seeing' is a strong word," Nick argued. "It wasn't as serious as all that."

"Mother of God." And Marc thought *he* got around. Fresh out of college and still in frat mode, these two made him look like an altar boy. "I assume she quit," he said.

"Yep," Pawpaw answered. "Called in this mornin'. But jazz singers are more common than mosquitoes in July round here. That's not why you need the sauce."

Marc brought the tumbler to his lips and belted it back, savoring the smooth, smoky burn of aged whiskey. He cleared his throat and clunked the crystal onto the table. "All right, I'm ready. Let's have it."

"Well, for starters," Pawpaw began, scratching his turkey neck, "someone double-booked the honeymoon suite. Now the head's busted in there, so neither of them can use it."

That wasn't so bad. "Call Herzinger Plumbing. He's expensive, but he's quick. Give the room to whoever booked it first, and offer the second couple the state suite. Then comp all their off-board excursions and give them a free bottle of champagne."

"There's more," Alex said from the other side of the table. "Lutz found an issue with the train linkage, and he says he doesn't like the look of the throttle valve."

"Shit." Now that was a problem. The city wasn't exactly overflowing with steam engine mechanics, or spare parts for an antiquated machine designed in another century. "Can he get it fixed in time?"

Alex shrugged. "Probably, if you make it worth his while. You know how it goes."

"Yeah, I know," Marc grumbled. "Offer a twenty percent bonus for his crew if they get it done by next week."

"And the Gaming Control Board called," Nick added. "They're auditing last year's income statements, and they said there're a couple pages missing from the general ledger."

"That's no biggie." Marc's sister could handle that. "I'll have Ella-Claire fax them over."

"Yeah, but the Mississippi permit still hasn't come through for the Texas Hold'em tournament."

"Son of a bitch." Marc was going to need another shot.

Licensing was an unholy nightmare when *Belle* crossed state lines, but nothing aboard the boat drew as much income as the casino. Nothing. And tournaments doubled their cash flow, because the participants tended to gamble damn-near around the clock. He'd bent over backward to book that event. Without those earnings, they were screwed like—well, like the jazz singer they no longer had.

Marc pointed to Nick and said, "This takes priority over everything. Drive up there yourself and make sure we get that permit. Turn on the charm—do whatever it takes. We won't cast off without it."

"Want me to go now?"

Marc nodded at the door. "I wanted you there five minutes ago."

"It's just . . ." Nick hesitated. "There's more."

Marc slid his tumbler to Pawpaw for another pour. "What is it?"

"Daddy called," Nick said.

"And?"

"He wants you to bring on Worm. Said to start him off busing tables."

"And who's going to look after him?" Their little brother wasn't a bad kid, but fourteen-year-old boys had a way of gravitating toward trouble, and Worm was no exception.

Instead of answering, Nick tipped back his beer.

"Let me guess," Marc said, accepting another shot from Pawpaw. "He expects us to do it for him."

"The boy'll be fine," Pawpaw promised. "Just like when y'all were that age. Family takes care of their own."

Easy for him to say. He wasn't the one responsible for keeping *Belle* afloat—both literally and figuratively. Still, it could've been worse. At least Daddy hadn't asked him to hire Beau. To say there was bad blood between Marc and his older brother was like calling Mount Fuji an anthill.

Marc tossed back his whiskey and wiped a hand across his mouth. "Fine, but we need to keep him busy.

I want that boy so worn out, he falls down dead in his cot each night by eight."

"That won't be hard," Alex said, "considering we're short staffed."

"What?" Marc's backbone locked. "Since when?"

Pawpaw laughed and gestured at Marc's empty glass. "Remember when I said you were gonna need that hooch? This is why. That shoddy employment agency that Alex used to hire the cleaning crew got shut down for forging work visas."

Marc pushed both palms against the air. "Hold up a minute." Everything had been fine when he'd left yesterday. "When did all this happen?"

The three shared a quick glance, and Pawpaw guessed, " 'Bout thirty minutes ago."

"It was the damnedest thing," Alex said. "Like a shit storm blew into town and opened up right on top of us. It all happened at once."

"All of a sudden," Nick added. "When it rains, it pours."

"Half an hour ago?" Marc whispered to himself.

Wasn't that about the time he'd crossed paths with Allie Mauvais? That's what he got for standing on the same side of the street with her. Maybe her great-great-grandma's spirit knew all the filthy things he'd wanted to do with Allie.

"We've got to have a full cleaning crew," he said, "or this trip won't last long." In such close quarters, sickness spread like wildfire, especially stomach bugs. All it would take was one bout of norovirus or E. coli to shut them down.

"No joke," Alex said. "Remember that one year?"

All four men cringed at the memory.

A few summers ago, their vegetable supplier had delivered a bad batch of iceberg lettuce. Within days, hundreds of folks had it coming out of both ends—even the guests who'd avoided the salad bar. There wasn't enough Pepto in the world to counteract a puke-fest of that magnitude. Just thinking about the smell . . . Oh, God, he was getting queasy. He quickly derailed that train of thought.

"If the press got wind of another outbreak like that, it would ruin us. Let's station hand sanitizer pumps near all the doors and stairwells," Marc suggested. "One inside every room, too." He addressed Alex and said, "Call another temp agency. While you're at it, see if you can snag us a few more servers."

When a few seconds ticked by in silence, Marc asked his family, "Is that it?"

Pawpaw snorted. "That ain't enough for you?"

More than enough. Marc felt the urge to knock on wood, toss a pinch of salt over one shoulder, cross his fingers, and tuck a rabbit's foot in his back pocket—and he wasn't even superstitious.

He dismissed the meeting and headed belowdecks to the boiler room. He wanted to see the valve "issues" with his own eyes and make sure Lutz wasn't screwing him over.

Halfway down the first stairwell, his cell phone vibrated against his left butt cheek. Marc pulled it free and discovered a text.

Are you free for some afternoon delight?

A smile formed on his lips. It was Nora, the perky redheaded waitress he'd taken home a couple of weeks ago. She was hotter than hellfire in the sack, with a carpet that matched the drapes. But despite that, he found himself texting, *Rain check?*

You at the boat? she replied. *I can be there in 10.*

No dice. Marc was wiped out, and Nora wasn't on his to-do list. *Will make it up to you after this cruise.*

It better be good!

Isn't it always?

She signed off with an *xxx/ooo*, and Marc shoved his phone into his pocket.

For the first time since he'd sprouted short-n-curlies, he didn't have the energy for sex. Hell, maybe he was jinxed after all.

One week and two dozen headaches later, Marc gathered his hair in a low ponytail and donned his captain's hat—pristine white with a gold-embroidered black bill. He straightened his tie and grinned at his reflection in the pilothouse window.

He'd waited a long time for this.

Through the port bay, he could see a flurry of movement as early-morning shipments of fresh food and last-minute supplies arrived for loading. In a few hours, guests would begin boarding, and there was plenty to do before then. Just when Marc had managed to weather last week's shit storm, the main chef had changed the menu and demanded a list of new ingredients.

Typically, Marc didn't tolerate that crap, but booking Chef Regale for this cruise had drawn a full house. The man was unarguably a ranting diva, but his name was legend. As a bonus, Regale had brought on his associate pastry chef, a bigwig in his own right. That was worth makin' groceries.

He buttoned his white suit jacket and headed downstairs for a walk-through of the main level, pleased to find the carpets freshly vacuumed and the brass handrails buffed to a shine. The new cleaning crew had mopped the deck so thoroughly, its wooden planks practically glowed, and each bench and lounge chair was clean enough for the most discriminating backside.

Satisfied, he touched base with his event manager and then strode outside to supervise the deliveries and greet any guests who might arrive early. He'd just stepped off the bow ramp when Worm waved one bony arm from the sidewalk and dragged himself over in a Hooters T-shirt, jean cutoffs, and a pair of Converse Chucks held together by a dying breath of glue.

Marc glanced around for Worm's mom, not too surprised when he couldn't find her. Their father didn't have the most discriminating taste in baby-mamas.

"What the heck are you wearing?" he asked his brother. "The *Belle*'s not a trash barge—she's basically a floating hotel. Even busing tables, you've got to look good."

"I know, I know." Worm tipped his shaggy brown head toward the duffel bag slung over his shoulder. "I'm fixin' to change. Didn't wanna get my good clothes all sweaty from walkin' over here."

"You walked all the way from uptown?"

"I'm not a kid," Worm protested with an eye roll, then swore, "Sweet Cheez-Its."

Teens and their attitudes. Was Marc ever this snarky? "Don't make me toss you overboard."

"We're not even *on* board," the smart aleck countered.

God bless, it was going to be a long couple of weeks.

"Well, let's fix that." Marc swatted his brother's scrawny tail, eliciting another nonswear. "Get on up there and find Alex. He'll take you to your bunk. After you change, come back here and be ready to help the porters haul luggage."

Worm hitched up his duffel and grumbled toward the ramp.

"Hey," Marc added, "and lose the attitude!"

"Yeah, yeah," came the retreating reply.

When Worm disappeared through the dining hall entrance, Marc pulled in a calming breath and turned his gaze to the tranquil blue sky and the leaves stirring above his head. It was perfect weather for boating—sunny and mild, with calm water to boot. The Mississippi could be a harsh mistress, but she'd decided to favor him with some sweet lovin' today, for which he was mighty grateful.

He strolled toward the sidewalk and paused when his cell phone rang. A glance at the screen showed *Phillip Regale calling*. Marc swiped a finger across the glass and answered.

"Bad news," Chef said, never one to mince words.

Marc hoped Regale hadn't changed the menu again. He'd already sent Nick to the market. "How bad?"

"I lost my pastry chef."

Marc damn near dropped his phone. "What do you mean, you lost him?"

"He's under quarantine with German measles."

"What?" Who the hell got German measles anymore? "Are you serious?"

"Of course I'm serious!" Regale bellowed, clearly insulted. "First documented case in a hundred years. If that's not some damned dirty luck, I don't know what is."

"Can you get someone to cover him?"

"That's the crazy part," Regale said in disbelief. "I've called every pastry master I know—even the ones I wouldn't ordinarily work with—and I can't get a single one to pick up the line. It's like they dropped off the planet. I half wondered if there was something wrong with my phone, but I reached you just fine."

"What are we going to do?"

"I left a message with an agency. If they don't come through, we'll have to use store-bought desserts. Maybe pick up a second chef when we stop in Natchez."

Suddenly, the wind kicked up, temperature dropping as clouds eclipsed the sun. The skin at the base of Marc's neck prickled into gooseflesh, and he shook off a chill. He glanced at the now-dark sky, wondering what had just happened. He had seen no storm systems on the radar this morning. He turned to jog back on board but stopped short, breath catching as he came face-to-face with Allie Mauvais.

Marc clapped a hand over his pounding heart while she stood there watching him—lips curved in a grin, raven hair whipping her cheeks, hands clasped behind her back as if she'd appeared by magic.

Which she probably had.

It took a few beats for Marc to find his voice. He told Regale he'd call him back and disconnected, then demanded, "What're you doing here?"

Allie gripped her waist with one hand, still smiling. "That's not very nice, baby."

Holding up his phone, he demanded, "Did you do this?"

"Do what?"

The answer formed on his lips, but it was too absurd to speak aloud. *Did you give my pastry chef an eradicated disease? Did you blow the throttle valve? And what about my old cleaning crew—did you get them deported?* Saints alive, it sounded ridiculous, even to him. He was losing his marbles.

"You okay?" she asked, furrowing her brow.

"Yeah, sorry." He rubbed one temple, hoping to restore his sanity. "It's not a good time for a visit."

"I know. I heard about your pastry chef. Does he really have German measles?" She shook her head and whispered to herself, "Who gets those anymore?"

His thoughts exactly, but he wondered how Allie had found out.

The question must have shown on his face. "The agency sent me," she explained.

He puzzled for a moment, and then the full meaning hit him like a sledgehammer to the skull: Allie Mauvais aboard his ship—for two weeks. No way in hell. He'd sooner wrestle a twelve-foot gator in a flaming vat of fish guts.

Before he had a chance to tell her no, she held her palm forward, revealing a small yellow pouch secured at the top with twine. "I also came to wish you luck and give you this."

Marc hesitated. He didn't trust Allie's gris-gris any more than he trusted her in the galley.

"It's dirt from Memère's tomb and a few pennies," she said, stepping nearer. "For good fortune."

He took a step back, licking his lips.

Allie tipped her head and studied him with those exotic eyes. "Are you afraid of me?"

"Of course not," Marc scoffed and plucked the sachet from her outstretched hand. He reminded himself that he wasn't superstitious, but made sure not to touch her. "But you can go back home. I can't use you here."

She heaved a sigh and narrowed her eyes at him. "You *are* afraid of me." Defensively, she folded her arms. "Grow up, Marc."

Despite her criticism, the words sparked a flash of pleasure low in his belly. He hadn't heard his name on Allie's lips since junior prom, and he liked the way it sounded. A little too much. He kind of wanted to hear it again, this time low and breathy with a moan behind it.

"I can help you," she pressed. "I don't have any catering jobs for the next two weeks, and I'm sure my sister will watch the shop while I'm gone."

"But the salary's not—"

"Doesn't matter," she interrupted. "This'll be a good way to get my name out there."

Marc scrambled for a valid excuse to say no. "Phillip's really hard to please."

"Wait," Allie said. "Phillip who?"

"Regale. He's cranky as—"

"*The* Phil Regale?"

"Yeah."

"The man who practically revolutionized flambé in haute cuisine?"

"I guess so," Marc said. "Is there more than one chef with that name?"

She shook her head, then bounced in place. "I've

been trying to meet him for years! I'd love to work with him!"

Marc tried warning her that Chef was a misogynistic prick who didn't like cooking with women, but Allie was too busy squealing and jumping in a circle to hear. Then she waggled one finger in the air and started dancing the Charleston. Marc couldn't help smiling. In her half-hysterical state, she'd never looked so . . . normal.

Allie Mauvais was human.

Of course she's human, you dickhead. What else would she be?

While Allie shimmied her hips, he considered her offer. He *did* need a pastry chef, and there were no other takers. In the end, what choice did he have? Before Marc had a chance to change his mind, he said, "Okay. Go home and pack, but be quick about it. We launch in two hours."

She didn't waste a second in turning and bounding toward the French Quarter, black curls springing freely down her back. She called over her shoulder, "You won't regret this!" and then vanished around the corner.

Marc wasn't so sure about that, but he was still grinning like a fool. He pocketed the gris-gris bag she'd given him and sauntered toward his ship. Then, as suddenly as it had begun, the wind died down, and the clouds broke, freeing the sun.

The day was perfect once again.

Chapter 3

"Marc Dumont is like the St. Charles trolley," Devyn complained. "Everyone in the city's had a ride." She grabbed a handful of socks from the dresser drawer and shoved them in Allie's suitcase with enough force to shake the bed. "Why would you want to spend two weeks trapped on a boat with a skeezeball like him?"

"He's not that bad," Allie told her sister, tossing her toiletry bag beside the socks. "And it's a really big boat."

"Not big enough for his libido." Devyn pushed a dark curl behind her ear and added, "Or his idiocy."

"You're missing the point," Allie said while scanning the bedroom floor for her work clogs. "I get to share an oven with Phillip Regale."

Devyn sniffed disdainfully and perched on the edge of the mattress. "I saw him on *Satan's Kitchen* a few years ago. He's an asswipe, and he spits when he talks."

"Hey." Allie waved a hand in the air as if dispersing a cloud of perfume. "Enough with the negativity," she said, laughing. "You're harshing my glow." The two sisters could pass for twins if it weren't for Dev's blue eyes and a few inches of height in her favor, but when it came to personality, they were like buttercream and rolled fondant—one sweet and fluffy, the other lovely but hardened. "Can't you just be happy for me?"

Devyn held up two nightgowns—a black lace teddy and a frumpy pink polka-dot sheath. "Which one?"

Allie pointed to the teddy.

"Aha!" Devyn cried, waving the lacy frock at her. "I was right. You want to get freaky with Marc!"

"I'm a grown woman," Allie reminded her ever so slightly older sister. "I can get freaky with whoever I want."

Devyn folded the long pink nightgown and placed it in the suitcase, then balled up the teddy and chucked it over one shoulder. "I'm just looking out for you. If Marc's anything like his big brother . . ." She pressed her lips together and smoothed a wrinkle from a pair of shorts. Dev didn't like talking about her short-lived romance with Beau, and today was no exception. "Well, let's just say there's a reason Memère cursed the Dumonts. Everyone knows they can't be trusted."

Allie paused midreach for a fistful of undies. "You don't really buy into that, do you?"

"Of course I do!" Devyn gawked at Allie like she'd sprouted a second nose. "They're practically sticking it someplace new every time the wind changes."

"No," Allie said, "I mean the curse. You think it's real?"

Devyn shrugged. "Sure. Why else would they be so screwed up?"

"Because it's all they've ever known. Kids think

dysfunction is normal when they see it every day. They learn by example; then they teach it to their own kids until someone breaks the cycle. It's basic psychology, not voodoo."

"Then explain why none of the men have gotten married in four generations," Devyn argued. "But the women have."

Allie didn't have an answer for that. It's not like marriage was truly permanent anymore. Thousands of feckless lovers married—and divorced—every day, no long-term commitment required. It *was* a little strange that no Dumont man had taken the vow since Memère's time, but that didn't mean a hex was to blame.

"I don't know," Allie conceded. "But I'm sure there's a logical reason."

"You and your logic." With a light bounce, Devyn stood from the bed and grabbed the hair dryer. She held it up in a silent *You taking this?* and tucked it beneath a sundress without waiting for a reply. "Funny that you're the one people come to see for charms, considering you don't believe in your own gift."

"I know I have a gift," Allie said. "It's just not rooted in hocus-pocus." She slipped her cell phone charger between a stack of shirts. "And more folks would ask for your help if you weren't so scary."

"Me?" Devyn pointed at herself, brows forming a V above a pair of pale blue eyes so cold they could frost the sun. "Scary?"

Allie laughed. "All your boyfriends end up in urgent care, and everyone assumes you jinxed them."

"Ex-boyfriends," Devyn corrected. "And that was a coincidence—all six times. I've never hexed anyone."

She considered a moment and tapped her bottom lip. "Though maybe I should. There are plenty of jerks I could practice on . . ."

"See?" Allie said. "Told you."

"You say 'scary,' I say 'public service.'" Devyn flapped a hand. "Potato, po-tah-to."

Allie leaned around her sister to peer at the bedside clock. "I've got to run. Any last-minute questions?"

"I don't think so. Let me make sure I've got the important stuff down." She began listing items on her fingers. "The alarm password is 1987; deliveries come on Tuesdays and Fridays; the credit card reader's broken, so cash only; don't take any checks from Mrs. Mason; and I need to be downstairs by four each morning to help the girls bake." Devyn fired a glare after the last bit. "You *so* owe me."

"I'll take you to Vegas when I get back," Allie promised. "But just for the weekend, and no tequila this time."

"Fine." Devyn zipped the suitcase, then held her arms out for a hug. "But you're more fun after a few shots."

"You say 'fun,'" Allie replied, squeezing her sister tight, "I say 'half-naked in the hotel fountain.'"

"Potato, po-tah-to."

"Thanks, baby." Grabbing her suitcase, Allie shuffled into the hallway and called, "See you in a couple weeks."

"Don't do anything I wouldn't do," Devyn hollered after her. "And I would *not* give Marc Dumont any nookie!"

"Can't hear *youuuuuu*," Allie teased as she rushed

down the stairs. On her way out the door, she paused to grab her backpack of gris-gris supplies: sacred soil, herbs, coins, flower petals, assorted fabrics, and twine. Her instincts—and Marc's stress level—told her she'd need to mix a few bags on this trip.

Though weighed down with twenty pounds of luggage, Allie's feet barely touched the ground as she made her way to the river. Good things were in store. She could sense it.

"Ahoy, sir." Allie set down her suitcase and stood at attention. "Private Allison Catrine Mauvais reporting for duty."

Marc turned from a crate of cargo, dark eyes smiling from beneath the bill of his hat. "Two things, Mauvais."

She gave her best soldier's nod. "First?"

The pages tacked to his clipboard ruffled in the breeze as he pointed it at the boat. "This isn't a naval vessel."

Of course it wasn't, but in his gallant uniform, Marc reminded her of Richard Gere in *An Officer and a Gentleman*. He'd even donned white gloves. It was a side of him she'd never seen before, and her tummy had fluttered when she'd caught a glimpse of him earlier that morning. Now she couldn't stop imagining herself as Debra Winger being scooped into his arms and carried off to his bed.

"And second?" she asked, corralling her imagination.

He flashed a smirk. "Allison Catrine?"

"Yeah." She folded her arms and stared him down. "What's funny?"

"Sugar, with that name, you leave me no choice but to call you Allie-Cat."

She smiled, not at the mocking nickname, but at the *sugar* casually tossed into the mix. Whether Marc realized it or not, his guard was slipping.

"I've been called worse," she told him.

Just like that, his smile vanished. An expression she couldn't place, hard and reflective, crossed his features, and she worried she'd said something wrong.

Nodding at the boat ramp, he ordered, "Go find my brother Alex—he's the personnel manager. He'll give you a staff shirt and take you to your room. I'll need you back out here in about thirty minutes to greet guests."

"Okay." She grabbed her luggage. "And thanks, by the way."

"It's just business." The warmth in his voice was gone, making her wonder what had happened. "I should be thanking *you*." But he didn't. Instead, he turned his attention to his clipboard, effectively dismissing her.

Allie refused to let his mood change bring her down. She had two weeks to chip away at Marc's shell, and contrary to what she had told her sister, the boat wasn't that big. Raising her chin, she clattered across the metal ramp and onto *Belle*'s main deck, then began searching for Alex.

She thought she'd spotted him through one of the dining hall entrances, but when she made her way inside, she discovered it was his twin brother, Nick. His blue eyes widened a fraction when he saw her approaching, followed by a face-splitting grin.

"Well, hey there, Allie," he drawled, taking in her suitcase. "You staying with us?"

Finally, a Dumont who wasn't terrified of her. "Yep. I'm your new pastry chef. You know where Alex is? He's supposed to show me to my room."

"Right here, hon." He hooked a thumb at himself and offered to take her bag, all the while looking her up and down like a hungry dog at the butcher store window. "I'll get you settled in, snug as a bug in a rug."

"Nice try, Nicky," she said. "Where's your brother?"

He wrinkled his mouth in disappointment. "Shoot. How'd you know?"

It was easy. Even as a kid, Nick had carried himself with more confidence than Alex. It was the slight arrogance in his gaze and the cocky tilt of his head that gave him away. That, and the name tag affixed over his left breast.

"You really have to ask?" she said. "I'm a Mauvais, baby. Now quit messing around and help me find your brother."

"All right, all right." He pulled out his cell phone, fingertips flying over the screen as he typed a text. "I told him to meet us at your room. C'mon." He pocketed the phone, grabbed her luggage, and took off across the room in long strides that had Allie jogging to catch up.

"Wait!" she called. "How do you know where my room is? Until ten seconds ago, you didn't even know I was here."

He pulled open the stairwell door and held it for her. "Easy. If you're taking the other guy's place, you're taking his room, too." Nodding ahead, he said, "Third floor. I'll follow."

She climbed the first flight, feeling his eyes on her caboose. A quick glance over her shoulder confirmed it.

"You're lucky," Nick said, not bothering to avert his gaze. "The pastry dude was some big shot, so he scored a suite next door to the head chef. The rest of us bunk three to a room down below."

"Lucky me," she said without a trace of sarcasm. She'd toured this boat years ago during a seventh-grade field trip, and she remembered how tiny the rooms were. "Sounds like you're on top of each other."

"You offering to share your room?" he asked. "'Cause I'd rather be keeping you company than one of my brothers."

They reached the third floor and stepped into a red-carpeted hallway that reminded her of an old horror movie she couldn't quite place. "Not happening." She pointed to her left and asked, "Which way?"

He dipped his head in the opposite direction. "313, the unluckiest number on the boat."

"That's all right. I make my own luck." Allie crossed the hall, glancing at each room placard as she passed. "Can I ask you something?"

"Fire away," came the reply. She was pretty sure he was still watching her butt.

"How come you're not bothered by the Mauvais-Dumont curse? I think sleeping with me is supposed to make your heart implode, or something."

Nick snickered. "You've got to admit, it'd be a pretty sweet way to go."

"So you're not afraid?"

"Honey, the only thing that scares me is a broken condom."

She wondered if Nick's bravery came from knowing he didn't stand a chance with her. Not that it mattered, because she had no intention of testing that theory. When she reached her door, she noticed Alex striding down the hall toward them. Unlike his twin, Alex kept his distance and ogled with his eyes, not his mouth.

"Hey, Allie." He gestured at the doorknob and waited for her to back up a step before moving in to unlock it for her. His fingers trembled, fumbling with the key while he darted glances up and down the hall. When he noticed her puzzled expression, he said, "We've got to hurry up and get you inside before Paw-paw sees."

"Oh, shit," Nick said from behind. "He's gonna blow a brain vein."

"Not if he doesn't find out."

"You'd better break it to him soon," Allie said, "because Marc wants me on the welcome line in thirty minutes."

Alex got the door open and ushered her inside a room the size of a generous walk-in closet. When the twins followed behind and shut the door, Allie inched along the double bed to give herself some space, which was in short supply.

She took in the slim dresser, each drawer cleverly latched to survive the rocking motion of the boat, and admired the netted shelves built into the wall. They'd forgone televisions and iPod docking stations in favor of a single digital alarm clock with AM-FM radio. She wasn't sure if the goal was to save money or maintain the historical feel. Maybe both. She made a mental note to ask Marc how they generated electricity on board.

A glance to her right revealed the bathroom, where beyond a tiny sink sat a plastic commode . . . smack-dab in the middle of the shower stall. She hadn't noticed *that* on the field trip. Allie blinked a few times to make sure she hadn't imagined it.

Nope, that was really a toilet. In the shower.

"There's something fundamentally wrong with doing your business while washing your hair," she said. And where did they keep the toilet paper—under the sink?

"Suck it up, buttercup," Nick said. "At least you're not sharing it three ways."

"True." Not even a night with Marc Dumont was worth that. Which reminded her—"Hey, Alex, I'm supposed to ask for a staff shirt."

"What size?"

"Medium, I guess."

He took an extra-long moment to appraise her chest before agreeing. "I need you to fill out some paperwork, too." Backing toward the door, he said, "Stay here. I'll be back in a minute."

As Alex walked out, the phone in Nick's pocket chirped and he glanced at the screen. "Duty calls. Let me know if you get lonesome, hon." He tossed her suitcase on the bed, and with a wink, he was gone, too.

Allie unzipped her suitcase and got to work unpacking. She'd just moved to the bathroom to freshen up when a man's voice boomed through the thin wall separating her from the next suite. A thrill ricocheted the length of her spine. She knew that gravelly bark. Phillip Regale had checked in.

The Phillip Regale!

Alex had told her to stay put, but there was no harm in a quick introduction, especially if Phil invited her inside his room and away from Pawpaw's line of vision. She rubbed some frizz-control between her hands and scrunched her curls. After a quick lipstick touch-up, she tucked her room key in her back pocket and checked the hallway, finding it vacant.

She tiptoed over and knocked twice beneath the peephole.

The door flew open more quickly than she'd anticipated. Allie flinched back while offering a shaky wave.

Phillip Regale greeted her with a curt, "What?" and tossed a handful of almonds into his mouth.

He was shorter than she'd expected, wearing a red *Belle of the Bayou*–embroidered polo instead of his typical white chef's jacket. But she recognized his salt-and-pepper crew cut and the trio of lines etched across his forehead and between his eyes. He was distinguished and broad-shouldered and clearly awaiting a reply.

"Hi, sir," she said and paused to swallow. "I'm Allison Mauvais, and I'll be—"

"No autographs." He started to shut the door, but on instinct, Allie wedged her sneaker-clad foot in the jamb. The hazel eyes narrowed at her were not amused.

"Can I come in for a second?" she asked, taking another quick peek up and down the hall.

Phillip wrinkled his nose like he'd smelled vinegar in his hollandaise sauce. "No, you most certainly cannot."

This wasn't going the way she'd planned. Allie

scrambled for damage control. "I just wanted to introduce myself. I'm your new pastry chef."

"Oh," he said, relaxing a bit. "Never heard of you." He opened the door an inch or two but didn't invite her in. "Where'd you graduate?"

"Cedar Bayou High."

"No," he said, snickering in a way that made her feel stupid. "Which culinary school?"

Allie hesitated, unsure of how to answer him. She had no degrees or formal training beyond what she'd picked up in her mama's kitchen. But deciding she had nothing to be ashamed of, she admitted, "I didn't go to culinary school. But I learned from the best."

"Yeah?" He munched his almonds, tipping back his head to look down his nose at her. "Who?"

"It's wasn't a formal apprenticeship, but my mama and my—"

"Oh, God." He pinched his temples between his thumb and index finger and regarded her with new eyes, taking in the exposed skin below the hem of her skirt and then raking his gaze over her breasts. "I get it. You're fucking the boss."

Allie's lips parted with a pop, heat rushing into her cheeks. Sheer mortification tied her tongue for several awkward beats, and just when she geared up to contradict him, Phil cut her off with a humorless laugh.

"I didn't just fall off the turnip truck, sweetheart," he said. "I've dealt with plenty of broads spreading 'em for a job. Just do what I tell you and stay out of my way. I'll hire my own guy as soon as we stop in Natchez."

With the toe of his shoe, he nudged aside her sneaker and clicked the door shut.

For a full minute, Allie's feet clung to the carpet as she stared at the oak barrier inches from her nose. The heat from her face spread downward, sparking a flame of anger inside her chest. Devyn was right. Phillip Regale was an asswipe. And when Allie blotted her cheeks, she discovered the jerk really *did* spit when he talked.

She balled one fist and pounded on his door. When he didn't answer instantly, she pounded three more times.

Alex turned the corner and bolted to her side. "What are you doing? Get back in your room!"

"Not yet," she said, pounding until her fist ached. "Not until he takes it back."

The door swung open again, and this time, Phillip's eyes were more than unamused. They were downright livid. "What now?" he demanded around a cheek full of nuts.

"Nothing, Chef," Alex said, wrapping an arm around Allie's shoulders and then releasing her just as quickly.

Allie shook her index finger at Regale. "I'm not sleeping with the captain!"

"Right." He tossed another almond into his mouth. "Then explain why I'm stuck working with an unqualified, hot piece of ass from the swamp."

Alex drew a sharp breath, flinging himself in front of Regale as if to take a bullet. "We need him, Allie," he said desperately. "Don't hex him!"

"Hex me?" Regale said with a snort. "Good God, what kind of Podunk shit is th—"

His voice cut off abruptly, hand flying to his throat while his watery eyes bulged wide. As seconds ticked by, redness crept into his face, followed by a shocked expression. He tried to cough, but no sound escaped his lips. With each new attempt, more color flooded his cheeks until he resembled an unripe plum.

Alex spun on her. "Undo it!"

"I didn't do anything!"

Phil bent at the waist and clutched the doorjamb, pounding his own stomach to free his airway.

"Please, Allie!" Alex begged. "Reverse it!"

She pushed Alex aside and skirted Phil's body until she settled behind him. Steeling herself, she wrapped both arms around his belly, situated her fist beneath his rib cage, clapped the opposite hand over it, and heaved backward.

Nothing happened.

"Oh, my God," Alex cried. "He's gonna die!" He frantically made the sign of the cross over Phil, mumbling a Hail Mary in disjointed Latin.

Allie tensed her muscles to try again. This time, she inched her fist upward and planted her feet hip-width apart for better leverage. With a mighty tug, she squeezed Phil's girth with all her strength and heard a light *oof* of air in response. She glanced over his shoulder just in time to see the dislodged almond smack an old man in the eye.

"*Couillon!*" the old man swore, clapping one hand over his injury. Then he turned his good eye on her and lowered the brow above it. "Is that a Mauvais? Aboard my ship?"

He had to be Marc's pawpaw. Allie hadn't seen him since she'd moved away from the bayou, but apparently he recognized her easily enough.

Before anyone could respond, Phillip growled and

shoved Allie into the hall, thanking her for saving his life by slamming the door in her face. Again.

Ten frantic minutes later, after she and Alex had tried tag-teaming his pawpaw into accepting her aboard the *Belle*, the old man stalked away.

"Over my dead carcass!" he hollered. "I'm havin' words with Marc. But first, I'm pourin' a line of salt at my door, so she can't curse the bed while I'm outside!" He pointed at Alex and warned, "You best do the same, boy!"

"That only works for those who mean you harm," she called after him. "I'm here to help."

As he charged down the hall, she thought she heard him mutter, "Damn straight. Help us all to hell."

Alex rushed after his pawpaw, leaving Allie alone to wonder if the Dumonts had it all wrong. Because if the day's events were any indication, it seemed Memère had jinxed her own line instead of theirs.

Chapter 4

Sliding on his sunglasses, Marc peered through the pilothouse window at the murky Mississippi, as the *Belle* sluiced through her currents like a hot knife through butter. Nice and smooth, just the way he liked it. He touched the throttle to open it up to a leisurely seven knots and enjoyed the manufactured breeze from a nearby oscillating fan affixed to the wall. Overhead, the clouds parted and bathed the deck in golden rays as if the Man Upstairs had personally blessed this voyage.

It was a good day.

The engine hummed flawlessly, propelling the newly repaired paddle wheel into a lazy rotation while his passengers milled about the multistory decks, sipping their mint juleps. Even the finicky sonar equipment had decided to play nice this afternoon in celebration of Marc's first day as captain. The only part of the *Belle* giving him any grief was of the living, breathing variety.

Which was usually the case.

"You're thinkin' with your tallywhacker," Pawpaw accused from his seat on the defunct side control panel.

"If you have a lick of sense, you'll drop that witch at the next port."

Marc cringed inwardly. *Witch, siren, devil, sorceress.* When Allie had said she'd been called worse than his teasing nickname, she was likely referring to the slurs his own family had hurled at her over the years.

And yet here she was, taking the abuse with a weary smile while saving Marc's bacon. Last he'd seen her, she'd stacked out a corner of Regale's kitchen to fix a batch of berry cobbler. Her bronze cheeks had been dewy with perspiration, her adorable nose smudged with flour, but despite Chef's demands to get the hell out of his way, she'd tossed a handful of blackberries into her mouth and soldiered on. Allie was a damned hard worker, and she deserved respect from the crew.

"Put a lid on that nonsense," Marc said. "I need a pastry chef a whole lot more than I need an *Onboard Historian*." He turned to Pawpaw and arched a brow at the old man's ridiculous title. As if the crotchety old coot were qualified to dispense knowledge beyond how to brew homemade whiskey.

Pawpaw pressed his wrinkled lips into a line, glaring at Marc in a way that warned he'd conceded the battle but not the war. As he stalked out the pilothouse door, he grumbled, "We're gonna need more salt."

Marc released a breath and tried to reclaim his perfect day, but it wasn't happening. Even the clouds knitted together, obscuring the sun and putting the kibosh on his grace from above. He called one of his copilots to man the controls, figuring he might as well head downstairs to mingle with the guests and check in with his sister, the head purser.

On his way to the main level, Marc turned a critical eye down each hallway, pleased to find uniformed maids shuttling clean towels and fresh ice water into each room. When he passed the reading salon, he nodded a greeting to a lone guest curled up on the plush chaise longue, romance novel in one hand and a cocktail in the other. That's what Marc wanted to see—his passengers relaxed and happy.

He descended the sweeping mahogany staircase and crossed the lobby to the main desk, where Alex was showing Worm how to operate the intercom system while Ella-Claire tapped at her keyboard.

The instant Ella-Claire's blue gaze darted up from her computer screen, her face broke into a wide grin. She skirted the desk and came running at Marc, chestnut ponytail swinging above her crisp white purser's uniform, sensible black heels clicking against the wood floor. She threw her arms around him and hugged his neck.

"Congrats, Captain," she said. "I'm so proud of you."

Marc gave her a squeeze and a smile to match. His little sister knew how much this day meant to him, and he loved her for it. They were half siblings—same mama, different daddies—but even though the *Belle* wasn't Ella's legacy, she'd spent every summer since her fourteenth birthday sweating right alongside him on this boat. Together, they'd towed luggage and scrubbed decks until his daddy had recognized Ella's talent for sweet-talking irate guests. He'd trained her for customer service, and now ten years later she practically ran the show.

"How's it going so far?" Marc said. "Any snags?"

She offered a reassuring pat on the forearm and returned to her station behind the polished wood counter. "Nothing I can't handle."

"What about the Gibsons?" Alex asked her.

Ella threw Alex a sharp look.

The Gibsons. Why did that name sound familiar to Marc? "What about them?"

"They're one of the couples who double-booked the honeymoon suite," Ella explained. "The bride's not happy with the stateroom."

"Even though we comped all their tours?"

Ella nodded. "I invited them to sit at your table for supper, but they didn't seem too excited about that."

No doubt. If you asked Marc, the best honeymoon was the kind where nobody left the bed. What was the point in going through all that wedding bullshit—not to mention the divorce that would inevitably follow—if you didn't get a week of nonstop sex out of it?

"I'll stop by their table tonight and see if I can smooth things over," he said.

"Thanks." Ella grabbed her clipboard and slipped a pencil behind one ear. "That reminds me, I've got to run to the dining hall real quick."

She asked Alex to hold down the fort until she returned, and after giving Marc a quick kiss on the cheek, she clicked off to her destination.

Worm leaned over the counter and pushed aside his shaggy brown hair to watch her leave, ogling her backside in clear appreciation while he murmured, "Sweet Cheez-Its."

Marc's jaw tightened. He swiveled his head and burned a warning glare into his kid brother's forehead. "Don't look at my sister like that."

"Why not?" Worm asked. "She's not *my* sister."

Alex tried to stifle a laugh, then clapped an arm around Worm's shoulders. "If you want to keep those 'nads long enough to grow hair on 'em, you'd better mind yourself around Ella-Claire. She's off-limits to all of us."

Damn straight she was.

None of Marc's half brothers shared a drop of blood with Ella, but he still expected the drooling horndogs to treat her like family. And to keep their quick-fingered hands to themselves. That was nonnegotiable, and they knew it. Not even his older brother, Beau, had messed with Ella, and that bastard nailed anything that moved.

Marc sent Alex an unspoken message in the tone of his voice. "If our little brother has time to scope out tail, maybe we haven't given him enough to do."

"I hear you loud and clear, Cap'n," Alex said. "I'll bet the cleaning crew can use his help. There are always a few motion-sick passengers yakking in the halls on the first day."

Worm groaned and muttered something under his breath, but apparently he knew better than to back-talk.

"C'mon," Marc said, grinning at his kid brother. "Let's go find you some man's work."

That evening, Marc changed into a clean dress uniform and combed his hair into a meticulous low ponytail for the formal dinner. He could smell the tangy, spicy aroma of caramelized chipotle chicken long before he entered the dining room. Once inside, he admired the presentation of tender chicken breasts and delicate chilies lacquered in orange glaze, his mouth watering in response.

Chef was one mean son of a bitch, but damn, the man could cook.

Marc assessed each table as he passed, greeting guests while assuring himself that their white tablecloths were starched to perfection, bone china was displayed properly above their platinum chargers, and silver was in the correct order from salad fork to soup spoon. The sounds of clinking crystal and easy conversation hung in the air, indicating a good time was being had by all.

Except the Gibsons.

Marc approached the newlyweds' table bearing a gift—a complimentary bottle of Dom Perignon Vintage—but when he presented the champagne, Mrs. Gibson sniffed and declared, "We don't drink."

Marc groped for a response. Experience had taught him how to spot a teetotaler from a mile away, and this pair of thirtysomething neogothic redheads didn't seem the type. The groom was sporting a visible neck tattoo above the collar of his dress shirt, and the bride had enough piercings in her face to trip a metal detector.

That'd teach him to judge a book by its cover.

"I apologize for the room mix-up," Marc said. "Is there anything I can—"

"Did you know Eric McMasterson?" the bride interrupted.

"Captain of the *North River Steamer*?" Marc asked, once again taken aback. "Only by reputation. Why?"

"He was my grandpa." The woman's shoulders rounded forward, prompting her husband to reach across the table and smooth a consoling hand over hers. "I spent half my childhood on his boat before they shut it down. Of all the historic steamers left, yours is my favorite. I planned our whole wedding around this cruise. And now . . ." She trailed off with a sad sigh.

If that weren't enough to make Marc feel like shit, a tear slid from the corner of her eye and plunked into her untouched garlic-mango rice.

Hell, what was he supposed to say to that—*Can I get you some sparkling cider instead?* Nothing short of snatching the honeymoon suite away from another couple would rectify the problem, and he couldn't very well do that.

"Beg pardon," said a familiar sultry voice from behind. "Are you the Gibsons?"

Marc turned to find Allie standing several paces back with a white bakery box cradled between her hands. She sashayed to the table, and Marc noticed half the heads in the dining room turn to watch the sleepy sway of her hips and the soft bounce of curls spilling wildly down her back. She'd removed her apron, but a dusting of flour on her polo shirt outlined its former shape. The effect drew his gaze to the clean red fabric stretched taut across her full breasts.

Mercy.

Even after twelve hours on her feet in those ugly white kitchen clogs, she looked so damned sexy Marc had to check the urge to adjust himself.

She placed the bakery box on the table and lifted the lid, revealing a miniature two-layer wedding cake iced in white buttercream. Dark pink piping encircled an elegant monogram of the couple's initials, just elaborate enough to commemorate the occasion without going overboard. The scent wafted up from the table and filled Marc's nose, and he pulled in a deep breath— sweet and sinful, much like the woman standing by his side.

"A little bird told me about the problem with the honeymoon suite," Allie said to the Gibsons. She leaned in and lowered her voice as if sharing a secret. "So I made this for you. It's my secret recipe butter cake with chocolate ganache filling." She added with a wink, "Don't tell the other newlyweds, because they're not getting one."

Mrs. Gibson's mouth had dropped open before she'd even glimpsed the cake. "Miss Mauvais?" she asked in plain disbelief.

Allie's back stiffened and she blinked at the other woman as if trying to place her. "Uh, yes. Have we met?"

"You don't remember me." Despite that, the bride's lips parted in a wide smile. "When I came to see you last year, you changed my life. You told me I had to believe to—"

"Receive," Allie finished with a smile of her own. "Sure, now I remember." She swirled a hand toward her own face. "But I didn't recognize you with all this."

"Oh." Cheeks flushing, Mrs. Gibson touched one of her nose studs. "Well, you said to be myself, so as soon as I left your shop, I went for my first piercing." She squeezed her husband's hand. "That's where I met Ryan."

Still grinning, Allie shook her head in awe. "Then it was meant to be, honey. My mama, God rest her, used to say there are no accidents. Same goes for your suite.

We might not understand it now, but there's a reason you ended up where you did."

"If nothing else," the bride said, standing to embrace Allie, "at least I get to say *thank you* in person. That alone is worth it."

When Allie returned the hug, tears welled in her mismatched eyes, clinging to her thick black lashes without spilling over. The sight brought a sudden heaviness to Marc's ribs.

He'd never seen Allie cry, not even in the sixth grade when a substitute teacher had flung holy water on her. With her gaze glistening and flour tangled in her curls, she seemed so gentle and kindhearted—words no one would use to describe a Mauvais woman. But the evidence was right in front of him. Allie had baked this cake without being asked—*after* she'd run herself ragged all day in Regale's kitchen.

Marc caught himself grinning at her, and he remembered his place, snapping into action.

He called for a server to assist the Gibsons in cutting their cake and summoned a photographer to capture a shot of the couple feeding each other the first bite. After a nonalcoholic toast to the newlyweds' future, Marc left them to enjoy their meal. He peered around the dining hall for Allie, but couldn't spot her.

Where had she run off to?

Allie gripped the cool metal railing, closing her eyes to savor the night air rolling off the river. She let the wind's gentle fingers lift the heavy curls from the back of her neck while she trapped a lungful of fresh oxygen and blew it out, nice and slow, imagining all her frustrations leaving her body with that breath. Then she repeated the process, because one breath wouldn't do.

Merde, what a day.

She'd dreamt of sharing a kitchen with Phil Regale since she'd watched him flambé a flawless Steak Diane on the Food Network a few years ago. Like all masters of the trade, he'd made it look easy, his instruments an extension of himself as he'd seasoned and seared that beef to perfection. She'd made it her goal to meet him, going so far as to drive to St. Louis for one of his restaurant openings, but she hadn't been able to wiggle her way through the crowd to even shake his hand.

Now she wanted to wrap her hands around his *coquilles.*

And tug. Really hard.

One insult hadn't been enough for him. All day long he'd lashed at her, undermining her authority with the kitchen staff by referring to her as "the captain's squeeze." *Tell the captain's back-swamp squeeze to get her oozing cobbler out of my oven!* Then he'd used his imposing size to shoulder her out of the way when their paths crossed, and he'd "accidentally" knocked her ingredients to the floor three times.

The worst part? When he'd left to circulate through the dining room, she'd snuck a bite of his glazed chicken. It tasted so good she wanted to cry. And she didn't cry easily. She'd learned to grow thick skin as a little girl.

What had this horrible man done to deserve such superior talent? Maybe she should have let him choke on that almond. Allie sighed and propped her elbows on the railing. Who was she kidding? She wouldn't have done anything differently. She couldn't stand to see anyone suffer, not even Phil Regale.

The outside door squeaked on its hinges and footsteps sounded on the wooden deck in long, sure strides approaching from behind. Soon the scents of soap and bold aftershave reached Allie on the breeze. She didn't have to turn around to know Marc had joined her, but she did all the same. Scrumptious as he was, why waste a moment in his company not looking at him?

She rotated her tired body and leaned back against the iron rail, tucking both hands in her pockets. The Louisiana moon illuminated one side of Marc's gorgeous face, casting a shadow beneath his lips and deepening the cleft in his chin. He rubbed a hand across his jaw while his dark eyes moved over her in a way that made Allie's pulse quicken.

Each of her ten fingertips begged to skim the contours of Marc's cheeks and tangle in his hair, but she shoved them deeper into her pockets and told them no. It was too soon—Marc wasn't ready.

"Nice night," she mused, tossing a glance over her shoulder at the leafy canopy of willows lining the riverbank.

"Mmm," he agreed, never taking his dark eyes off her. "Bet it was a long day, though. I know how hard Regale is on his staff." It wasn't a question, but he raised a brow as if expecting an answer.

Allie shrugged and told a teensy lie. "Nothing I can't handle."

Marc chuckled low and deep, his teeth a flash of white in the darkness. He propped an elbow beside her, settling so near that his dinner jacket brushed her bare arm and prickled her skin into goose bumps. "You sound like my sister."

Allie resisted the urge to lean into him. Marc would spook easily; she had to play it careful with him. "I like Ella-Claire. She's good people."

"Mmm-hmm," he agreed. "Way too good to have a jackass like me for a brother."

She slanted him a look from the corner of one eye. "That's not true."

"Aw, now, Allie-Cat," he murmured with a wicked grin that made her go all gooey inside. "You know I'm not an angel." The wind kicked up, tossing her curls into the air, and Marc captured one lock between his fingers. He smoothed it against his thumb for a moment before tucking it behind her ear.

Allie swallowed hard. She told her feet to stay put, but that didn't stop her face from inching toward his. "Neither am I."

Marc's gaze dipped to her mouth and held there. "No, I imagine you're not, sugar." He licked his lips, and just when Allie thought he might kiss her, he gave a regretful shake of his head and pulled back. "But you've been awful sweet around here," he said. "And I mean to thank you for that."

Allie stuffed down her disappointment and reminded herself that Rome wasn't built in a day. With a warm smile, she bumped his shoulder with hers. "Just doing my job, baby."

He returned her smile and ruffled her hair playfully. "Well, keep doing it. You saved my ass in there with the Gibsons."

"Aren't they adorable?" Allie brought a hand to her breast. The bride had come to the Sweet Spot over a year ago, looking for half a dozen cupcakes and a love charm. Well, mostly the latter. But the girl hadn't needed magic, just the courage to date the men she wanted instead of the trust-fund boys her mama had always pushed on her.

"Adorable," Marc said in a tone that implied the opposite. "I wonder if they take out their tongue rings before they get down and dirty."

Allie delivered a well-deserved elbow to Marc's ribs. "I imagine they leave them in, hon. When it comes to licking, tongue studs offer certain"—she stood on tiptoe and whispered in his ear—"*benefits.*"

Marc drew a sharp breath while his pulse pumped visibly at the base of his throat. His reaction told Allie he enjoyed her mouth at his ear just as much as she enjoyed pressing it there.

Good. She decided to leave him wanting more.

"I'd better go," she said, pushing off the rail. "Early to bed, early to rise. I want to beat Chef to the galley in the morning." Which meant waking up hours before dawn, but it would be worth it if she could bake her breakfast pastries in peace.

Marc didn't seem to like that. His forehead wrinkled and he held out a hand, catching her wrist to stop her, then releasing her just as quickly as if she'd burned him with her touch.

"Listen," he said. "I know Regale's kind of a tyrant, but if he's giving you any trouble beyond the usual assholery, I want you to come see me. Okay?"

Allie gave him a small grin, touched by his concern. No, she wouldn't bring those problems to Marc. She wasn't stupid. She knew the promise of Phil's mouth-watering cuisine had packed the *Belle* for the next two weeks, and Allie wouldn't put Marc in the position of having to discipline his most crucial staffer. Or worse, create so much resentment that Phil issued an ultimatum and forced Marc to let her go.

She'd find a way to handle Chef Boyardouche on her own.

"You got it." Allie threw him one last inviting smile and turned toward the door. As she walked away, she felt the heat of Marc's gaze on her body, so just for fun, she dropped her hair elastic and bent over—extra-slow—to retrieve it. When she stood, she heard a faint whisper in the background that sounded like "Mercy."

With a spring in her step and hope in her heart, Allie made her way upstairs to her suite—the unluckiest room on the boat—confident that tomorrow would be a better day.

Chapter 5

Allie pressed her lips together to choke back a yawn while she threw more weight behind her rolling pin, eager to finish this last batch of apple turnovers before the sun rose and Regale stormed the galley to reclaim his throne. The oven timer beeped, and Allie set aside her wooden roller in favor of a latex oven mitt. She pulled out a tray of golden brown pastries and set them on the metal racks to cool, then hurried back to her dough to cut strips, add cinnamon apple filling, and fold the turnovers on a clean baking sheet.

She darted a glance at the clock and brushed a glaze over the dough. Not only did she want to avoid working alongside Regale, but a secret part of her needed to prove she wasn't an "unqualified, hot piece of ass from the swamp." Maybe she'd never win Chef's respect, but if he saw how dedicated she was, he might quit threatening to replace her once they reached Natchez.

Twenty minutes later, Allie leaned against the stainless steel countertop and inhaled the delectable scents of apples and spice while admiring the fruits of her labor, no pun intended. This recipe was one of her most popular, with extra sugar and a squeeze of lemon. The four predawn hours she'd spent rolling and mixing and dicing would be worth it when she saw the looks of rapture on the passengers' faces.

And maybe Chef's, too. A girl could hope.

The kitchen staff began filing in, pulling waffle mix from the storage closet and chopping onions and peppers for the omelets. They greeted one another in cheery *good mornings* but brushed past "the captain's squeeze" as if she weren't there. Allie ignored the slight, arranging her pastries on serving trays until Ella-Claire strode into the galley with a clipboard and a smile.

"Smells amazing," Ella said, peering around Allie at the turnovers. "Can I steal one?"

Allie used a napkin to lift a still-warm pastry from the tray and hand it over. Ella was the only crew member aboard the *Belle* who didn't hate, fear, or want to seduce Allie, so she deserved the first bite.

"Mmm, thanks." Ella took the offering while lifting her clipboard for show. "Alex forgot to get your signature on these tax forms. As soon as you give me your autograph, I'll add you to the payroll."

"Won't the agency be paying me?" Allie asked.

"They didn't have you in their system." Ella shrugged. "Works out better for us anyway because now we get to hire you free and clear."

"Sounds good." Allie took the clipboard and scrawled her signature on the pages, then handed it back just as Ella sank her teeth into the first bite.

Ella's mouth curved in a preemptive smile. "Oh, Allie, this is so—" She cut off, eyes widening. Her expression of rapture transformed to disgust, and she snatched a clean napkin from the counter to spit her bite into it.

"What's wrong?" Allie asked. "Is it too hot?"

Ella's eyes watered as she spat two more times into the napkin to clear her mouth. "I think there's something wrong with this one," she croaked, handing it back.

Confused, Allie pinched off a corner of the turnover and popped it into her mouth. At first, the pastry seemed fine—light and flaky. But when the apple filling crossed her tongue, it tasted like a mouthful of ocean water, bitter and briny. Allie nearly gagged. She grabbed a napkin of her own and disposed of her bite. "Oh, God. That's awful!"

"It's so . . ." Ella began.

"Salty," Allie finished.

What had she done wrong? In her sleep-deprived state, had she incorrectly measured her ingredients? No, that couldn't be right. She'd made this recipe so many times she could do it in a coma. She lifted the steel bowl from its industrial-sized mixer and peered at the remnants of apple filling smeared on the inside. After running her finger along the rim, she brought it to her mouth and sucked it clean.

It was horrible.

Allie returned to her workstation to inspect the ingredients she'd used. One by one, she sampled the flour, cornstarch, and apples, finding them satisfactory. When she dipped the tip of a clean spoon into the sugar bin and brought it to her mouth, she found the problem. It was salt. She couldn't believe she hadn't noticed.

She rotated the plastic container until she found its label: *Granulated Sugar*. Allie knew for a fact there was real sugar in this cylinder yesterday when she'd made berry cobbler and chocolate-chunk cookies, because she'd sampled the finished products. That meant someone had sabotaged her workstation last night after she'd left—and ruined every single one of the turnovers she'd spent the last four hours preparing.

Who would do something so malicious?

"Look alive, people," Chef yelled, loudly clapping his hands as he strode into the room. When his gaze fell on Allie, a slow grin curled across his lips, telling her exactly who would do something so malicious. Looking right at her, he shouted, "Someone tell the captain's pretty little squeeze to get her breakfast pastries on the serving line. We've got early birds out there."

The staff shared uneasy glances, unwilling to pass along the message. Finally, a teenage boy asked Allie, "You want me to take them out?"

That's just what Chef wanted—for her to serve the guests contaminated food and ruin her reputation, and thus her career. What a coldhearted *cochon*. Allie's whole body scorched with fever, sending heat rushing into her face. She tried to steady her pulse, but her heart pounded so fiercely she felt it in her fingertips. The tingly burn of tears pressed her eyelids, but she forced them back.

She would bathe in acid before she'd let Chef see her cry.

"No," she said, glaring at Regale to let him know he hadn't won. Her own voice sounded foreign to her ears, eerie in its smoothness. "I changed my mind. I'm making coffee cake instead."

"Uh . . . Allie," Ella-Claire stammered, tossing aside her clipboard with a loud *clang*. "Let me help you."

"That's not your job." Allie had a small staff to assist her with the baking, and by God, they were going to back her up. "The pastry team will—"

"Be helping me," Regale finished. "I need all hands to run the omelet and Belgian waffle stations. Why don't you serve your pastries, sweetheart?" he asked with a sneer. "Something wrong?"

That did it.

Allie's tenuous hold on her temper snapped in half like a brittle lace cookie. Her vision went black for a moment, and when it returned, all she could see was Regale's smug smile and the hulking, bearlike set of his folded arms. She went deaf to everything but the rush of blood in her ears while an electric charge buzzed over her skin. Someone must have turned on the kitchen fan, because her hair blew behind her in waves that tickled the back of her neck. She felt her body trembling.

To calm herself, Allie closed her eyes and recited the Creole serenity prayer her mama had taught her. She chanted the words of peace, feeling her blood pressure drift down a few notches, and by the second verse she felt composed enough to open her eyes.

That's when she noticed the whole staff was staring at her in openmouthed horror.

Allie flashed a tight smile to defuse the tension in the room. "I'd better get to work on that coffee cake."

Ella's typically tanned cheeks had turned pale. She pointed at the teenage boy who'd offered to haul the turnovers into the dining room. "What's your name?"

The boy couldn't seem to tear his gaze from Allie's face. "Uh, Bobby, ma'am."

"Okay," Ella said in a voice a few decibels too loud. "Bobby, you assist Miss Mauvais with breakfast." When Chef geared up to complain, Ella cut him off with a lifted palm. "If you can't manage without him, I'll pitch in." Then she cocked an eyebrow, daring him to admit that he needed the head purser to assist him in making waffles.

Regale's mouth tightened, but he recovered quickly. "Thanks for the offer. I'll make do. Now, if you don't mind . . ." He swept one hand toward the door, basically telling Ella to get out.

Ella-Claire grabbed her clipboard and stalked from the galley with her head held high. She really *was* good people.

"Let's get to it," Allie said. She started by dumping over one hundred beautiful, flawlessly baked apple turnovers into the garbage.

That really hurt.

During the next hour, she and Bobby worked in a frenzy to mix, assemble, and bake three shallow pans of crumb cake. All the while Chef barked orders to *her* staff and resumed bullying her with comments like, "Tell the captain's voodoo squeeze that magic won't turn off her goddamned oven timer!"

Allie punched the END button, silencing the timer as she pulled her last pan of cake from the oven. She had to finish up and get out of here. A steady pressure had been building inside her head all morning, and she knew she couldn't hold it together much longer.

Once the pans cooled, she helped Bobby carry them out to the breakfast buffet, then thanked him for his hard work and dismissed him for a break. She didn't make eye contact with anyone inside the dining room. In strides a bit too quick, she made for the stairwell and took the steps two at a time to her room on the third floor.

After unlocking her door with trembling fingers, she stripped down naked, right there in the entryway, and stepped over her pile of clothes into the bathroom to run a hot shower. Safely behind the barriers of two locked doors and a plastic curtain, Allie hung her head beneath the steaming jets and finally let herself cry.

"You need to find her, Marc." Ella-Claire's big blue eyes grew impossibly wider as she slapped the purser's desk and leaned forward. "This is a full-on SOS."

"Now, calm down," Marc told her. "Chef's fine. I saw him ten minutes ago. And I'm sure Allie's fine, too. She probably needed some space."

Ella shook her head, setting her ponytail in motion. "You don't get it—you weren't there. Regale kept pushing and pushing, and then it was like someone flipped a switch. The lights flickered and wind came out of nowhere. Allie kind of blanked out and she started chanting a spell or—"

"Wait," Marc interrupted, his stomach dropping an inch. "What kind of spell?"

Ella bit her lip and admitted, "Well, I don't know. She wasn't speaking English."

Marc released the breath he'd been holding. Allie could have been reciting her grocery list for all they knew. He'd had his doubts before, but lately he'd glimpsed a brand-new side of Allie—compassionate and kind. He refused to believe she'd cause anyone harm. Even to Chef, who clearly deserved it.

"Look, I never believed in *all that*," Ella argued, "and I know Allie wouldn't hurt a soul, but the whole thing gave me chills." Ella lifted her forearm, where a dusting of translucent hairs stood on end. "I'm getting chills now just thinking about it."

Alex glanced up from his paperwork. "Allie made Chef choke on a nut yesterday." At Marc's dubious glare, Alex clarified, "She used the Heimlich on him, but still. He almost died."

"Let's see if I've got this right," Marc began. "You dragged me away from the pilothouse so I could track down our pastry chef and make sure she hasn't cursed the boat?" Marc expected this kind of idiocy from Pawpaw—maybe even from himself at one time—but not from his sister. Perhaps the Dumont crazy had started rubbing off on her.

"Oh, I don't think she cursed the boat," Ella said with a flap of her hand. "Just Phil."

"And we need him," Alex added. "So see if you can get her to undo it."

"Uh-huh." Undo it. Lord, it was too early for this mess. Marc heaved a sigh. "Fine. I'll go check on her."

"Nicky saw her take the stairs," Alex said. "So she's probably in her suite."

All alone with Allie Mauvais in her suite . . .

The idea should have scared Marc, but it put a small

bounce in his heels as he crossed the lobby to the main staircase. He was still springing when he knocked on her door, but the instant she answered, that buoyancy deflated faster than a leaky tire.

She looked like a drowned rat.

Her soaking-wet curls hung low and heavy, the locks dripping onto the lapels of her fluffy white guest robe. The oversized garment covered her from fingertips to ankles, dwarfing her body beneath yards of terry cloth. Mascara ran down her face in muddy streams as if she hadn't bothered to wipe away her tears.

Oddly enough, the effect was freaking adorable, but he still felt terrible for her.

"Aw, sugar," Marc said with a sympathetic tilt of his head. "That bad?"

"Don't!" She held up an index finger. "Don't do that! I'm a professional, not some hot piece of ass from th-th-th-th"—she gulped a hitched breath—"the swamp!"

Marc wanted to tell her the two weren't mutually exclusive, but it seemed like the wrong thing to say. "Of course you're a professional." He nudged his way inside and shut the door behind him, then kicked aside a pile of dirty clothes. "Honey, I tasted your coffee cake. It was so good, I had to take a cold shower when I was done."

That earned a weak smile. He wrapped an arm around her shoulders and led her to the foot of the bed. She plopped down, and when he lowered himself beside her, she leaned her soggy head on his shoulder. Marc didn't mind. He wanted to make her feel better, and besides, she smelled like warm vanilla sugar.

"Who told you?" Allie asked.

"Ella-Claire. She's worried you hexed the chef."

She sat up and faced him, her red-rimmed eyes softening in hurt. "Really?"

The look on her face sent an unexpected shock of pain through Marc, especially when he realized he'd contributed to the problem. Until now, he'd never put himself in Allie's shoes, never imagined how she might feel each time he crossed to the other side of the street when she walked by. He'd been an idiot to assume Allie was some unshakable force of nature. She bled like everyone else. How had he never seen it before?

"I'm sorry, hon," he said, pulling her close again. "Ella didn't mean anything by it."

Allie got quiet for a while, punctuating the silence with an occasional sniffle. When she finally spoke again, her voice sounded so small it tugged a knot in Marc's chest. "Do you believe that?" she asked. "That I curse people?"

"No, not really," he said. "But I'm not going to lie. I used to."

"Is that why you dumped me after junior prom?"

Junior prom. The memory brought an instant smile to Marc's lips, mostly out of embarrassment for his seventeen-year-old self. Talk about a blow to his ego.

He'd been so nervous that night he'd sweated through two dress shirts before he left to pick up Allie for the dance. Pawpaw had him half believing the devil would spring from the punch bowl and drag Marc straight to hell. His hands had trembled so hard Allie'd had to pin on her own corsage; his knees had knocked together so violently he could barely dance with her. It was a miracle he'd worked up the nerve to kiss her at the end of the night. Not his best performance, either—barely more than a shaky peck. She probably thought he was a lousy kisser, which he wasn't, thank you very much.

"Yes and no," he said with a chuckle.

She slid him a glare. "It's not funny." But one corner of her pink lips twitched in a grin. "I skipped a trip to the beach with my sister that weekend so I could stay home and wait by the phone."

Marc sucked a breath through his teeth. "And I never called."

"No, you didn't," she said, then added, "*ever* again."

"I'm sorry, hon." He dropped a quick kiss atop her head. "It wasn't anything you did. I was telling the truth that night when I said I wanted to take you out again."

"So what changed?"

He'd changed. More specifically, the skin all over his happy place. "The next day something happened that made me think the curse was real. I woke up with, uh . . ." Was there a delicate way to say *blisters all over my johnson*? "Well, an outbreak."

She glanced up at him with a question in her eyes.

"On my manhood," he clarified.

Allie gasped and gave him a playful shove. "And you thought that was my fault?"

Marc shrugged. "Daddy and Pawpaw kept telling me sex with a Mauvais woman would make my junk fall off, so . . ." He trailed off because the rest seemed obvious to him.

"But a rash could mean a dozen different things,"

Allie said, ticking items off on her fingers. "A reaction to your laundry detergent, a new soap, a food allergy, or—if that rumor about you and the cheer squad is true—a social disease."

"No way." Marc held up one hand in oath. "I've never gone bareback in my life, and I get tested on the regular. I'm cleaner than a priest on Sunday." He didn't mention that the old rumor was true. He had worked his way through the varsity squad—but always protected by a barrier of nice, safe latex.

"Still, I can't believe you blamed that on me."

"Not you," Marc said. He'd never believed Allie meant him harm. "The curse."

"Same difference."

"Not really." It was Allie's great-great-grandma who'd cursed the Dumonts, not her. "One is beyond your control and the other isn't."

"The other?" she asked.

"You know. Hexing people on purpose." At her piercing glare, Marc added, "Just speaking hypothetically. I don't pay a lick of credence to that stuff."

"Uh-huh," Allie said, clearly not buying it. "So you don't even believe the curse is real anymore?"

"Nope."

"Care to test it?" Her eyes—one the color of fine whiskey, the other grayer than a summer storm—twinkled with mischief and put a skip in Marc's pulse. "Because I know a way to find out for sure."

"What's that?"

"Easy," she said, raising one brow in a challenge. "Kiss me again."

Of its own volition, Marc's gaze flew to her mouth,

full and soft and still wet from the shower. He froze, unable to form a response to her proposal. He'd often fantasized about taking that pouty lower lip between his teeth and tasting Allie Mauvais—kissing her and doing it right this time.

So what was stopping him?

"What's the matter, baby?" she teased. "You scared?"

Maybe a little, but he'd never own up to it.

"Of kissing a pretty woman? Never." Marc accepted her dare, pushing up her robe sleeve and taking her hand in both of his. "But I think we should start small. You know, make sure lightning doesn't strike us dead."

"Mmm," she agreed with a mock solemn nod. "Baby steps."

"Yeah, exactly." He trailed an index finger along her wrist, all the way up to the inside bend of her elbow and back down again, then peered at her and asked, "Feel anything?"

The thumping vein beneath Marc's fingers told him Allie felt a whole lot, but she shook her head. "Nope."

"That's a good sign." Holding her gaze, he lifted her palm to his mouth and placed a slow, lingering kiss there, hiding a smile when she shivered and bit her lip. "How about now?"

Allie swallowed hard enough to shift her throat. "Nothing."

"Mmm, you don't say." It was time to dial it up a notch. Scooting nearer until their thighs touched, he swept back her dripping locks, then bent down and brushed his lips back and forth over her ear. He flicked his tongue along the rim before gently biting her lobe and whispering, "Now?"

A whimper was her only reply.

He was sure starting to feel something. Right behind his fly.

He worked his way down the side of her neck. When he found a weak spot at the top of her shoulder, he teased it—licking and sucking and nibbling until Allie's low moans vibrated the skin beneath his lips.

He'd always wondered what she tasted like, and now he knew. Clean and savory, like honeydew. Marc couldn't hide the lust in his voice when he tore his mouth away from her and asked, "Feel anything now?"

Allie's breath came in shallow gasps. She tilted her head for more of his touch and murmured, "Not a thing."

So he made love to her throat until she writhed in pleasure and leaned back onto the bed, sinking her fingertips into his shoulders to pull him atop her. A distant voice warned Marc he was going too far, but the blood drained from his brain and rushed between his legs, smothering his conscience with lethal force.

Distractions eliminated, he covered Allie's body with his own and pressed her soft curves into the mattress, then nibbled a path from her shoulder to her jaw. He reached the corner of her mouth and pulled back to look at her—sodden curls fanning out around her flushed face, eyelids heavy, lips parted in need. Lord have mercy, she was so gorgeous, he ached deep inside where nobody had stirred him before.

"If you still don't feel anything," he whispered, "we can probably try that kiss now."

"No lightning here." Allie reached up and unfastened his hair, sending it spilling down like a curtain.

"How about you, baby?" she asked with a seductive grin. "Anything scary happening in your pants?"

Chuckling softly, Marc aligned their hips and rocked, long and slow, against the terry cloth between her thighs to demonstrate exactly what was happening inside his pants. He must have hit the right spot because her eyes rolled back, mouth widening as she arched her neck and strained against him. Marc seized the opportunity and lowered his face to hers in a gentle kiss.

Or at least he tried to be gentle.

Once their lips met and she sighed into his mouth, he lost all control. A growl emanated from the back of his throat as he took her mouth with the force of nine years' pent-up longing. She fisted his hair and angled her face to take his seeking tongue, luring him deeper into her mouth in wet thrusts that mimicked the unconscious motion of his hips.

If he thought Allie's throat tasted good, it was nothing compared to her candied lips. He fed from her mouth, dizzy with the sensations of her warm scent and the noises rising from her chest. When she broke from the kiss and moaned his name, Marc quit caring whether or not the curse was real. If he woke up tomorrow with his head on backward it would be worth it.

"Marc," she repeated, bucking against his erection, her eyes closed in rapture.

His body heated, and he rushed to shrug out of his captain's jacket without leaving the decadence of Allie's embrace. With that accomplished, he gazed past his waist to the long, tanned leg wrapped around his hips . . . the very *bare* leg.

"You naked under there?" Marc asked in a husky

voice, not sure if he wanted to hear *yes* or *no*. It would be so easy to untie that white robe, unzip his fly, and slip right inside her.

But part of him knew it was a bad idea.

She answered by taking his hand and leading it up the length of her thigh, stopping where their clothed bodies met. He shifted aside so he could continue all the way to the top, and when he arrived at his destination he found her exposed, waxed baby-smooth, and already slick with desire.

God bless. He was going to burst in his drawers.

Bending to kiss her again, he ran one fingertip along the length of her slippery seam and stroked her with a whisper touch, teasing and tickling until she spread herself wide and dug her heels into the mattress in a silent plea for more pressure.

"How 'bout now, sugar?" he whispered against her mouth. "Feel anything?"

She only groaned and slurred a strand of incoherent Creole.

He didn't need a translation to know what she wanted, and he gave it to her—massaging circles over her slippery flesh and swallowing her cries of pleasure. She was petal-soft and hot beneath his touch. Marc wanted to watch his fingers as he worked more tension into her coiling muscles, but he couldn't bring himself to leave the sweetness of her mouth. So he let his fingertips send images to his mind, imagining the sheen of arousal glistening at the juncture of her thighs, the pink pout of her sex as he slid a finger deep and felt the first wave of orgasm clench around him.

Then in the worst imaginable timing, someone began pounding on the bedroom door.

"Don't get that," Allie gasped, thrashing her head from side to side.

"I have no intention of stopping," Marc promised. Nothing short of a fire would get him out of Allie's room—or her body.

He added a second finger and pumped deeper, then twisted his hand palm-up to massage her sweet spot. The next surge crested in a climax twice as hard as the first. Marc covered her mouth with his, smothering her moans of release. Her pleasure rang inside his head like music, pride washing over him until he nearly burst with it. He loved making Allie shudder in ecstasy; his only wish was to take her higher.

He had to join himself with her completely, to bury his throbbing erection where she was blazing hot and wet enough to take all of him in one hard thrust. Allie must have sensed his need, because even in her weakened state she reached for his belt buckle.

Oh, hell yes.

He helped her with the belt, then jerked free the button at his waist, his gut clenching in anticipation of finding his own release.

The pounding on her door grew louder, but Marc let the thumps and distant shouts fly to his mind's periphery. All he could think about was freeing himself from the confines of these damned pants . . . until the smoke detector split the air in a series of shrieks.

Only then did Marc lift his head and focus long enough to hear someone from the hall shout, "Fire!"

Chapter 6

"It's a miracle nobody was hurt."

Allie frowned at the snowy layer of fire extinguisher foam coating the surface of Regale's double bed. Thank God the flames hadn't spread beyond this room, or the *Belle*'s wooden decks could have caught like a tinderbox. Amazingly, the damage was contained to one ruined comforter and a few smudges of smoke staining the ceiling.

They were lucky.

Too bad no one else saw it that way.

"What rotten luck," Nick said from the hallway, still clenching the handle of the cherry red fire extinguisher.

Marc ran a shaky hand through his hair and studied Regale, who leaned against the wall by the open window, both arms folded over his barrel chest. Allie noticed from her position near the bathroom door that the hair on Chef's forearms was singed off, his only injury—remarkable, considering he'd awoken in a burning bed. The man could have been flambéed like the Steak Diane that had made him famous.

Talk about tragic irony.

"You sure you weren't smoking?" Marc demanded. "Because your story doesn't make a lick of sense."

Allie tensed, bracing herself for an angry tirade about "the captain's squeeze," and how Marc should have been doing his job instead of *her*, but it never came. Regale didn't mention Allie's bathrobe, nor did he criticize Marc's loose waves, tangled from her fingers, or the hastily buttoned jacket he'd used to conceal the enormous bulge in his trousers.

In fact, Chef didn't say anything at all.

He flicked nervous glances in Allie's direction but couldn't hold her gaze. Gone were the disdainful stares and the intimidating set of his shoulders. He lowered his forehead like a dog who'd been kicked by its master, afraid of another blow.

That could only mean one thing.

Chef thought she'd done this to him—burned him in his bed. How could he consider her capable of such cruelty? It was even more insulting than his belief that she'd earned this job on her back.

Allie could almost hear her sister's voice gloating, *I'll bet he won't mess with you now*, but this wasn't the kind of respect she'd wanted from Regale, the kind born of fear.

Chef glowered at the carpeted floor when he finally said, "I don't smoke."

"Well, beds don't light themselves on fire," Marc argued.

"I'm tellin' you," Regale ground out, regaining a hint of his former sauce, "I took a break to lie down and check e-mail on my cell phone. I dozed off. When I woke up, the goddamned bed was on fire."

"But that doesn't add up," Marc said.

"Doesn't it?" Regale scoffed and threw a glance at Allie. "The math seems simple enough to me."

Marc chewed his bottom lip and stared at the bed, no doubt mentally calculating *the math*. One voodoo priestess + one vengeful hex = Roasted Filet of Chef.

Allie hoped he wouldn't buy into Regale's paranoia, but her sinking heart told her that's exactly what he was doing. He couldn't help it. His family had ingrained superstition into him as permanently as burning a brand on his soul.

Darn it, she and Marc should be making love right now, starting a very different kind of fire. But judging by the way he dodged her gaze, she'd have to settle for one orgasm. Not that she was ungrateful—she'd never climaxed so hard in her life. The problem was, only ten minutes had passed, and already she wanted more.

So much more.

If her toes weren't still half curled in ecstasy, she'd cry.

"Well," Marc said with a sigh, "let's get it cleaned up in here so Chef can use his room tonight."

Regale pushed both palms forward. "Whoa, there. I'm not staying."

"*What?*" Marc froze in place.

"I'm getting off at the next port," Regale said. "I'll take a cab to the nearest airport and catch a flight home."

"No, no, no," Marc uttered, shaking his head in denial. "You can't do this to me."

"I'm sorry, but I can't stay here. Not with . . ." Chef looked at Allie and back down at the floor just as quickly in a silent message. *It's her or it's me.*

Allie's heavy heart sank another inch. This was what she'd hoped to avoid—forcing Marc to choose between her and his duty to the *Belle*.

Marc scrubbed a hand over his face, staring at the bed as if his dreams had burned along with the linens, clearly conflicted even though the choice was obvious. He had to do whatever it took to keep Chef on board. Nick seemed to know it, too. He furrowed his brow at his older brother as if to will the decision into him.

The seconds ticked by in silence until Allie couldn't take it any longer.

"You know what?" she said, faking her best chipper voice. "I heard Ella-Claire mention she's shorthanded at the purser's desk." Allie hugged herself with robe-covered arms to keep her disappointment trapped inside. Nobody needed to know how much this hurt. "We've got a fantastic galley crew. I'm sure they can get along without me if I leave recipes for them to follow."

Marc shook his head and chanced a peek at her from the corner of one eye. "Allie, you don't have to—"

"That's a great idea," Nick interrupted tightly, glaring at his brother.

Regale gave a reluctant nod, clearly preferring Allie left the boat altogether, but too chickenshit to say so. "We might be able to make that work."

"But your recipes," Marc said. "You sure you want to share them?"

Allie offered a smile. "It's not the recipe that matters, baby. It's the love I put into my desserts. I'm not afraid of anyone stealing my thunder."

"If you're sure . . ." Marc was giving her one last

chance to back out, but Allie saw the relief in his posture and in the gradual unclenching of his jaw.

"Sure as I'm standing here"—she released a shaky
laugh—"in my bathrobe." Hooking a thumb toward
her suite, she added, "I'd better get dressed and head
downstairs."

Then she turned and left without another glance in
Marc's direction, saving him the trouble of having to
placate her—and from seeing the hurt in her eyes.

An hour later, after she'd styled her hair to perfection
and spackled on enough makeup to pass for a televan-
gelist's wife, she strode to the head desk with her chin
tipped and her shoulders squared. She might feel three
feet tall, but she projected the confidence of a woman
who had the world on a leash.

Fake it until you make it, and all that.

When she approached the desk, she waved at Alex
and Ella-Claire, both huddled together over a stack of
paperwork. The youngest Dumont, a lanky teenage
boy whose name she couldn't recall, stood by sipping
a soda. He quirked a crooked grin, then ogled Allie's
boobs and mumbled something about Cheez-Its.

Strange kid.

"Hel-*lo*," the boy said, waggling his brows and eating her up with his eyes like a prepubescent Don Juan.
"I'm Jackson."

"But we call him Worm," Alex interjected. He ruffled
his little brother's hair. "Worm, this nice lady is Allie
Mauvais." He put extra emphasis on her last name, and
it didn't take long for the message to sink in. Worm's
brows quit waggling and shot up his forehead.

"Aw, balls," the boy swore, snapping his fingers in disappointment. "That just ain't right. I was in love for a few seconds."

Allie rolled her eyes. A true Dumont, that one. "Welcome to my world, kid."

"Did you really spark that dude in his bed?" Worm asked with a twinkle of admiration in his eyes.

"No," Allie said. "I'd never do anything like that." She fired a look at Ella-Claire to make her point, hurt that the woman had been so quick to jump on the blame-the-Mauvais bandwagon earlier that morning. She'd thought they were allies.

Ella blushed and studied her fingernails.

"I think it's cool," Worm said. "Wish I could do stuff like that. The asshole yelled at me last night while I was busing tables. Someone should tell him to say it, not spray it."

"I didn't . . ." Allie began, and then gave up the fight. There was no point in trying to get a Dumont to listen to reason. She plastered on that familiar fake smile and turned to Alex and Ella-Claire. "Never mind. Now that I'm out of the galley, I'm all yours. What can I do to help?"

The two folded their arms on the counter in a mirrored pose, shoulders barely touching. Their heads tilted toward each other in a way that caught Allie's attention. To the casual observer, the pair's body language might not have tripped an alarm, but to someone like Allie who studied minor cues for a hobby, that one action spoke volumes.

At the very least, they were close friends, but if the covert glances Alex kept sliding at Ella were any indication, he wanted more. As much as Allie enjoyed helping lovers find a match, she hoped Alex kept it in his pants. She liked Alex, and she'd hate to see him turned from a stallion to a gelding by his own brother.

"I'm sorry about all this, Allie." Ella-Claire fidgeted with a sliver frog pendant around her neck, smoothing a thumb over the amphibian's single emerald eye. "Marc told me you took this job to help promote your bakery, and now you can't do that."

Allie softened at the apology. She'd never been able to stay angry for long. "Not going to lie," she said, tucking both hands in her back pockets, "I'd rather be making pastries, but I can be a team player. Where do you need me?"

Alex's twin, Nick, approached the desk and jumped into the conversation. "I can use you in the casino." He tossed a gallon-sized Ziploc baggie onto the counter, revealing a rectangle of charred plastic sealed inside.

Allie grimaced at the remains. "What's that?"

"Chef's cell phone." Nick snorted in disdain. "We have to replace it, and of course he wants an upgrade for the trouble."

Allie scrutinized the half-melted device. If she tilted her head, she could see how it had once been a cell phone. "Hold on," she said to Nick. "You put out the fire pretty quickly, right?"

Nick nodded. "Only because I was in the hallway when it broke out."

"But look." Allie lifted the baggie and turned it over in her hands, studying the rippled screen. "This thing burned a lot longer than the bed did. I'll bet this is what started the fire."

The group shared a dubious glance before Nick threw her a bone. "Maybe. I guess."

"Never heard of a cell phone starting a fire," Alex added.

But it could happen—Allie didn't care what anyone said. Holding the phone toward Nick, she asked, "Can I have this? When we stop in Natchez I want to have someone look at it."

"Knock yourself out." Nick backed toward the lobby and motioned for her to follow. He glanced at her chest and a grin crossed his mouth. "Any chance I can get you to unbutton that shirt a little? It'd be great for business, especially if I put you behind one of the blackjack tables. My gamblers won't be able to count their own cards."

She gave him an answer in the form of a glare.

"Hey, no pressure," he said, lifting both hands like a robbery victim. "But you did say you were a team player. . . ."

Allie shook her head at him. Why couldn't it be Marc who thumbed his nose at the supposed curse? "I'm not feeling *that* generous."

While they crossed the lobby and made their way to the second floor, Nick snuck his usual glances at her rear end—clearly, he was an ass man—but he kept the come-on lines to himself. Which stuck her as odd.

"Not that I'm complaining," Allie said as they approached the casino, "but why aren't you hitting on me?"

"Ah." Nick nodded sagely as if preparing to discuss foreign policy instead of pick-up lines. "Despite what you might've heard, we Dumonts aren't total dogs. We never share women." After biting his lip, he corrected, "Except for the jazz singer, but that was an accident."

Allie cast him a skeptical look. To hear him tell it, you'd think they'd all tripped and landed inside the woman. "So I'm off-limits because . . ."

"Because you're Marc's," he said simply, opening the door for her.

Allie's heart squeezed as she preceded Nick into the gaming room. She wished she were as unaffected by his statement as she pretended to be. On the inside, she wanted more than anything to be Marc's girl—to warm his bed at night and feel the stubble of his jaw tickling her bare shoulder each morning.

To be the only woman who lit his fire . . .

She had her work cut out for her, though. Her sister had been right about one thing: the Dumonts had a raging case of emotional ADHD. They never stayed with one lover long enough to make it count.

Before long, the music of slot machine payouts stifled her thoughts, and Allie paused inside the casino to let her eyes adjust to the sensation overload. Flashing screens and twinkling lights competed for her attention, set against rows of gaming tables and roulette wheels. Quick-footed waitresses dodged stools to deliver drinks to sunglasses-wearing professionals and bucket-toting grannies alike. The scents of metal coins and excitement hung in the air along with the ring of electronic chimes, a few shouts of victory, and even more groans of defeat.

Yet despite the distractions filling the room, Allie's eyes found a lone white captain's jacket and fastened on Marc like a compass needle pointing north, drawn by an irresistible force of magnetism. She felt that pull deep inside and ordered her feet to remain rooted to the carpet.

Marc had removed his hat and let his chestnut waves hang loose against his shoulders, indulging in a moment of laughter with his pawpaw as they leaned against the bar that stretched along the back wall. The old man belted back a swig of amber-colored liquid while Marc spoke animatedly, talking with his hands.

Those hands.

Her body buzzed hot with the memory of Marc's touch. Heavens, the man could do things with his hands that should be illegal. If she lived ten lifetimes, she'd never forget the tease of his fingertips between her thighs, his warm breath in her ear asking, *Feel anything, sugar?*

Oh, yeah.

She'd felt it then and she felt it now. He possessed a magic more real than any curse, practically ruining her for all other men without ever moving past third base.

Gracious, she was going to get her heart broken. But knowing Marc, it would be worth it.

As if she'd called to him, Marc halted his conversation and met her gaze from across the room. His smile fell, his dark eyes growing stormy by slow degrees as he held her captive with nothing but a look. The intensity between them told her he wanted to pick up where they'd left off, but the firm line of his mouth warned he'd try his damnedest to resist. He stared her down for several heartbeats until Nick waved a hand in front of Allie's face and broke the connection.

"Earth to Allie," Nick said, snapping his fingers in front of her nose.

She blinked a few times and faced him. "Sorry. What?"

"Ever worked in a casino before?"

"No."

"Then I don't suppose you've got a gaming license." He pursed his lips as if brainstorming a way around that little roadblock, but he must have decided it wasn't worth the risk. With a small sigh he concluded, "Guess you can serve drinks."

The idea of slinging booze for the next two weeks made Allie's shoulders sag an inch. This wasn't how she'd pictured her trip. She was supposed to be in the galley alongside her professional idol, forming connections and wowing guests with her mouthwatering creations.

So much for that.

She saw Nick's sigh and raised him a groan. "Fine. Just tell me what to do."

He picked out a cocktail waitress in the crowd, a young brunette with fuchsia-painted lips and acrylic nails to match. "That's Christy, the head waitress. She'll assign you a zone; then you circulate it and keep a drink in everyone's hand. Alcohol tends to loosen the wallet, you know?"

"I bet," she said. "No pun intended."

"It's pretty easy. All the drinks are free, and everyone's carded at the door, so you don't have to worry about checking IDs." Nick gestured toward the bartender. "At the end of each day, split your tips with the barkeep. And don't stiff him. He'll mix your orders faster if you play by the rules."

Pay the drink pimp or suffer the consequences. "Got it."

"Once we stop in Natchez," Nick said, "we'll begin the Texas Hold'em tourney. Same rules apply, but don't be surprised if the pros refuse liquor."

"Because they'll want to keep a clear head."

"Exactly."

"But I'll be able to get off the boat for a while, right?" she asked. "I want to visit the fire department and have them inspect Regale's phone."

Nick offered a condescending grin, stopping just short of patting her on the head. "Sure thing. You just do what you gotta do."

Allie scowled at him, half wishing she could cast spells, then stalked off toward the bar. Once there, she met Christy, who outfitted her with a waist apron, serving tray, and an order pad. The girl had horrible taste in lipstick, but a generous smile that made Allie like her immediately.

"You take the nickel slots," Christy said, pointing to a dimly lit portion of the casino near the side wall. "It's the worst zone for tips, but I rotate the waitstaff to keep it fair. Tomorrow I'll give you the high-dollar blackjack tables." She grinned and nudged Allie with her pencil eraser. "Those are the big tippers."

Allie thanked her, trying to catch a bit of the woman's infectious enthusiasm, but without success. She tucked the round tray beneath one arm and strode toward the nickel-plunking, slot-pulling seniors. But just as she passed the first craps table, a hand reached out and snagged her by the wrist.

Allie paused in front of a man so pretty she had to fight the urge to flip her hair and bat her lashes. He was the living spit of that actor from the big vampire franchise. Allie squinted at his face to see if he sparkled, feeling a mixture of disappointment and stupidity when he didn't.

"Need somethin' to drink?" she asked him. *A vial of blood, maybe?*

He shook his head while his gaze took a leisurely stroll up and down the length of her body. Then he held out one hand. "I need a beautiful woman to kiss my dice. How about it?" The dance of amusement in his eyes led her to believe he wasn't referring to the white tossers.

Allie decided to give him the benefit of the doubt and play it friendly. "No way, baby. I don't know where your dice have been."

"Touché," he said, lifting his palm. "How about a blow, then?" He laughed in an easy, rolling chortle that saved him from being whacked upside the head with her serving tray.

Allie bent at the knees and blew on his dice, then shook her head teasingly. "And you didn't even buy me dinner."

"I can fix that," he said, tossing his dice without bothering to see what he'd rolled. "We could sneak off for a few hours when we stop in Natchez. What do you say?"

The question caught her off guard. If he'd asked last month, she might have said yes. He had a witty edge about him that she liked. But unfortunately for the both of them, a pair of soft lips and wicked hands had given her heart a case of tunnel vision. There was only one man on her mind now, and he was approaching from the bar, glaring at the back of the gambler's head hard enough to drill a hole into his brain.

"Afternoon," Marc greeted the man while pressing a possessive hand to Allie's lower back. "You'll have to excuse us. I need a word with Miss Mauvais." It wasn't a request, and he didn't seek the other man's permission.

With a stiff nod good-bye, Marc steered Allie away from the craps table. He led her behind the bar into the storage room, then kicked aside the doorstop and let the oak door swish shut.

Allie didn't know what to expect. Marc seemed angry with her, and the tension between them made the small storage space shrink by a few square feet. But she stood her ground, refusing to back against a row of beer kegs like her feet wanted.

One hand on her hip, she lifted her face to his and tried to ignore the intoxicating scents of aftershave and raw sex appeal that clung to the collar of Marc's dress shirt. If the Secret Service could bottle that smell, they'd scramble minds without lifting a finger.

Marc's mood shifted from irate to something resembling unease. He loosened the tie knotted at his throat. "Listen, Allie," he began, his gaze never fully connecting with hers. "We need to talk about what happened."

A cold weight settled in Allie's stomach. She knew where this was going. He was giving her the brush-off.

"When I came to your suite," Marc said, "it wasn't to take advantage of you. I didn't mean for anything to happen, and I'm—"

"Stop." Allie dropped her serving tray and whipped a finger in front of his nose. "Don't you dare say you're sorry!"

Immediately, he started backpedaling. "Now, don't go gettin' upset. It's not like that."

"Then what *is* it like?" she demanded.

"It's just . . . I only . . . We didn't . . ." He sputtered and stammered until he finally hung his head and muttered, "Shit. This isn't going how I planned."

Allie folded her arms. "Please tell me this isn't about some curse."

"Of course it's not. You know I don't believe in that mess."

But that was the problem—deep down in the recesses of Marc's subconscious mind, he did believe in that mess. She had to show him nothing catastrophic would happen if he let himself go. She released her frustration and stepped toward Marc, stopping when the tips of her breasts brushed his jacket lapels. His gaze widened and darted to the points of contact, but he made no move to separate himself.

That was a good sign. At least he wasn't afraid to touch her.

"Listen, baby," she said as she ran a finger down the length of his tie, "you didn't take advantage of me."

Marc swallowed hard enough to shift his Adam's apple. "Still, I—"

"Let me finish." Allie skimmed a thumb over his lips, choking back a surge of desire when his mouth parted to release a hot breath. "I asked you to kiss me, remember?"

He nodded slowly and licked his lips as if he could taste her there.

"And if you came to my room to make me feel better . . ." Allie straightened his tie and walked her fingers up the side of his neck to brush back his hair. "Well, it worked." She inched closer, near enough to feel the gradual thickening of his arousal pressed to her belly. Standing on tiptoe, she whispered against the edge of his jaw, "You made me feel *real* good, Marc."

He groaned and grasped her hips.

"And nothing big happened."

"Except this." He pushed his erection against her while nuzzling her temple.

"Except that," she agreed. She reached down and used a fingernail to trace the length of him. He hardened fully by the time she finished one rotation, his grip on her body tight, his breathing choppy. "But that doesn't scare me. And when you're ready to face your fears," she murmured, "I want to make you feel real good, too."

"Damn, Allie," he swore, thrusting against her palm.

"But . . ." She stepped back and put a few cold inches of space between them. "Not until then."

The lust-filled look he gave her sent wet heat pooling between her thighs. "That ain't fair, sugar."

A grin tipped one corner of Allie's mouth. Who said she played fair? "When you're ready, you know where to find me."

She turned and bent over—nice and slow, of course—to pick up her tray, then sashayed out the door, leaving Marc with something spectacularly long and hard to think about.

Chapter 7

By sunset, Marc had a residual cramp in his gut and balls the size of coconuts. If it was possible to die from sexual frustration, he'd be rocking a toe tag before dawn. He could barely walk upright as he climbed the stairs to the captain's suite, which of course was all the way on the top level.

Allie had damn near crippled him.

As if fantasizing about her for the past decade weren't enough, now his brain wouldn't stop refreshing his memory with the taste of Allie's throat, the feel of her silken heat pulsing around his fingers, the tickle of her nails teasing his johnson . . .

Mercy.

Thinking about it tugged the knot in his groin. He hunched over and gripped the handrail, then hauled himself to his quarters. It was going to be an early night for him. He'd arranged for someone else to pilot the *Belle* so he could grab a hot shower and a little relief. With any luck he'd be in bed by nine.

Lord, when had he become such a geezer?

He sank onto the bed and kicked off his shoes.

Checking his watch, he noted that Allie's shift should be over soon. Then she'd be free for the rest of the night—free to make him feel "real good."

When you're ready, you know where to find me.

Marc groaned and leaned over, cradling his head between both palms. His body was ready, no doubt about that, but the rest of him was slow on the uptake.

He wasn't sure what held him back. He'd always claimed he didn't believe in magic or hexes or any of that shit . . . but at the same time, he couldn't deny that some wonky stuff had happened since Allie reentered his life. She'd crossed his path and everything had started going south. Hell, right after he'd given her an orgasm, the bed next door had spontaneously combusted. Marc didn't know if he was cursed, but either way, something freaky was going on, and he couldn't ignore the signs.

But he wanted to. More than he wanted to breathe.

His cell phone buzzed from inside his breast pocket. He checked the screen and saw *Ella-Claire calling*.

"Hey," he said. "I was about to get in the shower. What's up?"

"We need you in the galley!" Ella's voice squeaked in panic. "It's an emergency!"

Marc sat bolt upright. "Another fire?"

"No, nothing like that," she said. "Chef won't serve dinner, and the guests are starting to complain."

"Son of a bitch." Of course the guests were pissed—supper should've been on the table an hour ago. "I'll be right down."

So much for finding relief tonight.

Marc put on his shoes, buttoned his jacket, and

headed downstairs, a surge of adrenaline propelling his aching limbs into a jog. He purposely avoided both dining rooms and entered the galley from the back door.

What he found in there could only be described as chaos.

Two dozen crew members ran circles around one another as they assembled plates of whipped potatoes and seasoned green beans. Chef hunched over the industrial-sized stove, sautéing rock shrimp and filling the air with savory steam. At first, Marc assumed they'd solved the problem, but then Chef sampled a shrimp and hollered a cuss. He threw his steel pan into the sink, where it clanked loudly and splattered the back wall with sauce.

"Damn it all to hell!" Chef yelled, then jabbed a finger at his staff. "Get me some more shrimp!" His workers collectively flinched. When they didn't move fast enough for him, he bellowed, "Get off your worthless asses and fetch my goddamned shrimp!"

The unfortunate bastards nearest to Chef wiped the spittle off their faces and scurried to the refrigerator to fulfill his request.

"What's the holdup?" Marc asked, gently nudging aside the crew to join Regale at the stove. He pointed toward the main dining room. "They're starving out there."

Regale always looked like he was two heartbeats away from an aneurism, but now his face turned maroon and his jaw clenched hard enough to break.

"What's the holdup?" Regale pointed to the pan he'd just chucked away. "My bourbon Creole lemon sauce, that's what." He jutted his chin toward the sink. "Go on. Try it."

Mentally rolling his eyes at the overgrown diva, Marc swiped a finger along the edge of Chef's discarded pan and brought it to his mouth. It tasted sour, like Chef had left it out too long and let it spoil.

"It's rancid," Regale said.

"So make a different sauce." Marc wondered how the idiot had managed to keep a restaurant franchise afloat. "You can't keep folks waiting all night for their supper."

Regale sucked a long breath through his nostrils while his face deepened to the shade of an eggplant. "I *did* make a different sauce. That was the tenth batch! Everything turns out rancid, every single time!"

"Did you check your ingredients?" Marc asked.

"What kind of fucking moron do you take me for?"

Marc elected not to answer that question, but he assumed Chef meant *yes*. "Then I don't know what to tell you. Sauté 'em in butter. You can't screw that up."

"Screw it up?" Chef drew back as if Marc had slapped him. "Are you implying this is *my* fault?"

Marc's patience snapped. "Who else's fault would it be?"

"I think we both know." Regale closed in on Marc until they were toe to toe. "One of us just doesn't want to admit it."

"One of us," Marc uttered, refusing to back down, "has no friggin' idea what you're talking about."

Regale's upper lip curled in loathing. "I'm talking about the back-swamp voodoo whore you keep around to polish your knob."

Marc heard a *pop* inside his brain like a blown fuse. Without thinking, he fisted Regale's shirt and slammed him into the stainless steel refrigerator. "You'd better shut the hole in your face before I shut it for you."

But he forgot Regale was built like a bull.

The man used one powerful arm to shove Marc away and the other to coldcock him in the eye. Marc's head snapped back as sparks of pain exploded behind his lid. He recovered quickly and delivered a left hook to Chef's kidney and a right jab to the gut.

It barely fazed Regale.

He growled and charged Marc, leaning down like an offensive lineman about to flatten him. Marc braced for impact, but just as their bodies connected, Regale lost his footing in a puddle of his own bourbon sauce and went down hard, knocking his forehead on the floor.

He lay there, out cold.

Good. Now the bastard couldn't run his dirty mouth.

Marc took a deep breath and glanced around the room at Chef's wide-eyed staffers. Since there was no chance of maintaining his professionalism after that display, he issued a command.

"Fry up some shrimp and serve it with something— anything—bottled cocktail sauce if you have to. I want dinner out there in fifteen minutes flat."

While the staff jumped into action, Marc dragged Chef's unconscious body out of the way and made a call to the pilothouse.

"Hey," Marc said when his man picked up. "Where's the nearest port?"

"Just passed one about a mile back," came the response. "Why'd you ask?"

"Turn the *Belle* around," Marc ordered. "We're dropping a passenger."

Marc tipped back a can of Coke, wishing it were a shot of Crown Royal, and pressed a bag of frozen peas to his eye. He winced when the contents shifted against his swollen flesh. He'd have one hell of a shiner in the morning, but it would be worth it. Already, he felt twenty pounds lighter with Regale off the boat. The chef had taken all his toxicity with him when the paramedics had wheeled him down the ramp and into the darkness.

Now there was the incidental matter of who would cook their meals.

"Gimme some of that, boy." Nodding at the bottle of Crown Royal, Pawpaw slid his tumbler across the table, and Marc used his free hand to pour two fingers of whiskey before sliding it back.

The executive bar had been deserted anyway, so he'd closed it down for an emergency family meeting. Nicky and Alex sat at opposite ends of the table, wearing the same worried expression, no beer bottles in hand.

Bad sign.

"Grab a Sam Adams and let's figure this out," Marc said to his twin brothers. When neither of them made a move for the cooler, he tipped his frozen peas in that direction. "That's an order from your captain."

Alex threw him a sour look and reached into the cooler for two beers, then handed one to Nick, who unscrewed the top and took a deep pull. He toasted Marc with his bottle. "You run a tight ship, Cap'n."

Marc knew it was a sarcastic jab, but he let it go. "Damn straight. I didn't take shit from Regale and I won't take it from you, so don't start." Okay, maybe he didn't let it go. But his blood was still boiling from the fight, and now wasn't the time to needle him.

"I still can't believe you cleaned his clock," Nick said. "That man was our bread and butter."

"That man was an unreliable dictator." Marc sucked in a mouthful of cola, and it slid down the wrong pipe. He coughed and swiped a hand over his mouth. "The guests won't be sorry to hear he's gone. Not after he held them hostage for an hour with no supper."

"You know who *else* should be gone?" Pawpaw said, pointing his tumbler toward the casino.

"Don't start." Marc wasn't in the mood to hear it. God help him once word spread among the crew that he and Regale had come to blows over Allie. Pawpaw would go apeshit. "She's got nothing to do with this."

It wasn't the truth, but he didn't much care.

"I second that," Nick said. "If anything, she's good luck. You should've seen her today. Every time she blew on someone's dice, they rolled a seven. The guys are nuts about her."

Marc's brows lowered. Just how many pairs of dice had there been? "Now that Regale's gone, I want her back in the galley doing what I hired her to do," he grumbled. "First thing." Alex snickered and Marc kicked him under the table. "I mean it."

"Aye-aye, Cap." Alex took a swig of beer, but he still had a smug smile on his lips.

Ella-Claire joined them and dragged over a chair to sit beside Alex. "Sorry I'm late." She grabbed Alex's beer, took a leisurely sip, and handed it back as if it were the most natural thing in the world to share a drink with him.

What was up with that?

He knew the two were buddies, but Marc didn't want Ella's mouth touching Alex's—not even by way of a beer bottle. Marc got up from the table and grabbed a Sam Adams from the cooler, then handed it to his sister. "Here, hon," he said, untwisting the top for her. "You don't want to go drinking after any of my brothers."

Alex scowled, first at Marc, then at the lip of his beer bottle. "You sayin' I have cooties?"

"Of course you do," Ella said with a friendly shoulder bump. "But they're sweet cooties." Just as Marc resolved to keep an eye on those two, Ella said something that shut down his mind to cohesive thought. "By the way, I took the liberty of calling Beau."

The men at the table drew a collective breath, and all eyes shifted to Marc. It took him a minute to find his voice. When it resurfaced, he sounded eerily calm despite the rush of anger in his veins. "Why would you do that?"

Ella rolled her eyes as if the answer should be obvious. "Because he practically cut his teeth in that galley. Didn't you tell me he started working in the kitchen before he could say his ABC's?"

Marc couldn't deny it. His big brother had always been a clever bastard and that, combined with his gargantuan size, meant any problem he couldn't solve with his brain had been solved with his fists. As kids, Beau had lorded it over him until Marc grew big enough to push back. They'd been at each other's throats ever since.

"No," Marc said. "He won't take orders. He's worse than Regale."

"He's family," Ella pressed. "And he's changed."

Marc cocked his head to one side and gave her a skeptical look.

"Really," she swore, holding up a hand in oath. "I don't know where he's been for the last couple of years, but he sounds like a new man." She sipped her beer, then lifted it toward Marc. "You know what he said when I told him you're captain now?"

Marc laughed without humor. "He probably asked if our liability insurance is paid up."

"He said *It's about flippin' time*."

"*Flippin'*?" Marc asked in disbelief.

"Okay, that's not the actual word he used, but still," Ella said. "He's happy for you."

Marc doubted that. "Doesn't matter. He's not a gourmet."

"His food is just as good . . ." Alex pointed out.

Nick added, "He works at half the salary."

"And he can meet us in N*aaaa*tch-ez," Ella sang, flashing an encouraging smile.

Marc tossed his frozen peas onto the table and wondered if it was too late to rehire Regale. Kicking a man's ass tended to burn bridges, but in this case it might be worth trying to get him back.

"Hire the boy," Pawpaw hollered, "and be done with it!" Then he muttered under his breath, "You'll bring a Mauvais on board, but not your own kin. It ain't right."

"Jesus, fine. Just do it." Marc reached for the bottle of whiskey but changed his mind. Liquor wouldn't cure what ailed him. Nothing would.

This trip was a bona fide disaster.

Allie shook her hips to the beat of "I Feel Lucky," singing along with Mary Chapin Carpenter from the iPod docking station in the galley. Regale had never allowed music in his kitchen, but this wasn't his kitchen anymore.

"I feel luck*yyyyyyyyy*, yeah!"

She whistled the rest of the song as she drizzled cream cheese icing over a batch of newly cooled breakfast Danish. Nobody else sang with her, but the galley staff had a collective spring in their step, a lightness that came from a total liberation from tyranny. Maybe Allie should play "Ding Dong! The Witch Is Dead." They'd probably dance a jig to that.

But it wasn't only Chef's absence that had Allie smiling. The *Belle* had finally docked in Natchez, and the passengers would soon disembark for a day of historic plantation tours and shopping—which meant the kitchen could operate on half staff.

Luxurious as the *Belle* was, Allie's feet itched for the firmness of solid ground. A flowery sundress and a pair of strappy sandals beckoned from her suite upstairs, and she couldn't wait to get out of this uniform and into something pretty.

After shuttling the Danish into the main dining room, she boxed up a dozen to take to the fire station and clocked out for the day.

Two hours later, Allie tucked the remains of Regale's melted cell phone inside her handbag, grabbed her box of Danish, and made her way onto the main deck, where Marc and his family lined the exit ramp to remind guests of the departure time and wish them a pleasant day. She waited for the passengers to clear out before approaching the ramp.

Marc shielded his face from the low morning sun, looking dashing as ever in his white captain's uniform. It wasn't until he turned to walk back inside that Allie noticed someone had blackened his eye—and done a thorough job of it. His upper lid was swollen half shut, the skin beneath it puffy and stained purple. His gaze widened when he noticed her, and for an instant, she thought she saw a spark there, excitement mingled with desire. But he snuffed it out just as quickly.

"What happened?" she asked him, pointing to her own face.

He grumbled to himself and tugged open the door to the side lobby, then left without another word. His pawpaw gave her the stink eye and followed.

Nick chuckled while taking a moment to appreciate the plunging neckline of her sundress. "Nothing he didn't deserve."

"Yeah," Alex added. "But you should see the other guy."

Allie started to ask about "the other guy," but decided she didn't want to hear any more. If Marc was going to ignore her, let him stay behind and stew all by himself. But before she had a chance to say so, Alex and Nick's heads swiveled in perfect synchronization toward the bow ramp. She glanced over her shoulder to see what had drawn their attention.

It was a striking young woman—no surprise there—

with hair the color of ripe strawberries and a smile that radiated easy sex. She wore a halter top and matching booty shorts paired with five-inch screw-me pumps. Allie wanted to ask how many pole tricks the girl could do, but Mama had raised her better than that. Instead, she darted a glance at Ella-Claire and raised an eyebrow.

"Can I help you?" Ella-Claire asked the girl.

"Yeah, I'm Nora." The woman popped her gum and nodded toward the pilothouse. "Marc's girlfriend."

Funny how two seemingly harmless, intangible words had the power to suck all the oxygen from Allie's lungs. Her lips parted, but she couldn't breathe through them.

Marc had a girlfriend?

He'd neglected to mention that small detail when he was lying on top of Allie with his fingers inside her. As the moments ticked by, the shock began to wear off, replaced by hurt. Allie thought she'd made progress with Marc—she believed they were friends. Was she fooling herself the whole time? Had she only seen what she'd wanted to see?

Nick and Alex exchanged a concerned glance, the kind men shared when one of their comrades was in trouble. Nick smiled and indicated the row of rocking chairs lining the side deck. "I can't let you inside, hon," he said. "But if you have a seat, I'll call Marc down to meet you."

Nora pouted her overly glossed lips but didn't argue. She strutted to the nearest rocker and sat in it sideways, slinging her bare legs over the arm of the chair.

Classy.

Allie told herself she'd dodged a bullet—any man

who had such lousy taste in girlfriends wasn't worth having. But there was no denying the slow ache opening up inside her like a sinkhole. If she stood there staring at Nora's infinite legs any longer, Allie might cave in on herself. She tightened her grip on the box between her hands and ordered her feet to move toward the metal ramp.

"Allie, wait," Ella-Claire called from behind. When she caught up, her blue eyes were full of sympathy. "I could use a break. Want some company?"

Girl time sounded perfect right now. Allie didn't trust herself to speak over the lump in her throat, so she nodded.

As she led the way down the ramp, she heard Marc's voice in the background, but she didn't turn around. She couldn't stand to watch him embrace another woman and lead her inside—and she especially couldn't think too hard about what the two of them would do once they were alone.

When had she fallen so hard? Allie figured Marc would break her heart; she just didn't expect it to happen so soon.

Once her sandals connected with pavement, she pushed Marc from her thoughts and scanned the road signs to orient herself. "We need Main Street," she told Ella.

"This way."

Ella seemed to know the lay of the land, and God bless her, she didn't say a word about what had happened aboard the *Belle*. They strolled through town at a leisurely pace, enjoying the gentle breeze on their shoulders as Ella filled the conversation with which movies she wanted to see next, and with which date. Turned out she'd been seeing a few different men, but none of them seriously.

Allie stopped at an intersection to wait for the crossing signal. "So there's nobody special?" she asked. "No one you like more than the others?"

The light turned green and Ella crossed, shaking her head and setting her ponytail into full swing. "Not really."

That wasn't a firm yes or a no. Allie's experience with matchmaking had taught her that *Not really* usually meant *Yes, kind of.* "My mama used to call that a liquid answer." She slid Ella an encouraging grin. "Sounds like you're not too sure."

Ella shrugged. She didn't say anything, but her hand darted to the frog pendant at her throat, and she worked it between her thumb and index finger. It was a nervous tell, sure as sunrise. Words lied, but body language didn't.

"That's a cute necklace," Allie said casually. "Where'd you get it?"

A reflexive smile curved Ella's lips. "Alex bought it for my birthday last year."

Bingo.

"It's an inside joke," Ella went on. "When we were kids, we used to sneak off to the creek to catch frogs. One day my mama found a toad in the washing machine. I must've left it in my pocket." Her smile widened at the memory. "It survived the washing, so Alex named it TIC, short for The Invincible Croaker. We put him in a shoebox and traded him back and forth for the summer—one week at my house, one week at his."

"Joint custody," Allie mused.

"Yeah," Ella said. "But he died in captivity." A wistful sigh escaped her lips, and she turned her gaze to a merchant's window as they passed. "I guess some things aren't meant to be caught and kept."

"Mmm," Allie agreed, then gave a nudge with her elbow. "Like Dumonts?"

A light flush stained Ella's cheeks. "You have to admit they don't have the best track record."

Allie thought back to Marc's surprise girlfriend, and the corners of her mouth turned down. "Ninety-nine years of lying, cheating, and running around? I'd say that's an understatement."

Ella shoved both hands in her pockets and peeked at Allie. "Do you really think they're cursed?"

The word *no* formed on Allie's lips, but she hesitated. Right now, some redheaded hoochie was wrapped around Marc like a horny squid. For all Allie knew, he had a different woman at each port. "They sure act like it."

After another block, they reached the fire department, and talk of curses and frogs turned to the science behind forensic investigations.

At first, the firemen shook their heads at Allie's request, but once they'd filled their bellies with her legendary Danish, they took Regale's cell phone and promised to call her in a few days with their findings. With a wave of thanks to her new admirers, Allie returned outside, where she and Ella made their way back down Main Street.

The temperature had ratcheted from warm to *whoa* in the last thirty minutes, so they kept to the shade and began looking for ways to stay cool. After browsing for antiques, they stopped at a hole-in-the-wall diner for lunch, then splurged on ice cream—a double scoop.

While they strolled along the river with their waffle cones in hand, Allie learned that Ella-Claire had secretly considered taking a job with a European cruise line, but decided against it when Marc's daddy had handed over the reins. When it came to her brother, Ella had a clear case of hero worship.

"Listen," Ella said when they'd come full circle and reached the dock. "I really like you, and I know my brother does, too. Don't give up on him yet."

Allie stared at the *Belle*'s vacant decks, seeing no sign of Marc or his girlfriend. Her heart pinched at the thought that the two might be holed up inside his quarters. "Thanks, baby. For you, the feeling's mutual." She licked a drip of ice cream from her wrist and frowned at the pilothouse. "But when it comes to your brother, I'm afraid he likes all the girls."

A deep male voice boomed with laughter. "Glad to see nothing's changed since I've been gone."

Allie spun around and came face-to-face—or rather face-to-chest—with a gray T-shirt stretched tight over the largest set of pecs she'd ever witnessed outside a WWF ring. She craned her neck skyward and recognized a familiar pair of green eyes smiling down at her from beneath a thatch of short auburn hair.

Merde.

The last time she'd seen this man, he'd left her sister holding the bag for two misdemeanors . . . and broken her heart. But that was on graduation night. No one had seen hide or hair of him since—and he was hard to miss.

"Beau Dumont," she breathed. It sounded like an

accusation, which it was. What in the world was he doing here?

"Hey, Allie." He flashed that crooked smile, the same one that had brought her sister to her knees, probably in the literal sense. "You're as pretty as ever, darlin'."

"And you've grown." Which she hadn't thought was possible. "Where've you been?"

Beau lifted one massive shoulder and ran a meaty hand over his buzz cut. "Joined the marines. They kept me fed."

And how.

"What's new with Dev?" Though he kept a hold on his lazy smile, Beau folded his arms protectively across his chest and held his breath while waiting for her answer.

So Allie made him wait a few more beats. "She's meaner than a sack full of rattlers, thanks to you."

That wiped the grin off his face.

"Uh, Allie," Ella-Claire said. "Meet our new head cook."

Allie couldn't help laughing. She wondered what Devyn would say when she discovered that Beau Dumont was not only back from the dead, but working in the *Belle*'s galley. She'd probably ask Allie to perform an "accidental" vasectomy with a dull butter knife.

"What's funny?" Beau asked, opening his arms to hug Ella-Claire.

Ella smiled up at him while wrapping her arms around his waist. "Allie's your pastry chef."

That slippery grin lifted one corner of Beau's mouth.

Keeping Ella tucked against his chest, he slung his other arm around Allie, then towed them both toward the boat ramp.

"Now, ain't that somethin'?" he said with pure sin in his voice. "I always wanted my very own pastry chef."

Chapter 8

Marc stood near the second-floor lounge window and watched Beau strut on board the *Belle* like he owned everything in his wake—including the two women squashed to his sides. Marc felt a headache pressing the walls of his temples, and he reminded himself to unclench his jaw. He'd have to jerk a knot in Beau's tail, and soon. The wily SOB had some nerve blowing into town and moving in on Marc's kid sister as well as his . . . well, *his Allie*.

He didn't know how else to label her.

Allie wasn't his girl, but he couldn't deny she was a lot more than an employee. He'd drifted into uncharted waters with her, someplace beyond simple lust but outside the boundaries of a relationship. They had no claim on each other, but damned if that meant he liked seeing her in another man's arms, least of all those of his asshole brother. Marc wanted Allie for himself, but he didn't *want* to want her.

It was fifty shades of fucked up.

Worse than that, she'd stolen his mojo, making it impossible for him to enjoy other women. When Nora had paid him a surprise visit that morning, he should have led the flame-haired vixen to his suite and released a week's worth of sexual tension.

But he couldn't do it.

The moment she'd thrown her arms around his neck, his body had rejected her like an old splinter. She'd felt all wrong pressed up against him, and she stank of stale cigarettes—something that had never bothered Marc before. Now it was a complete deal breaker. Nora didn't smell like sweet cinnamon. She didn't taste of clean honeydew.

Because she wasn't Allie.

"Up shit creek without a paddle," he muttered to himself.

He focused again on Beau, who'd just leaned down to take a bite of Ella-Claire's ice-cream cone. Cocky as ever. At least Ella had the good sense to give it to him afterward instead of sharing it. Allie glared at Beau as if warning him away from her ice cream, then ducked out from beneath his arm.

Good girl.

Marc grinned and turned away from the window. It was time for a little family reunion.

When he reached the galley, he found the door propped open by a twenty-pound canister of flour, so he paused a moment to gain his bearings.

In other words, to spy. No shame in that.

Beau was alone with Allie, but neither spoke as they busied themselves gathering ingredients for the evening meal. Despite the companionable silence in the kitchen, Marc sensed clear tension in their movements. Something in the wide berth they gave each other and the stiff set of their bodies reassured him that Beau hadn't succeeded in hooking Allie with that sticky "charm" of his.

Yet.

Beau had a way of wearing folks down. Marc knew firsthand. By way of introduction, Marc leaned against the doorjamb and folded his arms, then cleared his throat.

Allie glanced at him as a smile formed and simultaneously died on her lips. With a huff, she narrowed her mismatched eyes and turned her back on him, then flung her raven curls over one shoulder to rub it in. Marc suspected a certain redheaded waitress had put a burr in Allie's bra, but he kept mum on the subject and nodded a greeting at his big brother.

"Look what the cat dragged in," Marc said.

Beau's ugly mug split into a grin so wide it crinkled the tanned skin around his eyes. The reaction stunned Marc into a beat of silence. He'd seen a lot of smiles cross his brother's face—the *I'm faster than you*, the *I ate the last cookie*, and the ever-popular *I'm gonna pound on you when Dad's not looking*—but this one said *I'm glad you're here*.

That couldn't be right.

"Well, look at you." Beau wiped his hands on a dishtowel and scanned Marc from the bill of his white captain's hat to the tips of his polished black dress shoes. He shook his head in appreciation. "I don't know whether to hug your neck or salute you, little brother."

Neither of those options appealed to Marc. He extended his right hand, and Beau strode forward to shake it, his grasp firm but not overbearing. They pumped hands while sizing each other up. Beau appeared to have found four inches of height and twenty pounds of muscle while he'd been away. Marc wondered where his brother had been since he'd left the marines a couple years ago, but he didn't bother to ask. If Beau had wanted him to know, he'd have called or e-mailed.

Which he hadn't.

Finally the giant stepped back and nodded at Marc's black eye. "I believe you had a shiner the last time I saw you, too."

"Other eye," Marc said. "You're the one who'd given it to me."

Beau chuckled quietly to himself. "That's right. And you broke my nose."

Damn straight. That fight was the first time Marc had dished out more than he'd taken, disrupting the pecking order in their daddy's household for once. Marc grinned at the slight bend of his brother's nose.

"What were we even fighting about?" Beau asked.

Marc remembered like it was yesterday. Beau had been horsing around on the dock with his idiot friends and thought it would be fun to trash Marc's mama to score a few laughs. He'd said *Your mama's so broke, when she goes to KFC she's got to lick other people's fingers*. But his big brother hadn't talked any smack after that— kind of hard to do with blood gushing out of his nostrils. Every decent man knew better than to insult another guy's mother.

Besides, he and his mama weren't *that* poor.

Marc shrugged. "Don't remember."

"Probably something stupid," Beau said.

"Probably," Marc agreed.

A few beats passed in awkward silence before Beau changed the subject. "I talked to Daddy last month." He sniffed a laugh. "Is he really having another baby?"

"Yep," Marc said. "They're due around Christmas."

Beau stroked his jaw in disbelief, though Marc didn't see why he was surprised. This was par for the course when it came to their daddy. "When I left," Beau said, "Jack was still in training pants. I figured that'd be the last kid."

Jack? Marc furrowed his brow until understanding dawned. "Oh. We call him Worm. He's fourteen now—busing tables for the first time. I'll introduce you later."

"Appreciate that."

Allie made a noise of exasperation, standing on tiptoe to retrieve a stainless steel bowl beyond her reach. Just as Marc made a move to help her, Beau clopped over in two mammoth strides and plucked it from the shelf, then handed it over with a smile. Which she reciprocated with a bit too much warmth for Marc's liking.

His headache made a sudden reappearance. Before thinking better of it, he announced, "Miss Mauvais, I need a word with you in the hall."

She didn't reply. Instead, she ignored him and bent over to study a recipe card on the counter. Marc gave her a few seconds to acknowledge his request, and when she refused, he repeated himself more firmly. He wasn't about to let her disrespect his authority—not in front of Beau, who'd lead the crew into mutiny if given an inch.

But Allie only hummed an indistinct tune and sashayed to the pantry for a bin of confectioner's sugar. She didn't even spare a glance in his direction.

Marc gritted his teeth. If she thought he'd let this go, she was dead wrong.

"Allie," Beau said, resting an oversized hand on her shoulder. When she acknowledged *his* existence, Beau gave her a playful look and a squeeze. "The captain wants you. I think he needs to talk to you, too."

What an ass.

She huffed a sigh and threw down her bowl scraper, muttering to herself in Creole. Still refusing to meet Marc's gaze, she stalked across the galley and brushed past him into the hall.

Beau chuckled and began dicing a clove of garlic. "You must be losing your touch, little brother. They don't fall at your feet like they used to."

"Please," Marc said with a sneer. "Let's bring her sister on board and see how well you run your game."

That shut his piehole.

Marc followed Allie's trail of sweet perfume. When he didn't find her in the service hallway behind the galley, he continued to the utility stairwell and pulled open the door. There she was, stewing on the third step with both hands gripping her hips. She glared at him hard enough to melt his face, *Raiders of the Lost Ark* style.

"Well?" she demanded. "What do you have to say to me?"

Marc froze for a few beats. He'd only wanted to get her away from Beau, but he couldn't very well cop to that.

"Uh . . ." The only excuse he could pluck from his

foggy brain was, "You should be in uniform when you're on the clock. Especially when you're working in the galley. It's a hygiene thing."

He knew he'd screwed up, even before two lines appeared between her brows.

"Are you serious?" she asked sharply. "You dragged me out here to tell me to *change clothes*?"

"Now, don't go gettin' all—"

"Silly me," she ranted on. "'Cause I thought you might want to come clean about your girlfriend— maybe even apologize for using me and acting like a lying sack of pig innards!"

Marc pulled off his hat and hung his head in frustration. Whatever had been brewing between him and Allie, he could end it right here. All he had to do was let her believe the whopper Nora had told everyone when she'd snuck on the boat—that she was his steady girl. He knew Allie wasn't the type to pursue someone else's man. If she thought he was taken, she'd quit tempting him with her lush body and those exotic whiskey-and-gray eyes. Maybe he'd find a moment's peace then. But when he glanced up into those eyes, he saw pain shining there, and it hit him like a baseball to the chest.

Just like that, he broke.

"I don't have a girlfriend," he admitted.

Allie raised one skeptical brow. "But she said—"

"Nora lied."

"Why would she do that?"

"Stage-four clinger, I guess. We met in a bar last month and we had some fun. Nothing more than that."

He turned his hat over in his hands and took a seat on the step beside Allie's pretty little sandals. "Come on, you know me. The last time I had a real girlfriend was senior year." Because that was the only way the cheer captain would put out. "I don't do the whole 'girlfriend' thing."

While she processed that, Marc leaned back on his elbows and studied the slender curve of Allie's calves beneath the hem of that gauzy sundress. If he gazed upward and tilted his head at just the right angle, he could see the outline of her lacy French-cut undies. "Lord, sugar," he said. "You need to sit down before I start looking up your dress."

She laughed and finally relaxed, descending the stairs to take the spot next to him. She leaned forward to wrap both arms around her knees but sat near enough to fill his space with her heat. Curiously, she glanced at him over one shoulder. "Why is that, do you think?"

"Because you've got great legs," he told her. "I'd stare at 'em all day if you'd let me."

"No," she said, bumping him with her shoulder. "I'm not talking about my dress. I mean, why don't you 'do the whole girlfriend thing'?"

Marc shrugged and wondered if he should tell her the ugly truth. The reason he didn't do relationships was because there were only two possible outcomes when folks paired off—either they'd stay together until death, or they'd go their separate ways. And ninety-nine percent of the time, it was the latter, usually with a whole lot of tears and drama thrown into the mix. So why not be logical and avoid the hassle?

He decided to give it to her straight. Allie was a big girl—she could handle it. "Never works out anyway. Just makes sense to keep it casual."

She wrinkled her forehead. "I can see why you think that, given your family history. And I won't lie; dating can be painful. My last boyfriend moved up north for a job, and I spent the next week in bed with a gallon of fudge ripple."

Of their own volition, Marc's brows tugged down into a scowl. He didn't know Allie'd had a semiserious man in her life. He didn't like it, though he refused to ponder why he felt that way. "See? So what's the point if it never lasts?"

"The point is," she said, "you can't know if someone's a good fit until you try. As long as you keep nipping every relationship in the bud, you'll never smell the rose."

Marc's lips twitched in a grin. "Never been a fan of roses."

"You can't win if you don't play, baby." Allie leaned back with him, shoulder to shoulder. "You weren't afraid to take a risk on the *Belle*, right?"

He saw where she was going with this. But love and money were two different kettles of fish. "Apples to oranges."

"Not really," she argued. "By taking over your daddy's boat, you're risking bankruptcy, right?"

"Yeah," he said cautiously.

"So you're willing to risk your credit and all your cash, but not your feelings? Where's the logic in that?"

It made total sense to Marc. "The difference is I

know what I'm doing with the *Belle*. I have an actual shot at succeeding."

"And you don't at love?"

"Of course not."

Allie turned and peered at him as if she'd just learned Santa wasn't real. Her eyes overflowed with emotion, and it stirred something deep inside him—a warm swelling similar to the sensation he'd felt before kissing her. He couldn't decide whether he liked it or not.

"Aw, honey, that breaks my heart," Allie whispered, reaching up to cup his face. "You don't even know what you're missing, do you?"

Marc knew what he was missing.

One of his earliest memories was walking home from elementary school and finding his parents locked in battle because Mama had just discovered Daddy's pregnant mistress. A month later, the other woman had delivered twins—Nicky and Alex—and Daddy had taken a hike to create a happy home elsewhere. Marc would never forget the look of hurt and shame on his mother's face. *That's* what he was missing.

Or so he thought.

Now, with his cheek cradled in Allie's soft palm, her sweet breath mingling with his . . . he wasn't so sure. He saw a flash of what could be: an image of Allie tangled in his sheets, the satisfaction of having her all to himself. It felt good for a moment, until he realized how deeply it would burn when it all fell apart.

Because that's what would happen.

The concept of happily-ever-after was like finding

sunken treasure at the bottom of the ocean—sure, he'd heard stories about it, but he'd never actually seen it happen.

"I know what I'm missing." He took her hand from his face and placed it on her thigh.

With a shake of her head, Allie laced her fingers between his. The intensity behind that one innocent gesture sent an electric pulse buzzing along his flesh like a completed circuit—energy flowing in a circle back to where it belonged.

"No, you don't," she said. "Not yet."

Using her free hand, she grasped his tie and pulled him in for a gentle kiss, a taunting sweep of lips that obliterated his control and had him instantly falling into her arms. She ran her tongue lightly along his bottom lip and inched away, forcing him to chase her mouth, to admit to both of them how badly he craved her touch. He hated himself for his weakness, but that didn't stop him from wrapping an arm around her waist to draw her as near as she could get.

With Allie's mouth moving in sync with his own, the world fell away. There was no *Belle*, no staircase, no river, only the intoxicating press of her wet lips and the luscious taste of her on his tongue. He gave himself up to the swell of longing that radiated from deep within, devouring her mouth and taking as much as he could get. But no matter how tightly he crushed her to his chest, it wasn't enough. On an instinctive level, he knew one time with Allie would never be enough.

This was different from their last kiss—every bit as scorching but bigger somehow. Like he'd taken a piece of Allie and left a slice of himself with her in return. It was a foreign experience for him, equal parts wondrous and frightening, but as the seconds passed, the fear began to outweigh the pleasure. The sensations were too much.

He pulled back to escape the intensity, breaking their kiss but keeping his eyes closed to trap a bit of her inside him. When he opened his eyes, Allie was watching him from beneath heavy lids. The loaded smile that curved her lips made him grin in return.

"What?" he asked.

She untangled their fingers and used the stair rail to stand, then brushed off her backside. "Nothing." Nodding toward the next landing, she said, "I'd better go change. After all, I'm back on the clock, and there's all that hygiene to consider." Then she left him to admire the gorgeous curve of her legs as she climbed the stairs.

"We've got to stop doing this, you know," he called after her.

He couldn't quite hear her response, but it sounded like, "You'll be back."

And, yeah, he probably would be. It took all his control not to dash up the stairs after her.

Marc leaned to the side and shamelessly peeked up her dress before returning to his duties. He didn't know what to do about Allie, but he couldn't wipe the dopey expression off his face. It was still slanting his mouth when he returned to the galley.

Beau glanced up from his cutting board and gave Marc a smirking once-over. "So, did you set her straight, Captain?" The sarcasm in his voice could cut steel. "Show her who's boss?"

"Very funny." Refusing to be baited, Marc pulled a bottled water from the fridge. He unscrewed the top and chugged a few gulps, then leaned against the counter near Allie's workstation. "I'm here to set *you* straight before she gets back."

"Me?" Beau quit dicing onions and pointed the knife at himself. "What'd I do?"

Marc cocked his head and gave him the *don't be obtuse* look. "I saw you hanging all over Allie and Ella-Claire when you came aboard."

One corner of Beau's mouth lifted. "Oh, that."

"Yeah," Marc said flatly. "That."

Shrugging, Beau returned to his work. "What can I say? I'm an affectionate kind of guy."

"Affectionate, my ass." Marc darted a glance out the open door to make sure nobody was within earshot. He lowered his voice to deliver a stern warning. "Just remember you're here to scramble the eggs, not fertilize 'em."

Apparently, Beau thought that was the funniest damn thing he'd ever heard, because he broke into a heaving guffaw. He tossed down his knife and clutched his belly and doubled over, the annoying jackass. His braying reverberated off the walls, prompting Marc to close the galley door.

"Yuk it up all you want," Marc said, scooting aside the canister of flour that doubled as a doorstop. "I'm not screwing around."

"Shit, man." Using a handful of his T-shirt, Beau blotted his watery eyes. "You gotta warn me next time you drop a one-liner like that. I could've lost a finger."

Speaking of fingers, Marc raised an extra-special one at his brother to send a message not even *he* could misinterpret. "Keep your fly zipped. Or I might not wait for the next port to kick you off the boat."

"Keep it zipped, huh?" Beau folded his massive arms over his equally massive chest and stared down his nose at Marc. "You gonna follow your own orders, Captain?"

"Of course I am," Marc said. And since he'd never technically unzipped around Allie, it was true. "This is business."

"Uh-huh." Beau's tone made it clear he didn't buy what Marc was selling. He tapped an index finger against the corner of his lips. "You've got something right here. I'm no expert, but I think it's lipstick."

Marc scrubbed a fist against his mouth. When he pulled back his hand, Allie's bright coral gloss stared back at him, proving his brother right.

Shit.

A low chuckle shook Beau's chest. Nodding, he used his hand like a gun and fired it at Marc's heated face. "Busted."

"It's not like that."

"No? Were you trying on her makeup, then?" Beau immediately flashed a palm. "Not that there's any shame in that. I don't judge."

Maybe Marc should make good on that promise to dump his brother overboard.

"I've been gone a while," Beau said, "but I still know you up one side and down the other." Retrieving his knife, he approached the cutting board, but ignored the onions in favor of studying Marc with a critical eye. "Never seen you like this before, though."

Marc knew he should let it go, but curiosity took control of his vocal cords. "Like what, exactly?"

"Whipped." A satisfied grin unfurled across Beau's lips. "Harder than a rented mule."

"Bullshit," Marc said with a dismissive wave. He wanted Allie—no use lying to himself—but that didn't mean he was pussy whipped. It was attraction, plain and simple. "Maybe all those years of playing football rattled your brain."

"Hey, I took a few whacks to the noggin, but I can still tell Allie's got you sprung." Beau turned his gaze to the cutting board and began chopping onions at the speed of sound. "I get it, little brother," Beau went on. "Those Mauvais women have a way of sneaking inside your head when you're not looking, then digging in and never letting go." His blade never slowed, but Beau's voice took on a softer tone—one that sounded an awful lot like regret. "I'd know."

Marc dipped his chin in shock. "You mean Devyn? I thought she was a fling."

Beau huffed a dry laugh. "So did I."

"Wait a minute." Marc shook his head skeptically, pointing his water bottle at his brother. "You're telling me that Beau Dumont—the guy who *supposedly* lost his virginity to the Playmate of the Year—can't get over Allie's ice queen sister?"

"Hey, that totally happened," Beau said, jabbing a finger at Marc. "I was big for my age, and Miss July thought I was eighteen."

Marc rolled his eyes. Beau was still big for his age.

"And if Dev turned out prickly," he continued, "it's probably my fault, not hers. I screwed her over pretty hard."

"Damn," Marc swore under his breath. *Devyn Mau-*

vais. He'd have never guessed it. But the more Marc thought about his brother's ill-fated fling, the more he began to wonder if they'd experienced any anomalies during their . . . well, private time. "So," Marc began. "Did . . . uh . . ." He trailed off, drawing a sudden blank.

"*Did uh* what?" Beau asked.

What was Marc supposed to say? *Did the bed catch fire the first time you touched her? Was Pawpaw right—did your junk fall off afterward? Did you break out in boils south of the border?* Each question on Marc's tongue sounded more absurd than the last.

"The old legend," he finally said. "About the hex on our family . . ."

"What about it?"

Marc studied his shoes. "Did you ever get the feeling it was real?"

Beau didn't answer at first, but once he'd finished dicing his onion, he set down his knife and huffed a sigh. "Honestly? Yeah, I did."

"Really?" Marc asked. "Why?"

"Can't say for sure." Beau lifted a shoulder. "It seemed like something was keeping me from getting too close, like an emotional fence. Or hell, maybe I was just wasn't ready. But I do know one thing."

Marc nodded for him to go on.

"If I get another chance, I won't quit so easily." Beau grabbed another onion and picked up his knife. "I'll go after what I want, curse or no curse."

The response didn't alleviate Marc's confusion, but he felt relieved knowing that Pawpaw had exaggerated the consequences of tangling with a Mauvais. If nothing else, at least his manhood was safe.

"But it's different for you," Beau added. "I'm not in charge of the family business, and Dev isn't my employee. You've got no place chasing Allie's skirt."

Marc jerked his gaze to Beau's while his blood pressure hitched up a notch. Less than an hour on board, and already the pissing contest had begun. He should have known better than to assume they could have a peaceful conversation about women.

"No, you're not in charge," Marc agreed. "So go ahead and get that through your thick skull before we go any farther."

Beau snorted in derision. "I heard about the jazz singer."

"Yeah?" Marc said. "Then you probably heard I never laid a hand on her. That was Alex and Nicky's doing."

"What do you expect from two horny college kids, especially when you set the example for them? You're captain now. It's time to—"

"That's what this is *really* about, isn't it?" Marc interrupted. "That Daddy made me captain and not you."

Beau scoffed. "I don't want your job."

"Of course you don't—that would require you to stick around." Marc made a noise of contempt. "You want to give the orders and leave the work to the rest of us. Well, we've got it covered. Just do your job, and I'll cut your paycheck. Then you can disappear again."

Beau gritted his teeth and fell silent, but the redness rising into his face said that Marc had plucked a nerve. Good. It was about time someone took him down a peg.

But despite that, Marc couldn't take pleasure in delivering the perfect blow. If anything, he felt worse than before. He must be going soft.

The galley door swung open, and Allie drifted inside wearing a pair of hip-hugging khaki pants and a boob-hugging staff polo shirt.

She stopped short at the sight of Marc, probably wondering why he was in the galley instead of the casino, where he belonged. The Texas Hold'em tournament would begin soon, and if his head were screwed on right, he'd be helping Nicky with the last-minute preparations, not frozen in place and mentally undressing her.

"I should go," Marc said, more to her than to Beau. "The tourney starts in a few hours." But despite that fact, he couldn't seem to leave the kitchen. "Lots of loose ends to tie up."

"Mmm," she agreed, stopping to brush past him, never mind the six square feet of open space between Marc and her workstation. Her pink nails skimmed across his chest, leaving behind chills everywhere she touched. "And I need to make dessert." She peeked up at him, her lips still slightly swollen from their kiss. "I'm in the mood for something extra sinful—maybe a double-chocolate torte to add to the dessert buffet. What do you think?"

From nearby, Beau made a mock gagging sound. "Quit dancing around each other and shut up with that mess. I've got a weak stomach."

This coming from the two-time Fried-Pickle Eating Champion.

But he had a point. It was time for Marc to clear his head of Allie's perfume and see to the tournament. There was work to be done. No matter what his brother said, Marc wasn't whipped. Not even close.

The *Belle* came first—she was the only lady in his future.

Chapter 9

"So, did you take a three-hour tour on the SS *Manwhore* yet?"

Devyn's acerbic voice sounded even sharper through the cell phone, but the effect brought a smile to Allie's lips. She could picture her sister leaning against the back wall of the Sweet Spot, gripping one hip and glaring at any customers who dared to interrupt her call. But crankiness notwithstanding, Allie missed her sister like crazy. Growing up, she and Dev had been more than siblings. The avoidance of their superstitious classmates had made them best friends, too.

"Or," Dev continued, "have you finally regained control of your brain?"

Allie kicked off her kitchen clogs and reclined on the bed. As soon as her body sank into the mattress, her back muscles groaned in relief, thankful for a moment's reprieve after she'd spent all day on her feet. "I'm going to ignore that last question, since you're running the shop for me and all."

"That's right. And don't forget you're making it up to me in Vegas. I've earned that vacay a dozen times over."

"Is it that bad?" Maybe Allie should have checked in sooner. Dev had a good head on her shoulders, but she'd never run a business. "Did something happen?"

Dev snorted through the phone. "There's a lot of *something* happening. I swear your job is giving me gray hair. Crow's-feet, too." She paused as if checking her reflection in the metallic shelf brackets near the phone. "But we'll talk about that later. First things first—quit dodging my question. Did he hit it and quit it?"

"Dev!" Allie bolted upright in bed. A problem at the bakery—her livelihood and her dream—easily trumped sex talk. "Tell me what's wrong!"

"You first."

Allie made a frustrated noise and flung herself back onto a stack of pillows. "That's emotional blackmail." But she knew better than to attempt a battle of wills against her sister. Devyn was so stubborn, she could train a cat to bark.

"Fine," Allie conceded. "The answer's no."

"What?" Dev's reply was loud enough to alert the whole French Quarter. "You haven't banged him yet?"

"Shh!" Allie clamped a hand over the phone to muffle her sister's voice. "Please tell me nobody's in the store!"

She could practically hear the sound of Devyn's eyes rolling. "We're all grown-ups here."

"Still!"

"So what's the holdup?" Devin asked, totally nonplussed. "It's not like he's saving it for marriage."

"Do we really have to talk about this?"

"Did I wake up before sunrise to carve up a ten-pound block of butter?"

Allie sighed. "At least tell me everything's all right at the shop."

"Everything's all right at the shop," Dev parroted.

"Promise?"

"Pinkie swear."

"Okay. It's the 'curse.'" Allie used her free hand to make air quotes. "Marc won't say so, but I can tell he's afraid something will happen if we go any farther." Then she told her sister about Chef Regale's bed catching fire after Marc had kissed her . . . omitting the more torrid details of their romantic encounter. "And everyone thinks I did it because Regale sabotaged me in the galley."

"Hmm," Devyn mused. "Maybe you did."

"Wha—" The accusation stung like a slap to the face. She thought Devyn knew her better than that. "You can't be serious."

"You didn't do it on purpose," Dev clarified. "I know you'd never willingly hurt anyone. But you have Memère's spirit watching over you. That's more than enough to cause a reaction when someone like Regale does you dirty."

"If that's the case," Allie argued, "then why hasn't this happened before, like after last year's hit-and-run? Why didn't that pizza delivery guy's engine explode when he totaled my front end?"

"Because you're missing an important connection."

"Being?"

"Marc Dumont," Dev said as if the answer should be obvious. "He's the one carrying around Memère's curse, not the pimple-faced dick who hit your car. I think the bed igniting was a message from the spirits that you're playing with fire."

"Going for the literal interpretation, I see."

"I'm serious. Look, I know you're hot for this guy, but he's going to hurt you." Dev paused to let her words sink in. "You understand that, right? He's never been faithful—no Dumont man has. This can't end well."

That wasn't wholly true. Marc had never committed to a woman, so by default, he'd never been *un*faithful. But since that point wouldn't help win her argument, Allie kept it to herself. "I hear you, really I do, but there's more to him than you think."

A noise of disagreement echoed through the phone.

"No, really," Allie insisted. "His daddy's lying and cheating twisted Marc's whole perception of relationships. He doesn't believe in love because he's never seen it. Deep down, he's a good man." And before Devyn could issue another sarcastic grunt, Allie told her about how Marc had barely eaten or slept the past two days because the poker tournament had run longer than expected. He'd divided his time between the pilothouse, the casino, and the purser's desk. And every night without fail, he put on his most charming smile for the guests in the dining room, making sure to greet each table. "He could've pushed the responsibilities onto his staff, but he wouldn't do it."

"So he can't delegate," Dev said. "Color me unimpressed."

"You're not listening. He's invested in the *Belle*, not because it's easy money, but because it's keeping his whole family together." Which was something Marc had missed during his childhood. If it weren't for the boat, he and his brothers would barely know one another. "We take it for granted that Mama and Daddy loved each other, but their example set the foundation for the rest of our lives."

Dev softened a little at the mention of their parents. She released a nostalgic sigh. "Remember how he'd have tulips delivered the first Friday of every month?"

"To celebrate the day they met." Allie felt a pull at her stomach. The deliveries had continued after her parents died together in a car accident. One of the saddest moments of Allie's life was calling the florist to cancel Daddy's long-standing order. "He loved her so hard."

"And she felt the same way."

"But imagine how different it could have been," Allie said. "If Daddy had knocked up some other woman and left us for a new family, maybe we'd act like the Dumonts. Then people would call us cursed."

"Some already do."

"You're missing the point again."

"No, I get it." Dev lowered her voice in a reluctant concession. "But knowing *why* the Dumonts are messed up doesn't change the fact that they're messed up. It's just a matter of time before Marc lets you down, just like Beau did to me."

"Not necessarily." Not if Allie could reshape Marc's way of thinking—show him how it felt to trust and be trusted in return. In essence, show him what he'd been missing all these years. "I don't think he's damaged beyond repair. And if it doesn't work out . . . well, a broken heart never killed anyone."

"I'll remind you of that in Vegas when you're crying in your poolside margarita."

"I'm sure you will." And since Dev had mentioned her ex, Allie figured she should rip off the Band-Aid and warn her of his sudden reappearance. "Hey, speaking of Beau . . ."

"That's twice too many times I've heard his name today."

"Sorry, baby, but he's back. He finished his enlistment with the marines, and Marc hired him to replace Regale in the galley. I thought you'd want to know. It's just a matter of time before he shows up in Cedar Bayou or New Orleans." She braced herself for a tirade of obscenities, but the long silence that ensued prompted Allie to check the cell phone connection to make sure the line hadn't disconnected. "You still there?" she asked.

"We've been bombarded in the shop," Devyn finally said, shutting down like a liquor store on Sunday. "Apparently, your desserts are a hit with the passengers on that floating garbage heap. They've been calling and texting home to rave about your crème puffs, and now we can't keep up with the orders."

Allie wanted to press her sister to talk about Beau, but all thoughts of the man vanished, replaced by a hopeful tickle inside her chest. "Are you serious? That's fantastic!"

"Psh," Devyn said. "Fantastic for *you*. I had to hire three temps to help out. I can't pull the all-nighters like I used to."

"You're the best," Allie told her sister. "Just keep thinking of Vegas."

"For all the sleep I've sacrificed, you should hire me a stripper. One of those beefy cowboys whose chaps rip off with one tug."

"For you, I'll hire a whole posse." Before Allie could offer to throw in a bonus construction worker, her cell phone chirped to announce a text message. Glancing at the screen, she recognized the number to the Natchez fire department. "Gotta go. But thanks for holding down the fort. I owe you, big."

Dev grumbled, "It's a good thing I love you," and disconnected.

"Love you too, baby," Allie said into empty space. She tapped her cell phone screen, and it rewarded her with the message she'd been waiting for.

Hey, Allie. RE: the mobile device you supplied, it's possible that a faulty battery overheated and ignited the bedspread, resulting in a fire. But please note that without examining all the evidence, we cannot officially . . .

That was all Allie needed to hear.

She pumped a fist in the air and hopped off the bed to slip on her shoes. Finally she had proof that other-worldly forces had nothing to do with Regale's fire, and she couldn't wait to show Marc, even if it *was* ten o'clock at night. She tucked her phone in the back pocket of her jean skirt and headed for the door. When she slung it open, she stopped short at the sight of a gleaming nose ring.

Mrs. Gibson stood at the door with her knuckles poised to knock. The woman jumped in shock and pressed a hand over her heart. "How'd you know I was here?" she asked. "I didn't have a chance to knock yet."

Allie released a shaky laugh. "I didn't. I was on my way downstairs."

"Oh, well, I won't keep you." The woman lifted an

old hardback Bible for show. "I just wanted to share something real quick."

Allie hoped Mrs. Gibson wasn't one of those missionary types. "Thanks, hon, but I'm Catholic. My soul's already spoken for."

"Nothing like that," she assured Allie. "I found this Bible in our nightstand drawer. Usually I don't notice them when I travel, but I felt prompted to pick it up, and look what I found."

She opened the faded cover and showed Allie an inscription on the inside. In beautiful handwritten script, it read *May those who seek comfort find it here. —E McMasterson,* North River Steamer.

Allie didn't see the connection. She looked to Mrs. Gibson for understanding.

"That was my grandfather," the woman explained, her eyes welling with happy tears. "I don't know how it ended up here, but this belonged on his riverboat. If we hadn't lost the honeymoon suite and been reassigned to a different room, I never would've found it."

Allie felt her cheeks break into a warm smile. "See? I told you there are no accidents. This is a message of comfort from your grandfather's spirit."

Mrs. Gibson hugged the book to her chest. "Do you think the captain would mind if I took it home with me?"

"Not one bit," Allie said. "That's a gift, and it belongs with you. I'll replace it myself if I have to." Stepping into her room, she bent to reach into her backpack and pulled free a gris-gris bag for love and luck. "Here," she said with a wink, handing the sachet to Mrs. Gibson.

"Now get back to your room and enjoy that sweet husband of yours."

After sharing a quick hug, they walked together until they reached the stairwell and parted ways. Allie jogged down the stairs to the casino, figuring that's where Marc would be. She was right. She found him alone with Nick in the dimly lit room, the tops of their heads illuminated by a lone spotlight above the bar.

Marc had let down his hair and pulled off his tie, which rested atop a nearby barstool along with his captain's hat and jacket. He grinned at his brother while clinking his glass in a toast. When he tipped back his cola, a visible patch of tanned skin at the base of his throat shifted, trapping Allie's gaze for several long beats.

She couldn't stop imagining how his skin might taste beneath her lips or how he'd smell of sunshine and shaving cream. But more than that, she loved seeing him relaxed and happy for once. It lifted the corners of her mouth as she strode toward the bar.

"I take it the tournament went well," she called across the open room.

Nick whipped his head around and gave her a smile, then pointed behind her to the door. "Hey, Allie. Lock that, will you? We're closed till morning."

She spun on her heel and did as he asked. By the time she reached the bar, Nick had poured her a shot of something she couldn't identify in the dim lighting. Marc pushed out a stool for her and grabbed a nearby bowl of lime wedges.

"Tequila," Marc said with a mischievous grin.

Allie lifted a palm. "No, no, no. That's my kryptonite. A few shots of that and I start leaking IQ points out my ears. There might even be table dancing."

In response, Nick quickly procured a bowl of salt.

"C'mon, Allie-Cat," Marc said. "Celebrate with us. The tourney from hell is finally over."

She nodded at his glass of cola. "Why aren't you partaking?"

"Because I have to stay sober enough to pilot the boat in case of an emergency," he said. "You and Nicky don't."

"Go ahead, darlin'." Nick tipped aside his blond head and pointed to the spot below his ear. "I'll even let you lick salt off my neck."

Allie didn't have to tell him *thanks but no, thanks.* Marc did it for her in the form of a peanut hurled at his brother's head. After deftly batting aside the tiny missile, Nick hopped down from his barstool and backed toward the door.

"I know when I'm not wanted," Nick teased. "I'll leave you two alone . . . so you can find more interesting places to sprinkle that salt."

This time it was Allie who pegged him with a peanut. He took the abuse with a grin and vanished out the doors, locking the handles behind him.

"I didn't mean to break up your party," Allie said, pulling her cell phone from her back pocket. "I just wanted to show you this." She tapped her *message* button and turned the screen to face Marc.

Squinting, he leaned in and read, *If that overgrown weasel asks about me, remind him that the quickest way to a man's heart is through his chest with a sharp knife.* Marc wrinkled his forehead. "I don't get it. Is that supposed to be a threat?"

"What?" Allie glanced at her phone and discovered a new text from Devyn. "Oops, wrong one. My sister's not exactly turning cartwheels at the idea of running into Beau." She pulled up the message from the Natchez fire department and handed Marc the phone. "Read this one."

Marc scanned the text and nodded thoughtfully. "Huh. Faulty battery." Then he added a casual, "Good to know," and went back to sipping his Coke.

Good to know? How did he not see what a big deal this was? Allie shook the phone in his face. "This proves I didn't cause the fire."

Marc sucked a drop of cola from his bottom lip. "Nobody said you did."

"Oh, come on. You were all thinking it."

He shook his head. "Not me."

"Liar," she said, lifting the shot glass to her lips. "I saw it all over your face that day in Regale's suite."

"Naw, honey, that was pain," Marc said with a grimace. "I had a raging case of blue balls."

Allie sputtered tequila into her fist and choked on a laugh, doing her best not to snort liquor up her nose.

"But Regale believed it," Marc went on. His impish twinkle faded as he dropped his gaze into the glass of cola. "And you stepped up and left the galley to keep him on board." He peeked up at her with respect in his eyes. "That was mighty big of you."

Allie threw back what remained of her shot, wincing at the burn. She cleared her throat. "I know how important the *Belle* is to you." The dark circles beneath his eyes proved he'd run himself ragged this week. "You look exhausted. Why don't you turn in?"

He flapped a hand and poured her another shot, waiting until she downed that one, too. "I'm all keyed up. I need to unwind first."

At least they agreed on one thing. Marc needed to blow off some steam, and Allie was happy to help—they were even in the perfect place for it. "Then let's play a game."

Marc glanced over her shoulder to the rows of dormant slot machines and empty roulette tables in the darkness. He pressed his lips together as if weighing her suggestion and finding it intriguing. "What'd you have in mind?"

"Well," she began. "You're probably tired of poker."

He nodded in agreement. "Especially the Texas variety."

Which left blackjack, but then they'd have to take turns representing the house, which didn't sound like much fun.

"I don't know a lot of card games," Allie admitted. "We could play Go Fish." She'd meant it as a joke, but Marc's lips tugged in a wide smile that drew out the cleft in his chin. He seemed to take it seriously for a moment, then laughed in a low, masculine chortle that turned her thoughts from gaming to sinning.

"Haven't played that in a while," he said, nudging another tequila shooter in her direction. "What should we wager?"

"Do we have to bet?"

"Of course," he said. "That's half the fun."

In general, Allie didn't carry much cash, and what little she had was in her suite. "I don't have any money on me."

"That's okay. I don't want your money."

She glanced around the bar for ideas, then pointed at a bowl of salty snacks. "We could play for pretzels."

"Pretzels?" He scoffed in offense. "What are we, twelve?"

Allie scowled at him. "Well, what do you want?"

His gaze took a slow trip down the length of her body, from shoulders to toes and back up again. Her skin heated as she began to understand the stakes he had in mind. "I wouldn't object to seeing what you've got on under those clothes."

Reflexively, Allie darted a glance at the strong contours of Marc's chest, barely visible as shadows beneath his white dress shirt. Truthfully, she wouldn't mind seeing what he was hiding either. "Are you suggesting we play Strip Go Fish?"

He answered by toasting her with his Coke and eyeing her shot in a silent message to drink up.

"Right here in the casino?" she added.

"The door's locked, and the cleaning crew isn't scheduled to come around till third shift." He nodded to a dark corner on the opposite side of the room. "We can sit back there if you want. That way nobody will spot your bare-naked backside through the glass doors."

Allie pointed at him. "I think you mean *your* bare-naked backside." Which she was going to enjoy ogling—immensely.

"Sugar, you're going to be very cold, very soon," he teased. "So you'd better take another shot."

"I *will* have another, but only to prove I can still trounce you half-drunk."

She tossed it back, then slid off her barstool, feeling

warm and floaty as she led the way to a round table in the corner. Marc found one of those battery-operated candles that mimicked a flame's flickering glow and set it on the table, so he could "see what he was winning." They continued their Go Fish trash talking until they'd found a pack of cards and settled in their chairs.

"Wait," Allie said while Marc shuffled the deck. "First we should make sure we're starting out with the same number of clothes." She counted her polo shirt, bra, skirt, panties, and clogs. "I've got five."

"Are we counting socks and shoes as one item?"

She shook her head. "Separate."

"Then I've got six."

He quickly remedied the injustice by unbuttoning his dress shirt and pulling his arms free. Beneath it, he wore a white T-shirt that fit him like a second skin, stretched unmercifully tight across his broad shoulders. Even in the dim light, his bunching chest drew Allie's eye and watered her mouth.

She swallowed hard. "That's better." So much better.

Marc caught her staring and faked a stretch to show off the inside curves of his biceps, then turned it up a notch, flexing them so they strained the hem of his T-shirt sleeves. A hint of dark ink peeked at her from beneath the fabric.

Oh, heavens. Allie loved a good tattoo, especially on a properly muscled body. She wanted to see all of it . . . and hunt for more.

"You're not distracted, are you?" he asked with a smirk.

"Not one bit," she lied. "Prepare to lose your other shirt, Captain."

Chapter 10

"Got any fives?"

"Go fish," Allie said, twirling her hand in a *take it off* motion. She hoped Marc would remove his T-shirt this time. When she'd rejected his request for threes, he'd simply shrugged and kicked off his shoes, mirroring her first move. Shoes and socks were always the first things to go in stripping games.

"Whatever." He set down his cards and reached below the table to peel off his socks. "Now we're both barefoot."

Allie's mouth pulled into a frown, but she reminded herself that he didn't have any more barriers left. By default, it would be the shirt or the pants next. "Got any twos?"

His teeth flashed white in the darkness, a wicked grin providing his answer. "You get a line; I'll get a pole. We'll go fishin' at the crawdad hole." He waggled his brows at her shirt. "Lose that top, sugar."

She reached for the deck to draw a card and accidentally knocked the pile askew. Maybe she'd overdone it with that last tequila shot, especially on an empty stomach. After drawing a ten, she placed her cards on the table and pushed to standing. "I'll keep the shirt for now."

"The skirt, then?" he asked, his voice thick with teasing. "You think you're safe because we're sitting down, but I can always peek under the table."

With great deliberation, Allie unbuttoned her denim skirt and lowered the zipper. She didn't intend to play it seductive; the tequila had simply clumsied her fingers. But when she glanced up to find Marc transfixed by her labored movements, his neglected Coke poised at his lips, she took extra care to roll down the waistband and smooth the fabric over her hips inch by meticulous inch. By the time the skirt dropped to the floor and revealed her black satin panties, Marc looked ready to choke on an ice cube.

Even though she'd lost an article of clothing, she felt victorious. She ran her hands over the tops of her thighs and let him get an eyeful before lowering herself to her seat and telling him, "Go ahead and peek, baby. I'm not shy."

Marc kept his gaze above the table's oak rim, but he seemed to have trouble swallowing his cola. "Nah. I'll wait for the full monty." He fanned out his cards and studied them for far too long before asking, "Nines?"

Allie sat straighter and smiled. "Nope! Say good-bye to that T-shirt."

He muttered a curse under his breath. "Lucky for you, I'm not bashful either."

Marc reached behind his head to grab hold of his collar and pulled off the thin garment with one brisk motion. He shook back his hair and followed with some more trash talk, but his words faded into obscurity as Allie stared at his naked chest.

God bless, he was a sight to behold.

She'd seen him shirtless a time or two, back in high school when he'd run track and played on the soccer team. He'd turned her head then, all lean and solid and tanned. But gorgeous as he'd been, there was no comparison between that boy and the man sitting before her now.

Marc's shoulders had broadened with time and hard work, rounded with muscles that made her want to hold on tight for a wild ride. She could almost feel the heat of his smooth, hard chest against her own, the ripple of his abs pressed to her flesh.

It was suddenly too hot inside the casino. Allie fanned herself with her cards.

"Like what you see?" he asked with a grin, clearly pleased with himself. When he leaned back in his chair, the tattoo on the inside curve of his tight biceps winked at her—a fleur-de-lis symbol. Allie's gaze traveled across his torso to another tattoo directly over his heart. This one was burgundy and poorly formed, like a splash of wine staining his skin.

She pointed at it, ignoring his teasing. "What's that?"

He glanced down at himself and chaffed a thumb over the spot. "This right here?"

Allie nodded.

"A birthmark," he said. "Must be hereditary, because my daddy and brothers all have it. Pawpaw, too."

Allie tipped her head and studied the mark, finding

it odd that the Dumont men would share the same skin irregularity. Allie didn't remember much from her high school genetics lessons, but she didn't think birthmarks ran in families. "All in the same place?"

"Yep." He shrugged. "Same shape, same color, same location."

She didn't recall seeing it when they were kids. "Has it always been there?"

"Since the day I was born." Marc leaned forward as if to get down to business. "Now quit stalling and move it along. I want that top on the floor."

"Fine," she said. "Got any queens?"

Grumbling, he handed over the queen of hearts, but when Allie asked for an ace, he released a low chuckle and pointed at her polo shirt. "Go fish."

"Don't get too excited," she told him while unfastening the buttons below her collar. "I have bikinis that show off more goods than this bra."

She pulled the polo carefully over her head so as not to snag a curl and placed it in the chair beside her. True to her word, two stretchy panels of black satin covered her breasts, displaying nothing but a deep line of cleavage.

Apparently, that was enough to render Marc speechless. He held up three fingers in a wordless request for cards while shamelessly eyeballing her boobs.

A few moments later, it was Allie's turn to gape at the sight of Marc in a pair of tight gray boxer briefs that left absolutely nothing to the imagination. They hugged the tops of his strong thighs and drew her gaze upward to the trail of dark hair encircling his navel and dipping below a waistband of cotton so thin it should be a crime. Allie caught herself biting her lip in disappointment when he sat down, something that didn't escape Marc's notice.

He teased her until the time came for Allie to remove her bra. Then his words died as he watched her slide each strap down the length of her shoulders with deliberate care. She held his gaze while unfastening the back, then flashed an impish grin and shook her hair in front to conceal both breasts when she pulled off her bra and let it fall onto the next chair.

Marc glared at her. "That's evil, right there. Pure evil."

"Quit whining and give me your queens," she said on her next turn, right before remembering she'd already asked for that card.

Marc's glare transformed into a triumphant glow that enlivened his entire face. He sat back in his seat and tossed his cards onto the table, mouthing the words *Go fish*.

Allie closed her eyes, mentally kicking herself for being so careless. This was it—the game was over. He'd won.

If only she hadn't been so distracted by Marc in his underwear . . .

"Want some help?" Marc asked, his voice thick with anticipation. "I'm an expert panty remover with years of dedicated experience. I can have them around your ankles, lickety-split."

Allie took a deep breath and stood from her seat. After taking a moment to fortify herself, she let her lids drift open. But when she glimpsed Marc again, something in him had shifted.

He wasn't bragging now, instead watching her with a wolfish hunger that tightened her stomach and sent it dipping south. Clearly this was no childish game to him—not anymore. He wanted her, and her body responded to him at once, flushing with warmth despite the fact that she was practically naked in an air-conditioned room.

"Why don't you come on over here," he murmured, dark and husky, "and let me do the rest?"

Allie didn't have to tell her feet to take a step forward. They moved toward Marc of their own volition and didn't stop until she reached his chair. For a pregnant beat, he used his eyes to take her in, scanning her legs while holding his breath in a charged anticipation she felt as tangibly as static electricity.

He let out a lungful of air and brought both palms to the outside swell of her hips, then simply held her like a man savoring a moment he'd waited a lifetime to experience. Allie knew that wasn't the case—Marc could have any woman he wanted—but it made her feel special all the same.

He used his work-roughened hands to skim the length of her thighs, all the way down to her knees and back up again until he reached her backside. There, he tucked his fingers beneath the satin fabric of her panties and took two handfuls of flesh, groaning appreciatively at the weight of her in his palms.

"Goddamn, Allie," he swore and moved in to kiss her navel. "You're a walking wet dream."

While he nuzzled and tickled her with the fine whiskers peppering his jaw, she tangled her fingers in his chestnut waves and held him nearer to her core, pulling him in as close as they could get. They stayed like that for a while, touching and stroking, savoring the quiet intimacy until Marc hooked his thumbs around her panties and tugged them down over her hips and to the floor. She stepped free and kicked them aside, standing before him completely nude for the first time.

Marc's gaze didn't linger. In the span of two heartbeats, he placed a gentle kiss between her thighs. Allie felt a ghost of warm breath, and the next thing she knew, Marc had run his tongue fully up the length of her femininity.

She wasn't prepared for the shock of pleasure that tore through her. Breath catching at the top of her lungs, she clutched the back of his chair for support. He only gave her a moment to recover before he did it again—flattening his tongue in a lazy assault that left her knees weak. Next he used the tip to flick and tease, sending her pulse rushing between her legs.

"Marc," she began, not sure whether to ask him to stop or keep going. It felt exquisite, but she wanted more from him. She wanted all of him.

When she remained silent for too long, he made the decision for her by positioning her left heel atop his knee and deepening his erotic kiss. Between nips and licks, he groaned decadently and made torrid promises of what he'd do next. Allie could hardly stand the intensity. Her limbs grew weak and heavy, her eyelids sinking as the pressure built inside her.

He latched onto her most sensitive spot and drew it into his mouth with gentle suction, eliciting a loud moan from her in response. Allie tipped her head forward and tried to keep standing upright, but with each wet tug, she sank farther into his lap. Finally, Marc conceded the battle and let her drop down to straddle his thighs.

He pulled her against his bare chest and slid his mouth against hers in a kiss that tasted of sweet cola and her own salty arousal. She twined both arms around his neck and explored his mouth while her hips sought friction against the massive erection straining the front of his Jockeys. Their mingled breaths grew choppy until Marc slowed things down, pulling back to gaze at her, his lips wet and swollen, eyes dark with lust.

"You're so beautiful," he whispered while brushing her long curls behind both shoulders to expose her breasts. Tenderly, he took one in each hand and admired them, skimmed his thumbs across her nipples while repeating, "So beautiful."

Allie bit her lip to contain a moan. She had a feeling where they were headed, but she needed to ask anyway. "Are we really going to do this?"

Marc took her by the hips and rocked against her. "Jesus, I hope so. I might die if we don't."

Smiling, Allie skimmed her palms over his strong shoulders, down the firm curves of his biceps, and across his smooth, hard chest, wishing she had another pair of hands to feel all of him. She'd fantasized about this moment for so long, but making love with Marc wasn't enough for her now. She refused to be just another notch on his bedpost.

She deserved more.

"I want to be the only one, Marc," she said, using her index finger to trace the birthmark over his heart. "Or we need to stop right now, before we go any farther."

He froze. Judging by the terror etched into his face, you'd think she'd demanded a two-carat solitaire and a minivan.

"Calm down, baby." Allie resisted the urge to roll her eyes. "I mean the only one sharing your bed. If you're sleeping with me, you're not sleeping with anyone else." When his shoulders unclenched in relief, she added, "I don't like to share. Do you?" She tossed back her hair and arched against him. "Do you want me doing this with another man?"

"No." Possessively, he tightened his grip on her hips. "No sharing."

She stifled a grin. "So we're clear?"

He moved in to kiss the side of her throat, stopping just below her ear, where he whispered, "Crystal clear. You're the only one I want, Allie." Then he took two handfuls of her backside and pulled her against his steely length as if to show exactly how much he wanted her. Which seemed like a whole lot.

"Good," she managed. "Then it's sett—"

She gasped when he latched onto her nipple and tugged it deep into his mouth. As soon as she gulped a breath, he turned to the other nipple and caught it gingerly between his teeth, barely grazing her until he'd teased it to a tight point.

Allie couldn't wait any longer. She reached into his Jockeys and freed him, taking a moment to stroke his long, thick shaft from top to bottom, then used her thumb to spread a bead of arousal over his velvety tip. Eagerly, she poised herself above his erection. She was on the Pill, they were both clean, and she wanted him inside her five minutes ago. She sank an inch onto him, her eyelids fluttering shut with fulfillment, but just as she opened her thighs to take him deeper, he halted her movements.

"Stop," he said, contradicting his words with an expression that pleaded for more. "Let me grab my wallet so I can suit up."

"We don't need a condom," she told him. "I'm on the—"

"I use one every time, sugar. It's not worth the risk."

He reached down to snag his pants, and in less than sixty seconds he had the condom rolled on and firmly in place. Allie reminded herself this was the responsible thing to do, but she couldn't help it—she wanted to feel the warm friction of his naked skin inside her.

But she didn't pout for long.

Marc took her by the hips and seated her atop his rounded head, then dipped into her from below, working inside by gradual degrees and stealing every coherent thought from her mind. By the time he was buried to the hilt, she could barely recall her own name.

He held her still for a while and fed her gentle kisses while she stretched to accommodate his considerable girth. Patience waning, Allie grasped Marc's shoulders and began a slow rock against his base. When she felt ready, she dug her toes into the carpet and lifted halfway up the length of his shaft before sinking down again.

Foreheads tipped together, they shared a blissful groan, each delirious with rapture. Allie kept going, setting an easy rhythm that Marc occasionally slowed by wrapping his arms behind her and crushing her to his chest. She knew what he was doing—delaying her climax and prolonging the pleasure. But though she wanted to make it last, the tension coiling low in her belly warned she couldn't hold off much longer.

Marc filled her ears with half-incoherent whispers of how good she felt, how gorgeous she was. He sat back in his chair to admire her while alternately kneading her breasts and running his palms along her thighs. Allie decided to give him a true eyeful. She leaned back and rested both elbows on the table, opening her legs wide to display their joined bodies while she rode his hips.

At the sight, Marc's lips parted and his face glazed over.

"Mercy," he groaned, scrubbing a hand over his jaw. "That's the hottest fucking thing I've ever seen."

Spurred by a new passion, he clutched his chair base, gaining purchase to thrust hard into her. The table shook with each pump, ice cubes rattling inside Marc's neglected glass of Coke. For a split second Allie worried they might topple it over, but then he used a thumb to massage circles into her swollen bud, and her mind shut to every sensation beyond the pure delight building between her legs. Like an electric current, it traveled down both thighs and back up again.

She extended her arms and gripped the table ledge while rolling her hips to meet each powerful thrust. Her lips parted, breath coming in shallow gasps. The room was thick with the noises of skin slapping skin, the frenzied squeak of the table joints, and the hysterical moans rising from her throat.

Her control was about to snap—she couldn't last another second.

Allie tipped back her head as her inner muscles shuddered against Marc in an orgasm so fierce she had to clench her jaw to contain a scream. He never relented, slamming harder between her thighs until Allie sobbed a curse without a care for who might overhear. The waves of ecstasy took her again and again for what felt like days. When they finally stilled, she lay boneless in his lap, more satisfied than she'd ever been in her life.

"Again," he commanded, wrapping her legs around his hips and standing from the chair. He lifted her pliant body and set her on the table, where she sprawled on her back, still weak and trembling. "I want to feel you come again."

Allie didn't think she could do it. She tried to tell him so, but then he ground against her in a circle and sparked to life every nerve ending below the waist.

"Yes," she whispered as his arm hooked around her knee and lifted it over his shoulder. The position opened her to take him even deeper, something she hadn't thought possible. "Yes," she repeated, eyes rolling back at the delicious invasion. He filled her so completely, bumping her cervix in a shock of pain that somehow heightened the pleasure.

He slowly rotated his hips and plunged into her hard enough to send his glass of Coke and half their playing cards sailing off the table. Allie held tight to the lacquered wood and rocked with him. Marc chanted her name like a prayer and branded her with his gaze. When the next wave of sweet agony hit, he came with her, bucking against her flesh with a long, low groan. From within, Allie felt him pulse in a staccato of release. He held there for several blissful moments until they both collapsed into a heap of sweaty tangled limbs.

"God bless," she whispered.

That was *so* much better than a brown sugar pecan scone.

Allie was in heaven. She wanted to bear Marc's weight forever. It felt like the most natural thing in the world to lie beneath him—like this was where she belonged. But he rested atop her only long enough to catch his breath before gently pulling out and tucking himself back into his Jockeys, condom intact.

She bristled at his abrupt withdrawal.

Seconds ago, he'd turned her world on its axis, and now he was shoving both legs into his pants while scanning the carpet to find the rest of his clothes. He picked his way through the pile, grinning to himself when he lifted her panties off the floor.

"Hurry up and get dressed," he said, tucking her underwear into his pocket.

Allie's heart turned cold while her sister's words rang inside her head, *Did he hit it and quit it?* Is that what was happening here? She hated to believe Marc would do that to her, but it was starting to look that way.

Propping on one elbow, Allie peeled a few playing cards off her back while watching him tug on his T-shirt. When he came across the spilled cola, he scooped the ice cubes into the glass and replaced it on the table.

"What?" he asked, catching her staring at him.

Allie struggled to force the words though her throat,

which was growing thick with welling tears. If he was about to ditch her, she'd have to get off at the next port and ask Devyn to pick her up. She couldn't stay aboard the *Belle* and pretend none of this had happened.

On frail limbs, she pushed to her feet. Marc peeled the jack of clubs off her butt, then pocketed that along with her panties—souvenirs of his conquest.

"Here, put this on." While handing over her skirt, he paused to study her expression and asked, "What's the matter?"

"You tell me," Allie said, bending down to snatch her bra off a nearby chair. She shoved her arms through the straps and latched the trio of hooks at the back. "We just made love, and now you're gearing up for the fifty-yard dash."

Marc's forehead wrinkled in confusion. Allie stepped into her skirt, and by the time she secured the button, understanding dawned on his face. "Oh," he said, lips twitching in a grin. "Is that what you think—that I'm fixin' to make a clean getaway?"

She provided her answer in the form of a glare.

"Come here." When she stayed rooted to the floor, Marc sauntered over to her and snaked both arms around her waist. He nuzzled her ear through thick curls and murmured, "You didn't actually think we were finished, did you?"

Allie's resolve was weak. All it took was the heat of his breath to unravel her.

She tipped aside her head to welcome the brush of his lips on her neck. He kissed his way down to her bare shoulder and spoke against her bra strap. "The cleaning crew will be here soon. Get dressed so I can take you back to your room and strip you naked again. I'm going to do filthy things to you, Allie. And I won't stop till the sun comes up."

Allie's breath hitched. Hopeful once again, she pulled back to look him in the eyes. "Are you sure? Don't you need a couple hours to . . . recuperate?"

He gave her that signature smile—the one that deepened the cleft in his chin and sent her heart *ping*ing against her rib cage. There was a promise in his gaze, of more than just a few moments of sin.

"Sugar," he said, "we're just getting started."

Chapter 11

The next morning, Marc awoke to the soft snuffle of feminine snoring, an unexpectedly adorable sound that parted his lips in a sleepy smile. Allie's pretty little head rested on his chest, a beam of low sunlight from the window dancing over her raven curls, picking up bluish hues he'd never noticed before. There was a lot about this woman he hadn't noticed before last night, but now he knew every inch of her curves by heart. He'd taken great care to explore her—inside and out—and he'd loved every minute of it.

Lord, she'd blown his mind—catapulted him to a whole new level of heart-quaking, lung-bursting volcanic climax. Marc had been with a lot of women over the years, but Allie made him forget every last one. No joke. He couldn't recall a single name but hers. Sex with Allie was so damn good, it didn't seem natural.

Maybe because it's not, warned a distant voice that sounded an awful lot like his superstitious pawpaw. *If you lie down with the devil, you're gonna get burned, son.*

Marc pushed those bullshit thoughts right out of his head.

The girl in his arms was more angel than devil, the perfect mixture of tenderhearted sweetness and sultry siren. But that assurance didn't stop him from peeking beneath Allie's bedsheet to make sure his manhood was still intact after a night of debauchery with a Mauvais woman. Thankfully, it was—and *very* happy to see Allie stirring beside him.

"Stand down, soldier," Marc whispered. "Let's give her a break."

Besides, if the sun was up, that meant he was overdue in the pilothouse and Allie was late for her breakfast shift. But damned if the general would listen to reason. His helmet stood at full attention, refusing to surrender until he'd divided and conquered the lean tanned thighs curled around Marc's hip.

With a sigh, he checked the clock on her nightstand. They were already late. A few more minutes wouldn't hurt.

Burying his nose in Allie's scented curls, Marc murmured a husky "Good morning," while letting his hands travel down her back to her naked ass, where he grabbed two firm, delectable handfuls of flesh. He loved the way she filled his palms. She had the kind of butt that made him want to thank her mama—her daddy, too, rest their souls.

Allie stretched her spine and made a noise of contentment, blinking awake and squinting against the early-morning light. She rested her chin on his chest and flashed a smile that warmed his heart.

"Mornin'." She started to say something more but gasped and tore her gaze to the alarm clock. "Oh, no!" Muscles tensing, she moved to launch out of bed.

"Hold up there, sugar." Marc threaded his arms around her waist and pulled her back against him, spoon-style. "Where's the fire?"

"But my breakfast pastries," she objected. "I should have started them hours ago."

"I'm sure your staff is on top of it."

He could feel her answering smile in the way she melted into his embrace. "You're just saying that because you want to be on top of *me*."

"Not true." He reached around and cupped her breast, thumbing her nipple until it pebbled beneath his touch. When she released a soft moan, he nibbled her shoulder and thrust against her glorious backside. "I think I'll take you from behind this time."

"You're so bad," she whispered, pulling aside her hair to give him better access to her neck. He sucked the sensitive skin there and reached between her legs, pleased to find her more than ready for him. "So very bad," she breathed, opening for his fingers.

"Mmm, and you like that, don't you?"

He didn't need a reply; her body answered for her.

Marc closed his eyes and focused on spreading the slippery heat over her folds. Occasionally, he dipped a finger inside to find more lubrication. And there was always more. He loved this evidence of how badly she wanted him—the feel of her, absurdly slick, made him so hard it hurt. To ease the ache, he pushed his erection between the dampened passage of her upper thighs, stroking the outside of her hidden entrance. His breath hitched at the wet friction, his body begging him to ease in where she was blazing hot and tight as a fist. But as much as he wanted to indulge in bare contact,

Marc had never left himself unprotected, and he didn't intend to start now.

"Don't move," he ordered, shifting onto his back to grab a condom from the nightstand. After rolling it down the length of his shaft, he settled behind Allie and slipped into her with liquid ease.

They shared a long groan. "God," she swore, gyrating in time with each lazy pump of his hips. "You feel so good I almost can't stand it."

Chest rumbling with male pride, he wrapped both arms around her, holding tight as he drove into her again and again. Allie covered his hands with one of hers and whispered in broken Creole while reaching down to touch herself where they joined.

Marc watched over her shoulder and went half delirious at the sight of her circling fingers. He wanted to make it last, but when her inner muscles contracted in orgasm, she milked a climax out of him that he felt clear to the pit of his soul. Gritting his teeth, he thrust upward one last time and spilled inside her.

They lay there, sweaty and satisfied, their flesh glued together in a way that made it all the more difficult to part from her.

"Damn," he said, still panting for air. "Every time we do this I think it can't possibly get any better, but it does. What's your secret?"

Allie drew his palm to her mouth and placed a kiss there. "I could tell you, but then I'd have to kill you."

He laughed. "If we keep up this pace, you'll be the death of me anyway."

Glancing over her shoulder, she suggested, "We can slow down anytime you want, baby."

Right, like *that* was going to happen. She made him hornier than a parolee on release day. He'd made love to her six times in the last nine hours, and it still wasn't enough. Even now, a tingling of blood flow to his jock warned he'd grow hard again if he didn't pull out—which he needed to do so they could bathe and get dressed.

Probably a bad idea to suggest they shower together. Soaping up Allie's wet, naked body would surely lead to more naughty shenanigans.

Yeah, definitely a bad idea . . .

"C'mon." Grinning, he gestured toward her bathroom. "Let's get cleaned up. I know a fun way to conserve water."

When Marc finally reached the pilothouse, he threw open the door and nearly collided with Pawpaw, who speared him with an icy glare. The scrunching of the old guy's brows said he had a bone to pick with Marc, but he stewed silently in the corner while the second-in-command delivered a brief report. Afterward, Marc thanked his backup pilot and dismissed him for a day's rest.

The door had barely closed behind the man when Pawpaw lit into Marc.

"Where the hell have you been, boy?"

One hand on the wheel, Marc sipped his coffee and suppressed the urge to snap at his grandfather. "I got a late start this mornin' is all. No reason to get your britches in a twist."

"Late start?" Pawpaw stammered. "We've been tryin' to track you down all night!"

That sounded bad. Marc's stomach tightened, and he took his eyes off the river just long enough to face his granddaddy, whose typically tawny cheeks had darkened to the shade of a summer raspberry. "Why? What happened last night?"

Pawpaw laughed without humor. "What *didn't* happen?"

"You going to tell me or not?"

"Where should I start?" asked the man, lowering his saggy bottom onto a folding chair and clearly enjoying Marc's unease. "How 'bout with the theater show? One of the actors in the second performance broke a leg—literally. Poor bastard slipped on a Twinkie wrapper, of all things, and went down harder than a prize heifer."

Cringing, Marc drew a sharp breath through his teeth. "He okay?"

Pawpaw lifted a shoulder. "Guess so. The EMT said it looked like a clean break."

"The EMT?" As far as Marc knew, there were no medics on board. Just the staff nurse, who treated stomach bugs and the occasional scrape. "Where'd you dig up one of those?"

"I didn't. We stopped around midnight."

"Stopped the boat?" Marc damn near dropped his coffee. "You docked the *Belle* last night?" *And I didn't notice?*

Pawpaw raised one bushy brow and leaned forward in his chair. "Twice."

"And nobody bothered to tell me?"

"Not for lack of tryin'," Pawpaw said, shaming Marc with a bitter glare. "You wouldn't answer your phone."

Marc set his coffee on the console and patted himself

down, searching for his cell but coming up empty-handed.

"Lookin' for this?" Pawpaw pulled the cell from his shirt pocket and handed it over. "Found it on the casino floor . . . in a patch of dried Coca-Cola."

Avoiding his granddaddy's eyes, Marc took the sticky device and shoved it in his jacket pocket.

"When I went to your suite," Pawpaw continued, "you weren't there. We tore the boat apart looking for you, 'specially the second time."

Marc returned his gaze to the water, barely seeing a thing as guilt clawed a jagged trail into his skull. He was captain of the boat—directly responsible for the *Belle* and every soul aboard. How could he be so irresponsible as to go off the grid all night? And how was it possible they'd docked twice and he'd never noticed?

He knew the answer, just didn't want to admit it. He hadn't detected the stops because Allie's bed was rocking, even when the boat wasn't. Making love with her felt so incredible he probably wouldn't have known if the boat were on fire.

Marc cleared his throat and refocused on the controls, slowing the throttle to bring the old girl down to six knots. Unfocused as he was right now, he probably shouldn't be piloting at all. "What happened the second time?" he asked, not sure he wanted to hear the answer.

"Domestic dispute," Pawpaw said, hooking his fingers in sarcastic air quotes. "That's what the cops called it, anyhow."

Marc pinched the bridge of his nose. "You're telling me the law was aboard my boat?"

"Naw," Pawpaw said. "Beau stepped up and handled it. He carried the perp down the ramp and the officers stayed on the dock."

"What'd the guy do?"

Pawpaw snorted in amusement. "Crotchety son of a bitch nearly took off my head with a wine bottle."

"He attacked you?"

"Sure as I'm sittin' here. His wife sent me one-a-them dirty text messages and he—"

Marc whipped his head around. "You were sexting with a *guest?*"

"Hey," he said, pushing both palms forward, "I didn't encourage her. I was just minding my own business when her old man came at me swingin' a 1982 Merlot."

"Oh, yeah?" Marc smelled bullshit. In his younger days, Pawpaw had made a reputation for himself as the bayou's number-one backdoor man. "Then how'd she get your number?"

Pawpaw's gaze dropped to the floor. "That ain't the point."

"God help us," Marc muttered under his breath. "Sometimes I wonder how we're still afloat."

"It all worked out for the best," Pawpaw said with a dismissive wave. "Once they left, I had the maids turn down the room so the folks from 116 could have it."

Marc hated to ask. "What happened in 116?"

"Pipe burst in the head." A low whistle puffed Pawpaw's cheeks. "When the maintenance crew came, they found a dead opossum in the toilet."

"Fan-damn-tastic." Marc noted the sonar equipment was on the fritz, too. "That's all we need—a critter invasion."

"If it ain't one thing, it's another," the old man mused.

No doubt. And it didn't escape Marc's notice that the figurative downpour had occurred precisely when he'd taken Allie Mauvais to bed. He tried telling himself it was a coincidence, but it felt like a lie.

The stakes seemed to escalate with each touch. An after-prom kiss had earned him a boxer-full of blisters. The first time he'd crossed Allie's path since high school, half his cleaning crew had been deported and his pastry chef had contracted German measles. He'd given Allie an orgasm, and the bed next door had burst into flames. Now after a night of lovemaking, all hell had broken loose.

What would happen next?

Marc was afraid to think about it, because he wasn't ready to stop seeing Allie. Not even close. He'd always known one night with her wouldn't be enough, and sure as dawn, he'd be back in her arms tonight.

But regardless, he needed to keep his priorities straight. The *Belle* came first, not Allie . . . even if he did love making her come. In the end, she was just a woman, flesh and bone, and his time with her was fleeting. The *Belle* would be here long after Marc was gone, serving a new generation of Dumonts. He had to keep her thriving.

"So where were you last night?" Pawpaw asked. When Marc ignored the question and resumed sipping his coffee, the old guy scoffed and added, "Whoever she was, I hope she was worth it."

Marc grinned above the rim of his Styrofoam cup.

She was.

He spent the rest of the day perched behind the wheel, staring out the front window at the mighty Mississippi but seeing Allie's face reflected in each wave and shadow. Every wooden creak and groan of steel transported him back to last night when she'd moaned his name in a litany of pleasure. Even the warm jasmine breeze tormented him with reminders of her scent.

He hadn't caught a glimpse of Allie all day, and yet there was no escaping her.

Touches of her presence were everywhere—in the abandoned gris-gris bag on a hallway table outside his suite; in the ramekin of crème brûlée on the lunch tray Worm had delivered to the pilothouse. Marc had never been a fan of that particular dessert, considered it nothing more than glorified pudding, but the buttery custard and crisp caramelized topping Allie had created were so delicious he'd sent Worm back to the galley to fetch seconds.

Whether in bed or in the kitchen, one taste of Allie's sweetness was never enough.

Marc checked his watch, wondering what she was doing right now. The dinner shift had ended hours ago, so she was probably in her room getting ready to catch up on all the sleep he'd denied her last night. His mouth pulled into a frown. He wanted to see her, but he didn't know what the proper protocol was for their "relationship." He'd promised not to nail other women while he was sleeping with Allie, but that didn't make them a couple. Or at least he didn't think so. Allie wasn't his girlfriend, was she?

Hell, he didn't know. This was foreign to him.

He pulled his cell phone from the control panel and

tapped a hasty text. *What are you up to? Would love to see you later*, then shook his head and inwardly chided himself. No, that sounded needy. Plus, he shouldn't be putting any form of the L-word into Allie's head. The last thing he needed was for her to get the wrong idea and assume their arrangement went any deeper than simple lust. He deleted the message and shoved his phone into his pocket, deciding to let her make the first move.

As long as she made a move soon.

About an hour later, when he'd resorted to pinching himself in order to stay awake, two quick knocks sounded from the pilothouse door, and the object of Marc's obsession peeked her curly head inside, giving him a smile that made his heart leap into his throat while a swarm of moths took flight in his belly.

Lord help him, his brother was right. Marc was whipped like a rented mule.

"Hey," he said, doing his best to play it cool. "This is a nice surprise."

Allie nudged her way inside and shut the door with her hip, then held up a steaming cup of coffee and a few cookies on a napkin. "I don't mean to bother you, but I figured you could use some sustenance."

"You read my mind." Caffeine, sugar, and a heaping dose of Allie Mauvais were exactly what he needed. His mouth watered, partly from the scent of roasted coffee beans and chocolate chips and partly from the candied perfume clinging to her throat. "Thanks, hon."

She handed him the offerings and pointed at the folding chair by the wall. "Want some company? I can stay for a while and help keep you awake." The dirty thoughts collecting inside Marc's head must have shown in his eyes, because she pushed forward both palms and clarified, "No hanky-panky while you're at the wheel, Captain. All I'm offering is a little lively conversation."

He laughed and brought the coffee to his lips. The dark roast was rich and heady, sweetened with something that reminded him of pumpkin pie. Damn, she even made good coffee. Was there anything she couldn't do?

"No worries," he said. "I'd never slack off at the helm."

She lowered herself onto to the rickety chair and studied him for a moment. "I know you wouldn't. The *Belle* is your whole world." There wasn't an ounce of resentment in her words. When Marc turned to regard her lovely face, he saw a glimmer of respect shining there.

"She is," he agreed. "That doesn't bother you?" Over the years, most women he'd tangled with had complained that he'd spent too much time on the *Belle* and not enough in their beds. He wondered why Allie felt differently.

She shook her head. "Not at all."

"Why?"

A slow smile lifted her cheeks and her eyes softened as if she wanted to give him a hug. It looked a lot like empathy, which caught him off guard. "Because I know the real reason you've invested your heart and soul and all your money in this boat."

He lifted a questioning brow.

"It's about family," she said simply. "As long as the *Belle* stays in business, everyone you love is here—Alex and Nicky, little Worm, Ella-Claire, and your pawpaw. Even Beau."

While he processed that, she went on.

"Plus, you had an . . ." She trailed off, searching for the right word. " . . . An *unusual* childhood. You didn't grow up in the same house with your brothers—some of you didn't even go to the same school—so your only chance to be together was on the *Belle*. She's the single thread that ties together the most important people in your life."

Marc stared out the front window and considered Allie's words. He'd never thought about it that way, but he supposed she had a point. If it weren't for summers slaving aboard this boat, he'd never have seen his brothers. The one time they'd tried to organize a family barbecue, Worm's mama had "accidentally" stabbed their daddy in the thigh with a wooden kabob skewer. After that, they gave up on yearly reunions.

He might consider his brothers idiots, but they were *his* idiots, and he liked having them around—even Beau, despite the fact that he busted Marc's chops on a daily basis. The only Dumont missing on board was their daddy, and until now, Marc hadn't realized how quiet the boat seemed without the man barking orders at them. Almost too quiet.

"So," Allie continued, "by making the boat your priority, you're putting your family first. How could anyone fault you for that?"

"Believe me," Marc grumbled, "plenty of women have tried."

"Then they didn't know you at all."

He grabbed a cookie and threw her a teasing glance. "And you do?"

With a shrug, she crossed her long legs at the ankles and folded both arms behind her head. "Better than you think."

Marc laughed and dug into his cookie, but deep down he figured she was right. Her observations about the *Belle* had proved Allie understood him better than he understood himself.

Truth be told, that scared him a little.

He didn't want her to get under his skin or inside his head and take up residence there. Allie was more than a red-hot lover. She was quickly becoming a friend too, and if he allowed their connection to grow stronger, it would sting all the more when everything fell apart. Which it would. People weren't meant to mate for life—the divorce rate clinched it.

Logically, Marc knew he should pull back, but that's not what he did. Allie enchanted him with her infectious cheer and her kind words, and he couldn't ask her to leave.

They spent the next hour talking about her bakery, the Sweet Spot, and how she'd ended up there. Turned out she'd spent several years as an office manager for a New Orleans dermatologist until her parents had died and left her a small inheritance.

"That's when I realized how short our lives are," she said, peering into the darkness. "Way too short to spend my waking hours getting paid minimum wage to run someone else's business."

"But why a bakery?" Marc asked. "Why not a voodoo shop or a haunted graveyard tour? With the last name Mauvais, you'd have an edge over the competition."

Allie frowned. "Because I'm more than my last name. All my life, people have seen me as Juliette Mauvais's great-great-granddaughter. I want my own identity, separate from hers."

Marc understood. The Dumont name had its own muddy reputation, which had never really bothered him until recently. But he was captain now, and he wanted folks to take him seriously, not see him as another liar or player or cheat. Once you'd been branded, a reputation was hard to shake. He and Allie had that in common.

"And I love to bake," she went on. "My mama was big on comfort food. Anytime I had a bad day, she'd make her special bread pudding with an extra dash of lemon juice, just for me." She smiled to herself. "It always made me feel better. There was a lot of love in her kitchen, and I like to think I'm keeping her memory alive through her recipes. It feels good to know I can lift someone's mood with something as simple as a cruller."

"Brave move," Marc said, knowing full well the challenges of managing a small business. "Especially doing it on your own."

"I'm not alone—not really. At first I was going to open the shop in Cedar Bayou, because it was all I could afford. But Devyn knew I'd do better in the city, so she insisted on chipping in her half of the inheritance for the camelback store."

That surprised Marc. "She's part owner, then?"

"Mmm-hmm. A silent partner, and you'd never know

it. She hasn't asked to see a single income statement." She pursed her lips for a moment. "Not that there's much income to speak of, but still."

As talented as Allie was in the galley, she should be in the black by now. Maybe Marc could help. "Let's add your contact information to the *Belle*'s Web site," he suggested. "We'll mention you in the newsletter, too. I've heard the guests raving about your desserts. Let's give them a reminder—maybe a recipe. A way to relive part of their vacation when they get home."

Smiling, she drew her knees to her chest and wrapped both arms around her legs. "I like it. With any luck, soon my real customers will outnumber the fake ones."

"Fake ones?"

"You know, the folks who only come around for love charms." With a wistful sigh, she rested her chin on one knee. "They think I'm the reincarnation of Memère because we look alike. But I'm not. I have her eyes, not her so-called power."

She seemed so defeated that Marc handed her a cookie. "Then why don't you quit making gris-gris?" That would put an end to the steady flow of traffic from the old wives and starry-eyed teenagers. "Just cut them off. Eventually word will get around, and they'll leave you be."

"I don't know," she said around a bite of chocolate chip cookie. "Sometimes it's annoying, but the people who come to me are lost, and I get to steer them in the right direction." She reached for his coffee and took a sip, then handed it back. "That makes me feel useful."

Marc scoffed. "Honey, you're plenty useful without all that mumbo jumbo."

Allie grinned with a far-off look in her eyes as if re-playing a memory. "You don't get it."

"Then enlighten me."

So she told him the story of opening day at the Sweet Spot, when a college coed had come looking for a love charm to win back her cheating boyfriend. "She was insecure and terrified of being alone," Allie said. "I could see the desperation in her eyes, and I knew she'd never listen to reason. So I lied. I pretended to read the bones, and I told her the spirits of her ancestors de-manded she stay away from the boy because she was destined for someone better. I said they were angry that she was willing to accept so little from a man."

"Did it work?"

Allie nodded, her whole face lighting up in a smile. "I passed her on the street a few years later. I don't know if she ever met anyone, but she strutted down that sidewalk like she owned it. She's not that same scared little girl anymore." She pointed her cookie at him. "Tell me that wouldn't make your day."

Marc had to admit she was right.

From there, the conversation returned to him, specif-ically what he'd been up to since they'd graduated high school and lost touch. Talking with Allie was easy, and before long, he found himself confiding his ma-ma's bout with cancer—how he and Ella-Claire had taken turns living at home to help out after each round of chemo.

"She's been in remission five years," he said. "Health-ier than ever."

Allie stared at him with a grin tilting her lips.

"What?" he asked.

"You can tell a lot about a man by the way he treats his mama."

"Whatever." Marc waved her off. She was making a big deal out of nothing. Any decent human being would have done the same. "My daddy really put her through it. Someone had to look out for her."

Tossing her half-eaten cookie onto his napkin, Allie stood from her chair and settled behind him. She wrapped both arms around his waist, and after giving him a tight squeeze, she stood on tiptoe to whisper in his ear, "I like you, Marc Dumont."

The tickle of warm breath in his ear made Marc shiver. Before he could return the sentiment, Allie abruptly released him, then let herself out the pilot-house door.

Marc listened to her retreating footsteps, missing her already. He liked her, too—perhaps more than he should.

Chapter 12

Allie grabbed a towel and stepped out of Marc's shower, careful to avoid the creakiest floorboards and risk waking him. Just because she had to be up before the sun didn't mean he should suffer, too. The poor thing needed his sleep. They'd kept each other awake with near constant lovemaking for the past several nights, and it was starting to catch up with them. A peek in the mirror at the dark circles shadowing Allie's eyes reaffirmed it.

She opened the medicine cabinet for a tube of concealer, instantly grinning at the sight of her cosmetics occupying shelf space with his Gillette foam and Scope mouthwash. She liked seeing the merging of their toiletries. There was something so homey about their deodorants and razors hanging out together.

Marc had caught her off guard a few days ago when he'd suggested she keep some essentials in his suite to save time in the mornings. Most men would balk at the idea, probably fearing that today's toothbrush would become tomorrow's colease. This was a big step for a commitmentphobe like Marc, and she'd accepted his offer casually, hiding how much it had meant to her.

No need to spook him. He probably hadn't admitted to himself that she was his girlfriend yet. That was okay with Allie. What they had was real, regardless of how Marc defined it.

After towel-drying her hair, she scrunched her curls with a dollop of antifrizz serum and dressed in the spare uniform she'd stashed in Marc's chest of drawers. When she was ready to go, she slipped on her kitchen clogs and crouched at Marc's side to watch him sleep by the light of the digital alarm clock. She told herself she'd only stay a moment, but she lingered to listen to his rhythmic pulls of breath and his occasional murmurs. She smiled and figured he must be dreaming.

It looked like a pleasant one.

A corner of his lips kept twitching as if in laughter, the adorable cleft in his chin barely visible beneath a dusting of golden brown whiskers. In sleep, his dangerous edge softened into childlike innocence. She could watch him like this for hours and never tire of it. He was spectacular, filling her chest with a warm, tingling sensation that told her she'd moved far beyond mere attraction to Marc.

God help her, she was in love with him—a rambling Dumont man.

Gathering her hair to one side, she leaned down and kissed his forehead, pausing to take in his masculine scent. His skin was warm beneath her lips, and she wished she could crawl beneath the covers and into his powerful arms.

He stirred at the contact, and with a long groan, blinked awake. "Hey," he said in a sleep-thickened voice. "I was just dreaming about you." He smiled and made a grab for her waist. "Come back to bed and help me finish it."

Allie danced away before he could catch her. If she allowed herself to indulge in one moment of Marc's caress, she wouldn't be able to leave until noon. "Hold that thought," she said and glanced at her watch, "until about ten o'clock tonight. Then I'm all yours."

He wrinkled his forehead in confusion. "I can't see you till ten? Don't we dock in St. Louie today?"

Allie gasped and brought both hands together. She'd forgotten about that! A day in St. Louis meant the boat could operate on a skeleton crew, freeing them both for some alone time.

Marc rubbed his eyes. "I was hoping we could sneak off somewhere after the guests leave for their tours."

The prospect of spending a full day with Marc made her want to turn cartwheels, but she curbed her enthusiasm, not wanting to appear too eager. Folding both arms, she threw him a teasing smile. "I suppose that can be arranged. We'll have to lie low, though." She'd spent so much time insisting she wasn't *the captain's squeeze* that she'd look like the mother of all hypocrites if anyone discovered them together.

He focused on the bare skin beneath the hem of her skirt, licking his lips like the hungry wolf he was. "How low do you want to lie? We can hole up in here all day. I can think of plenty of ways to keep busy. . . ."

Tempting as that was, Allie longed for a little terra firma. "Down, boy. You're taking me on a proper date for once. Pick me up at my room when you're ready."

"Mm-kay." He waggled his brows as she backed toward the door. "Wear that flimsy sundress I like." Pointing at the bottom of his rib cage, he added, "The one that's cut down to here."

Allie dragged a finger down the length of her cleavage. "Down to here, huh?" She bit back a grin. Marc had exaggerated the revealing nature of her dress, but if he loved it that much, she'd wear it every chance she got. "It's a deal." With a wink, she told him, "And I might not wear anything underneath it."

Marc's eyes glazed over. He made a move toward her, and Allie hastily turned the doorknob and stepped into the hall before he could leap out of bed and drag her back in with him. She blew him one last kiss and shut the door, then peeked up and down the hallway to make sure nobody had seen her sneaking out of his room.

Fortunately, she was alone.

When she made her way down to the galley, she was surprised to find Beau and the entire kitchen staff darting around one another to prepare breakfast, the air already thick with the scents of sizzling sausage and baking biscuits. A lump of guilt settled in her tummy when she realized she was the last to report for duty. Beau glanced up from his cutting board. He didn't say a word, but his eyes darted to the clock on the wall.

"Morning," Allie said as she rushed to the sink to wash her hands. She donned her apron and spun toward the refrigerator, where she reached for the goat cheese Regale had bought but had neglected to use. She'd never considered including it in her berry torte, but inspiration had struck that morning when she'd awoken in Marc's arms, and she suspected the blend of flavors would complement one another perfectly— bold and sweet, kind of like herself and Marc.

She couldn't stop smiling while she crushed ginger-snaps for the crust, and by the time she slid her pans into the oven, she'd made half a dozen impromptu changes in the recipe that had her mouth watering just thinking about them. While the tortes baked, she jotted down the modifications in a spiral notebook so she could replicate it at the Sweet Spot.

The aroma of mixed berries and gingerbread drew Beau's gaze away from his cutting board. After the tortes had cooled, he joined Allie in helping her separate the crust from the pans and cut the pastries into individual servings.

"This looks amazing," Beau said, admiring the creamy filling. When he lifted a slice and positioned it above a dessert plate, he let the spatula slip to the side, sending a small portion down in a sloppy heap. He slid her a glance. "Oops, that one's ruined."

Allie laughed. It was obvious he'd done it on purpose. "Guess you'll have to eat it, then."

"It's the only logical thing to do," he said. "It'd be a crime to let it go to waste."

She handed him a fork. "I took some liberties with my mama's recipe. Let me know what you think."

Beau shoveled a heaping bite into his mouth. Seconds later, he closed his eyes and pressed a hand over his heart. His noises of rapture drew a few curious gazes from the staff, and as soon as he swallowed, he uttered a good-natured curse. "I don't know what got into you, but that's goddamned incredible."

Allie blushed and hid a grin. "There's a little extra love in my cooking today, that's all."

"That's all?" he repeated. "Allie, this is the best berry torte I've ever tasted." He clapped her on the shoulder. "You're at the top of your game. Keep up the good work."

While Beau returned to his station, Allie beamed and finished slicing her pastries. Regale never would have complimented her baking. Ever the diva, he'd wanted the spotlight for himself.

Beau Dumont was good people.

When the breakfast rush had ended and the galley workers finished cleaning up, Allie and Beau stayed behind to inventory ingredients.

With his head in the refrigerator, Beau observed, "We could use more butter."

Allie scrawled it on the list. "That's a general rule in life."

He pointed at her notepad. "Write down *shallots*, too." After shutting the fridge, he assessed the contents of the pantry. "And pork rinds."

"Pork rinds?" she asked, trying to imaging how he'd incorporate those into a recipe. "You going to crumble them as a topping?"

"No." Beau shrugged. "I'm gonna eat 'em."

If personal snacks were going on their grocery list, she was adding Junior Mints. When she'd finished jotting down everything they needed, she held up the notepad. "Want me to pick this up? I'm heading into town anyway."

"No, I'll get it," he said, taking the pad from her. "I'm picky about my veggies."

"Suit yourself; I'm heading upstairs to change. See you at four."

Allie returned to her room, noting that the same set of unused folded towels sat on her bed. The maids had probably noticed she hadn't been sleeping here. She wondered if they'd begun gossiping yet and whether anyone had linked her to Marc. To be on the safe side, she shook out the towels and mussed her bedsheets, then scattered the pillows.

She applied some light makeup and styled her hair, twisting it into a loose updo that cooled the back of her neck. Smiling, she pulled Marc's favorite dress from the closet. As promised, she didn't wear a stitch beneath it. The silky fabric felt decadent against her bare backside, like a sinful secret. By the time she'd strapped on her sandals, a trio of knocks sounded at the door, sending her pulse rushing with excitement. She grabbed her handbag and met Marc in the hallway.

His eyes went wide, scanning her from the top of her head to the tips of her open-toed platforms. "Wow," was all he said, but his tone spoke volumes.

"Wow, yourself." She took a moment to appreciate the sight of Marc in a tight black T-shirt and faded jeans that cupped him in all the right places. He wore his hair in loose waves that brushed his broad shoulders. He looked relaxed and happy and criminally sexy—a lethal trifecta.

He wrapped both arms around her waist and greeted her with a kiss that said he was just as excited about their date as she was. He traced her curves, then slid his palms over her rear end and froze.

"I don't feel any panties under here," he whispered against her mouth.

"No," she whispered back. "You sure don't."

Groaning, he lifted her into his arms and took a step toward her door. "Let's go inside for a minute."

"Forget it." She squirmed out of his grasp and smacked away his hands when he tried to capture her again. "I'm not giving it up until you take me out and show me a good time."

He winked at her. "I can show you a good time right here." But despite his teasing words, he laced their fingers together and led her toward the stairwell. He brushed his thumb affectionately over her wrist as they descended the stairs, occasionally bringing their linked hands to his lips. Once they reached the main level, he let go of her and instructed, "You head to the bow ramp—I'll be right behind you. If anyone asks where we're going, I'll say we're picking up supplies."

"Okay, sounds like a plan." She'd just begun to push open the door when Marc's pawpaw stepped into view from the stairs leading to the boiler room.

Allie's heart lurched. How long had he been standing there?

Pawpaw narrowed his eyes at her, then at Marc. "Where you goin', boy?"

"Into town," Marc said without missing a beat. He patted his side pocket. "And I've got a long list, so I'd better get to it." He nodded ahead in a signal for Allie to hurry up.

She obliged, stepping onto the main deck, then making a beeline for the bow ramp. The clicking of her sandals drew the attention of twins, Alex and Nicky, and their big brother Beau, who leaned against the deck rail, watching the last guests depart.

In true Nick fashion, he whistled at Allie as she passed. "You sure look nice. Got a hot date?"

"No!" she said a bit too loudly. "Just picking up some fresh fruit from the farmer's market."

"Hey," Marc said from behind. "I need to go into town, too. Want to share a taxi?"

Judging by the muffled laughter coming from his brothers, their act wasn't fooling anyone.

Beau followed them down the ramp. "I'm stopping at the farmer's market. I'll split a cab with you guys." When Marc fired a glare over his shoulder, Beau returned it with twice the fury. "Is that a problem?"

Marc didn't object, probably because his pawpaw was still watching, but the instant the three of them crowded into the backseat of a taxi, he let Beau have it. "You're enjoying this, aren't you?"

"Like hell I am." He shot Allie a chiding glance from the opposite end of the bench seat. "You two are the worst pair of liars I've ever seen."

Allie bit her lip and linked her arm through Marc's. "Do you think your granddaddy suspects anything?"

"If he saw the way you two looked at each other," Beau said, "then, yeah. He's old, not blind. That goes for the rest of the staff, too. They're gonna think the captain's playing favorites, and that's the last thing we—"

"Enough," Marc ordered. "Shut up or get your own taxi." He wrapped an arm around Allie and told the cabdriver to take them to a place called the Hill, then turned the topic to the Italian restaurant where he'd made lunch reservations. "The best in the city," Marc claimed.

Beau frowned but let the subject drop. He asked Allie, "What's your sister up to these days?" Though he used a casual tone, he shrank a few inches into the vinyl seat. "She ever get that education degree she talked about?"

Allie laughed at the idea of her sister leading a classroom of children. She'd forgotten that Dev had wanted to become a teacher. "No, she dropped out of college freshman year. She's kind of a Gypsy now—just a short-term gig here and there. She gets bored easily."

Beau didn't seem to like that. He spent the rest of the ride in silence, staring out his window. When the taxi pulled up beside an adorable Italian bistro, Marc tossed his brother a twenty-dollar bill to cover the fare and ushered Allie onto the sidewalk. Before the cab pulled away, Beau rolled down his window and asked, "Hey, will you tell Dev I said hi?"

Allie wished she could help, but any communication from him would only make matters worse. "I'm sorry, baby. That would be a bad idea."

Beau nodded and rolled up his window. With a wave, he was gone.

"After you." Marc's touch returned Allie's attention to present company. He held open the door for her and settled his hand at her lower back while leading the way to their table. Once there, he pulled out her chair like a gentleman and ordered a bottle of chilled white wine.

"This is nice," Allie said, taking in the cozy dining area of a dozen round white-draped tables, each anchored by a duo of candle tapers. The tangy scent of marinara and baking bread set her mouth watering. Marc had chosen well.

He opened his menu and began perusing its offerings. "Only the best for my gal."

The offhanded statement set Allie's heart fluttering. She raised her own menu so he couldn't see her smiling. When the waitress returned, they both ordered the chicken parmesan, and Marc poured their wine.

Lifting his glass in a toast, he began, "To . . ." and trailed off in deliberation.

"To old friends and taking chances," she suggested.

"Agreed."

He clinked her glass and took a long sip, locking eyes with her from above the rim. She detected something new in his gaze, more than the wicked desire she'd seen burning there for the past week. This seemed tender, like he wanted to pause time and live in this moment for a while longer. Was it her hopeful imagination, or had Marc actually fallen as hard and as fast as she had?

"You're the prettiest girl in here," he said, instantly bringing a blush to her cheeks.

Allie stared into her lap. "Don't be silly."

She'd never felt shy around him before, but now her palms were starting to sweat. She blotted them on her linen napkin and took a few gulps of wine. The alcohol helped loosen her tongue, and by her second glass, she felt like herself again.

They talked about their hobbies, and when the topic of favorite movies came up, Marc's response was, "*Unforgiven*, with Clint Eastwood. It's about a—"

"A retired gunman who gets revenge for a mutilated prostitute," Allie finished. "Yeah, I liked that one, but not as much as *A Fistful of Dollars*. That was Clint's best work, if you ask me."

Marc's eyes widened. "You like Westerns?"

"No," Allie said, leaning forward for emphasis, "I *love* Westerns."

"Oh, my God." He looked ready to marry her on the spot. "You might be the world's most perfect woman. Do you know that?"

"Real funny."

Allie had her flaws, and so did Marc. But as the hour passed, she couldn't help wondering if they were perfect for each other. The longer they talked, the more they discovered how much they had in common. They both hated collard greens and the Chicago Cubs, they felt equal pressure to keep their businesses afloat, and they each pictured themselves moving back to Cedar Bayou one day.

"I like the city," Marc said. "But sometimes the bayou's the only place I can hear myself think."

Allie nodded. "I miss the way the air back home smells in the summer—like lavender and honeysuckle. Outside my shop it mostly smells like car exhaust."

They spent a few minutes gossiping about old friends, and when they'd finished lunch, Marc hailed another taxi and told the driver to take them to the Missouri Botanical Garden.

"You're going to like this," Marc promised during the ride. "Especially if you miss the flowers."

And he was right. She loved it.

Marc led her on an easy stroll through the Japanese

garden—fourteen acres of lush green lawns and wind-ing paths leading to an expansive lake with four tiny islands of stone jutting proudly from its depths. Lan-terns hung from the lowest branches of blossoming trees, and the air was heavy with floral warmth.

Marc held her hand the whole time, releasing her only to wrap an arm around her waist. They crossed an arched wooden bridge and paused in the middle to gaze into the water. Allie thought she spotted a turtle, but she couldn't be sure. When she glanced up to ask Marc if he'd seen it, she found him watching her. He had that soft look in his eyes again, but before she could ask what he was thinking, he cupped the back of her neck and drew her in for a gentle kiss.

His lips moved in perfect sync with hers while his fingers traced the contours of her face. This kiss was different from the hundreds of others they'd shared, so full of tenderness that Allie's throat grew thick with emotion.

There was love in this kiss—she felt it.

She locked both arms around his neck and melted into him without a care for the passersby on the bridge. She let herself get lost in Marc's embrace until his cell phone vibrated against her thigh.

With a reluctant moan, Marc pulled away and reached into his pocket for his phone. His brow fur-rowed as he read the message on his screen. "Uh-oh."

"What's wrong?" Allie asked, leaning to peer at his phone.

The text was from Nicky. *Hurry back to the* Belle. *911!*

"Sorry, hon," Marc said. "We've got to go."

They rushed to the parking lot and hailed a cab.

During the ride to the dock, Marc's body was so stiff, he could have posed as one of the sculptures in the Japanese garden they'd just fled. He spoke on the phone with Nick, and though Allie was only privy to one end of the conversation, she could tell something major had happened to the boat's engine.

"How bad is it?" she asked when he'd disconnected.

Marc drew a deep breath and let it go in a loud puff. "Bad enough that we'll be stuck in St. Louis another day." He leaned forward and cradled his head in both hands. "Maybe two. And that's assuming I can find someone to fix the train linkage."

Allie didn't know what a train linkage was, but it sounded complicated. She scooted nearer to Marc and rubbed his back. "I'll work with Ella-Claire to keep the guests happy during the layover. Maybe we can throw together a quick gala—everyone loves a party." When he didn't reply, she promised, "It's going to be okay."

He took one of her hands and held it tightly. "Thank you." He didn't say anything more until they reached the *Belle*.

When they stepped out of the cab and approached the boat ramp, Marc's pawpaw greeted them with folded arms and a scowl. He stood at the head of the ramp, blocking their entry as Marc's brothers loitered behind, looking uneasy.

Allie's internal alarm blared when she realized nobody would make eye contact with her. Then she recognized her luggage heaped into a pile at Pawpaw's feet, including her backpack of gris-gris supplies.

Allie's ribs tightened around her sinking heart. They were kicking her off the boat.

Marc noticed, too. He pointed at her suitcase. "What's all this?"

"It's your wakeup call, boy," his granddaddy spat. He nodded toward Allie without giving her the courtesy of a glance. "We've had nothin' but trouble since you brought her on board. Now the engine's half-busted, and we're about to get shut down. She's a blight on this family." He jabbed a finger at the ground. "It's gonna end right here."

Allie's face burned. She was no stranger to rumors and scrutiny, but this was different. This was personal. But she wouldn't fight back—she knew how important Marc's family was to him. Blinking away tears, she took a step toward her bags, but Marc reached out an arm to stop her.

"Miss Mauvais isn't going anywhere," he said in a low firm voice that dared anyone to disagree. He locked eyes with Beau. "You all go on and take Allie's things back to her room."

Nobody said a word.

Beau scratched his neck and studied the tips of his shoes. "Listen, little brother, I get where you're coming from. Allie's a damn fine pastry chef, but folks are starting to talk. I'm not saying this is right, but maybe—"

"When I want your opinion, I'll give it to you." Marc's voice cut like steel, causing his younger brothers to glance nervously at each other. "I said, take Allie's things back to her room. So either do it, or pack up your own shit and go." When nobody moved, he added, "Now."

Slowly, Beau grabbed her suitcase and gave his brothers an encouraging nod. The twins took the rest of her luggage and Worm slung her backpack over one shoulder. They made their way toward the stairs while watching the storm brewing between Marc and his grandfather.

"She's entranced you, son," Pawpaw said. "You can't see it, but I can."

"Save it. I've got enough to deal with." Marc stepped forward until he was toe-to-toe with the man. "Move aside."

Pawpaw raised his jaw. "I won't let you bring her on board my ship."

"Last time I checked," Marc ground out, "it was my name on the deed, not yours."

"If your daddy knew what you were up to, he'd tell you to get your priorities straight."

Marc didn't back down. "And I'd tell him to mind his own damn business. Allie's saved my ass more times than I can count. She stays. I'm your captain—whether you like it or not—and I'm going to give you one last chance to move before I haul you out of the way."

Pain flashed in his granddaddy's dark eyes, so much like Marc's they could pass for father and son. "We're kin, boy. I spent my whole life building this legacy for you and your brothers. You gonna turn your back on me for a *woman*?"

Marc clenched his teeth and fell silent, scrubbing a hand over his face and clearly beginning to waver.

"It's time to choose," Pawpaw said. "It's her, or it's me."

Shit.

As if Marc didn't have enough trouble on his hands with the train linkage, now he was facing a full-on mutiny from his own family—the people who were supposed to have his back.

So much for blood being thicker than water.

They could learn a lesson from Allie. She didn't owe him a damn thing, and yet she'd worked harder than anyone to make this trip a success. The curse wasn't her fault, and he had no intention of abandoning her in St. Louis.

He'd rather sever his own arm.

"I'm not choosing anything," Marc said to his pawpaw. "If you can't support my decisions as captain, then you're the one turning your back on me, not the other way around."

Pawpaw's glare shifted to Allie. "You don't know what she's done."

"Yeah, I do," Marc said. "Let me tell you what she's done." He looked the old man in the eyes while he recounted the story of the Gibsons' wedding cake and how Allie had stepped aside to keep Chef Regale on board. "She didn't complain once while she was in the casino, because Allie's a team player. When she heard about the problems in the engine room, she started planning a party for the guests. I didn't have to ask—she took the ball and ran with it." Then Marc said, "What have *you* done, aside from criticize Allie and call her a witch?"

Pawpaw didn't have an answer for that question.

"That's what I thought." Marc hitched a thumb toward the dock. "Either apologize to Miss Mauvais and get back to work, or fetch your things and call a cab. I've got to see to the train linkage." He pushed around Pawpaw and strode onto the bow ramp, leaving his grandfather to make his decision.

Chapter 13

Allie gripped the deck rail, watching Marc's pawpaw fade into the distance as the *Belle*'s massive paddle wheel turned a lazy rotation and left the old man behind. A faded yellow taxi pulled into view near the dock, and Pawpaw loaded his duffel bags into the trunk. He shook his head one last time, then climbed into the backseat. Moments later, he was gone.

She couldn't believe it. Marc had chosen *her* over his grandfather.

Allie didn't know what to think about that.

Most women would feel flattered, but she wasn't most women. Allie cared for Marc, and she hated causing a rift in his family. He'd stormed off to the boiler room an hour ago, but she could sense his pain from a distance—a steady ache beneath her breast that likely wouldn't let up until she'd helped set things right with his grandpa. And if the ugly words the men had hurled at each other were any indication, peace wouldn't come easily.

At least the boat's engine had given them a reprieve, humming to life thirty minutes ago as unexpectedly as it had quit. Releasing a breath, Allie faced the setting sun, a smudge of tangerine glowing through bubble gum clouds. It was a beautiful evening, but there wasn't time to find a rocking chair and explore her thoughts.

The guests were waiting for dessert.

She returned to the galley and helped serve the eight-layer Peach Decadence cake she'd spent the afternoon baking, then added cookies and bread pudding to the buffet. She cleaned her station and prepared tomorrow's breakfast menu. When her work was done, she lingered in the kitchen, unsure of where to go next. Should she visit Marc or give him some space?

Deciding to follow her instincts, Allie climbed four flights of stairs to the pilothouse door. After knocking twice, she peeked inside and found him sitting at the helm in his tall captain's chair.

"Hey," she said softly. "Just seeing if you need anything before I turn in."

He swiveled to face her, a pout tugging the corners of his mouth. "My shift's done in an hour. Can you wait up for me?"

"If that's what you need." She stepped inside and slung an arm over his shoulder. With her free hand, she tugged off his hat and brushed her fingers through his loose hair. "Are you sure you don't want to be alone? I'll understand."

Marc pulled her onto his lap. "Sugar, nothing relaxes me like you do." A shadow seemed to pass over his stunning features, his hands tightening around her hips. "I don't want to waste one minute of the time we have left by sleeping apart."

Allie lowered her brows. The time they had left? What was that supposed to mean? "I'm not going to turn into a pumpkin when we dock in New Orleans, you know."

The irritation must have shown on her face because Marc started backpedaling. "Don't get the wrong idea—I'm not saying this is just a vacation fling."

"You sure about that?"

"Positive."

She gave him a skeptical look. "Then what's with the ticking clock?"

"Come on, Allie," he said, turning toward the front window. "You know me." His tone was thick with self-loathing in a way she didn't like. "Not just me. My whole family—we have a way of ruining everything we touch. Even one another. Today proved that."

Allie cupped his cheek until he met her gaze. "And you think you'll ruin me?"

"Not you," he told her. "You're too strong for that. But *us*?" His dark eyes said the rest. *I'll ruin what we have together.* "I don't want to screw up, but I have to admit I don't have the best history."

"Baby, you don't give yourself enough credit." Marc needed to see that he wasn't doomed to follow the same path as every Dumont man who came before him. "You're not your daddy. You won't make the same mistakes he did."

"That's why I always use protection."

He was missing the point. "I'm not talking about birth control. I'm talking about mastery over your life. You're not destined to fail, and you're not cursed."

He smiled, but it didn't reach his eyes. "I know, hon.

Sorry. I'm just in a weird mood tonight. Forget I said anything." He scooted her off his lap. "Why don't you head back to my suite and get the bed warmed up, okay? I'll be there in a jiff."

Reluctantly, she left him with a kiss. She hoped she'd gotten through to Marc, but when he came to bed later that night, he made love to her like a soldier headed for war . . . with one exception. He wouldn't look her in the eyes. His lips scarcely strayed from hers, his hands brushing her face as if to memorize each freckle and eyelash, but no matter how many times she tried to hold his gaze, he refused the emotional connection.

She understood what he was doing—avoiding intimacy and preparing for the inevitable breakup, because that was all he'd ever known. A chill settled in Allie's soul when she realized she'd lose Marc unless she changed his way of thinking.

And fast.

The next morning, she served her breakfast pastries and set off in search of Ella-Claire, hoping an estrogen-enhanced brainstorm session would yield some ideas. She found Ella standing behind the purser's desk with Alex, the two of them engaged in an intense thumb war that rendered them oblivious to her approaching footsteps.

"Hey, back off, cheater," Ella said, pushing Alex's chest to put another inch between them. With her other hand, she gripped his fingers and hooked a thumb around his. She had him pinned for an instant, but he wriggled free. In clear desperation to win, she crowded him and launched a new attack.

Alex chuckled. "Who's cheating now?"

"All's fair in love and thumb war. I'm taking you down, buddy."

She used her free hand to tickle his ribs, and Alex retaliated in an assault on her tummy. Seconds later, the thumb war gave way to a full-on tickle fight, the echo of their laughter reverberating through the lobby. It didn't take long for Alex to overpower his opponent.

Securing both of Ella's wrists behind her back, he pinned her against the counter and smiled in victory. Alex moved forward until nothing but a sliver of air separated them. He swallowed hard, the mood shifting as his gaze dropped to Ella-Claire's mouth and held there.

Gracious, these two had it bad.

Just when Alex leaned down for a kiss, Allie cleared her throat.

Alex glanced up, his eyes flying wide. "Allie!" He released his *buddy* and jumped back as if she'd caught him doing something wrong. Which she had. Marc would pummel Alex six feet under if he discovered his brother putting the moves on Ella-Claire.

"Hey, there," Allie said, folding her arms on the countertop. "Whatcha up to?"

"Nothing!" Alex glanced around the desk until he found a clipboard, then snatched it with a shaky fist. "Uh, I should run. I've got . . . uh . . . *stuff* to do."

"Mmm," Allie said with a knowing look. "Sounds important."

Ella-Claire casually handed him a sealed envelope. "While you're out, will you drop this by room 215?"

All too happy to comply, Alex grabbed the letter,

skirted the counter, and took off down the side hallway like a felon on the run. *There goes a man with a guilty conscience*, Allie thought. His partner in crime straightened her sleek brown ponytail and pretended nothing had happened.

"What's going on with you two?" Allie asked.

Ella made doe eyes and blinked in ignorance. "Nothing. We're just friends."

"Liar," Allie scoffed. "What if it'd been Marc instead of me who walked in here and broke up your little tickle fight?"

Ella dropped the innocent act. "You're not going to say anything to him, are you? Because I swear nothing would've happened."

"He was about to kiss you."

Ella dismissed the argument with a flick of her wrist. "I wouldn't have let him." She leaned in and rested both arms on the counter, mirroring Allie's pose. "Look, I like Alex. He's my bestie. But he's a player—always has been. No matter how much we flirt, I keep him in the friend zone. I'm not stupid enough to fall for a Dumont."

Allie's face went slack. Even Marc's sister knew it was lunacy to try to tame his wild heart. That didn't bode well.

Ella-Claire realized her mistake, instantly stammering to correct herself. "I don't mean Marc—he's different from his brothers. I've seen the way he watches you, Allie. He's totally smitten."

Allie caught her bottom lip between her teeth. "Really?"

"I swear," Ella said, holding up one hand in an oath. "I've never seen him like this. You've given me hope."

Allie raised a brow in question.

"That he might actually slow down and let himself be happy," Ella said. "I think you're good for Marc—and that he can be good for you, too."

"I want that to be true," Allie said. "But there's a lot of baggage in the way."

Ella-Claire gestured to the extra chair behind the purser's desk. "I need to finish the billing. Want to help me stuff envelopes while we chat?"

That sounded perfect. Talking always came easier for Allie when she busied her hands. She sat side by side with Ella, working while she explained the recent change she'd noticed in Marc.

"He's already pulling away," Allie said. "I can feel it."

Ella licked an envelope, making a *yuck* face at the glue. "Are you sure? Because it seems like he can't get enough of you."

"Positive. Ever heard of a self-fulfilling prophecy?"

"I think so," Ella told her. "Is that where you believe in something so much that you make it happen?"

"Sort of," Allie said. "But on a subconscious level. Like if a person is convinced he's going to lose his job, he might pull back from his coworkers, then start slacking off and showing up late."

"Which results in him getting fired."

"Exactly." Allie folded another room service bill, creasing it with her fingernail. "On the surface, Marc says he doesn't believe in the curse. But I think he buys into it just enough to set low expectations for himself. Last night he basically told me our days are numbered. Now I can barely get him to look at me."

"You think he's going to break it off?"

"No, not yet," Allie said. "But I think over time he'll sabotage his happiness. Just like his daddy and his pawpaw. People learn what they live. The curse isn't real, but it might as well be, because the Dumonts keep perpetuating the cycle."

Ella went silent for a while, gazing at the lobby ceiling as if the answer might appear up there among the chandelier crystals. "So how do we undo a lifetime of superstition, bad habits, and even worse examples?"

"That's the million-dollar question, isn't it?"

And Allie didn't have one red cent toward the answer. She scowled at the framed photo of Marc's great-great-grandfather that hung on the wall inside the purser's office. Edward Dumont bore a slight resemblance to Marc, but his chin was weak and his eyes were cold. He looked like the kind of man who hadn't taken many risks, despite the fact that he'd made a thriving business of the *Belle*.

Ella-Claire followed Allie's gaze to the portrait. "He's the one who started this mess. I heard he had a fiancée but left her at the altar. He never got married after that, not that it stopped him from having a gaggle of kids with three different women."

Something compelled Allie to study the portrait more closely. She stood and approached it, not sure what she was looking for, and gripped the frame to pull the picture down from the wall. It was bolted in place, but the backing budged just enough to dislodge a piece of paper that had been wedged behind it. Onion-thin and yellowed with age, the page drifted to the floor. When she picked it up, she saw a letter to Edward dated 1915. It was signed by someone named Silas Dumont.

"Check this out," she said, returning to the desk to show Ella-Claire. "There was an old note stuck behind the picture."

Ella scooted her chair closer, and together they read the letter in silence. It was brief, but impactful, shedding light on the origins of the Dumont *curse*.

"Wow," Ella said. "That explains a lot."

"Edward and Memère." Allie shook her head. "I had no idea they were lovers."

"Not just lovers. *Engaged*."

Allie glanced down to find her forearm covered in goose bumps. Carefully, she folded the note and tucked it inside a book for safekeeping. "Do you mind if I hold on to this? I want to show my sister." Devyn was going to eat this up.

"Be my guest," Ella said. "But you might not want to let Marc see it. Nothing will convince him the curse is fake if he reads that."

Marc's right arm tingled, the blood flow interrupted by Allie's sleeping head resting on his shoulder. But he made no move to wriggle free. He lived for these quiet moments alone with her when they lay so close, he felt the thump of her heartbeat against his chest. If he shut his eyes and concentrated, he could slow his pulse to match hers. Then they were like one person, connected on the most basic levels—body to body, heart to heart.

Cheesy, but true.

Carefully as possible, he stretched to turn off the alarm before it woke her, then pulled the sheet over her breasts so she'd stay warm. He didn't care if he made her late. Today they'd dock in New Orleans and the trip would end. They'd resume their separate lives, connecting just as much as the curse would allow. Instinctively, he knew his time with her was finite.

Work could wait. Allie couldn't.

Until recently he hadn't understood guys who lost their shit over a woman. Years ago, he'd taken a date to see *Jerry Maguire*, that sappy-ass movie starring Tom Cruise. When the actor had uttered his famous line "You complete me" to his onscreen girlfriend, Marc had laughed out loud and suggested that Tom surrender his Man Card.

But Marc wasn't laughing now.

The joke was on him. He never imagined a person could complete him the way Allie did. She understood his twisted family dynamic and held her own around each of his brothers—even Beau. She supported the *Belle* and earned the respect of guests and crew alike. She was more than just a lover, and Marc finally knew what he'd been missing all these years.

His other half.

Truth be told, that scared him. Because losing Allie would do more than hurt; it would leave him incomplete— torn and worthless. He could barely stand to think about life without her.

Reflexively, his arms tightened, rousing her from deep slumber. An adorable whine rose from her throat, and she burrowed her cheek deeper into his shoulder.

Right before drifting off again, she murmured, "Love you, baby."

Marc's breath locked inside his throat.

Allie loved him?

Had she really meant that, or was she just talking in her sleep? And did he feel the same way? Having never been in love before, he wasn't sure, but he couldn't imagine feeling anything stronger than the swelling behind his ribs. He wanted to whisper it back but couldn't manage to shake the words off his tongue.

He thought about the conversation they'd had a few nights ago in the pilothouse, how Allie had promised he wouldn't turn out like his daddy. Part of him wanted to believe he could keep the flame alive if he tried hard enough. The other part of him warned that everyone felt that way, especially in the beginning. Nobody got married expecting to divorce.

Besides, Marc had never spent more than a few weeks with one woman. Was he capable of monogamy? He'd never forgive himself if he ran around on Allie like his father had done to every woman he'd ever "loved."

But what if they *could* defy the odds? Shouldn't he at least try to make a go of it?

Hell, he didn't know. At this point he was thinking in circles, and he knew a better way to spend his time than brooding. He nuzzled his way to the side of Allie's throat and woke her with openmouthed kisses, suckling the weak spot beneath her ear until she writhed against him and moaned his name.

The day could wait.

*   *   *

When he escorted her to the galley an hour later, Beau glanced up, his head covered in a ridiculous do-rag. He frowned and pointed an egg at Marc. "You made my pastry chef late, Captain."

Marc grinned at him. "My apologies, Chef. I can personally guarantee that it won't happen again."

"Yeah," Beau grumbled. "Only because we dock before lunch."

Beau cracked the egg against his stainless steel bowl and began whisking in a blur of movement, but amusement sparked behind his eyes. And he wasn't the only one.

It seemed the entire staff wore a collective smile this morning in anticipation of returning home. The lone man out, Marc didn't want the voyage to end.

But he gave himself a mental kick in the pants and remembered his duties. If he didn't make his guests feel special, they might spend their future vacation dollars elsewhere. With a nod good-bye at Allie, Marc left to make his rounds.

He'd just crossed the lobby when a flash of metal caught his eye. A quick glance over his shoulder showed the Gibsons approaching from the stairs. The bride beamed brighter than her glinting lip rings and tackle-hugged him.

"Thank you," she spoke into his lapels as her arms squeezed his waist. "I can't tell you how much that book meant to me."

Marc didn't have the foggiest idea what she was talking about, but he patted her shoulder and played it cool. "My pleasure. I hope you had a nice honeymoon."

"The best," she said, gazing at her husband. "We'll be back for our anniversary."

That was exactly what Marc wanted to hear. The newlyweds drifted toward the outside deck, allowing him to continue to the service desk.

Ella-Claire dashed around the counter when she spotted him and threw both arms around his neck. Folks sure were in a hugging mood today.

"What's this for?" he asked.

She clucked her tongue at him. "Can't a sister be proud? You officially rocked your first trip as captain."

A prideful smile lifted his lips. "I wouldn't say I rocked it . . ."

"Don't be modest." Ella straightened his tie and brushed a bit of lint off his jacket. "It wasn't all smooth sailing, but you handled everything like a pro. You were born to do this, Marc."

He shrugged her off and gave another grin. "At least I didn't sink us."

"There you go again with the modesty." She stood on tiptoe to kiss his cheek, then linked their arms and led him toward the counter. "And I know it's none of my business, but I think there's another reason you've looked so happy lately. . . ." Her voice trailed off, thick with romantic implications.

Marc didn't bother to deny it, but he didn't take the bait either. Not that his silence stopped Ella from meddling.

"Can I give you some sisterly advice?" she asked, blinking those big blue eyes at him.

"Fine."

Ella took his face between her palms. "Allie's good for you. I like her. Don't mess it up."

Marc sniffed a laugh. She made it sound so easy. "Is that all?"

"Listen," she said, "once we get home, it'll be easy to slip back into old habits. If Allie's important to you, then tell her. Make her a priority. Because as much as you love the *Belle*, this boat won't grow old with you or care for you when you're sick."

"I've got health insurance, and the *Belle*'s already old. She'll outlive us all."

Ella-Claire frowned at him. "You know what I mean."

Yeah, Marc understood what she meant. "I know."

"So talk to her," Ella pleaded. She tapped him on the cheek. "It wouldn't kill you to make a commitment, either. Prove that you want her—make a grand gesture. Every woman wants to feel wanted."

"Deep thoughts," Marc teased. "You're a real Plato."

Ella shoved him, knocking him back a step. "Don't be an ass."

Marc drew her in and dropped a kiss on the top of her head. Ella was a sweetheart, even if she was bossy. "I'll do my best."

He spent the next several hours laughing and schmoozing, but his brain had one foot out the door. His sister was right. When they docked in New Orleans, Allie would tow her little wheeled suitcase back to her camelback store, and he'd sleep alone tonight.

Marc frowned.

He didn't want to sleep alone. He'd grown accustomed to the warmth of Allie's body draped across his, the soothing rise and fall of her chest, and the scents of sugared vanilla and sex on his sheets. Of course he'd keep seeing her, but at this point, dating would be a step backward.

Ella had said he should make a grand gesture. Maybe he should ask Allie to move in with him—they'd practically lived together these past couple of weeks anyhow. It seemed sudden, not to mention a little terrifying, but the more Marc thought about it, the more he liked the idea. An excited flutter tickled his stomach when he pictured Allie moving in her things, filling his closet with her pretty sundresses and his bureau with her lingerie—even that silly polka-dot nightgown she'd worn last week.

Yes, he decided. He'd ask her to live with him. It seemed like the right move.

The afternoon passed slower than a geriatric slug. Marc found himself growing more nervous with each minute, and by the time the guests departed and he dismissed the nonessential staff, he had to run upstairs to change his sweaty shirt.

He damn near had a heart attack when he noticed Allie had cleared out all her bottles and tubes of girlie products from his bathroom. She wouldn't leave without saying good-bye, would she?

Buttoning his shirt as he went, he tore down the hallway to the stairwell, then rushed to her room on the third floor. He knocked several times, but she didn't answer.

"She's gone," said a maid working in the adjacent room. The woman pointed toward the opposite stairs. "But you can probably catch her."

While jogging down the hallway, Marc replayed their morning together to see if he'd done something to upset Allie, but he came up empty. There was no reason for her to rush off like this.

Eventually, he found her stacking her bags on the deck near the bow ramp.

"Hey," he called.

She turned and greeted him with a warm smile, and Marc released the breath he'd been holding. In three quick strides, he joined her, settling both palms around her waist without a care for the stragglers looking on. Let them gawk. He wanted everyone to know Allie belonged to him.

She shielded her eyes from the afternoon sun and settled a hand on his chest. "Miss me already?"

"You weren't going to sneak off, were you?"

"Of course not," she said. "I was just getting my bags together; then I figured I should get out of your way."

Marc bent his mouth to her ear. "Sugar, I like you in my way."

She pulled back and gave him a seductive grin. "Do you, now?"

"Mmm-hmm," he said. "In fact, I was hoping we could talk about that." His heart thumped and his palms were growing damp. "I've had a lot of fun these past couple weeks . . ."

"Me, too."

"So . . ." he began, barely able to speak over the pulse pounding in his ears. "This might sound crazy, but hear me out. I think we should . . . um . . ." He trailed off, a sudden lump of fear rising in his throat.

He tried to swallow it, but he lost his nerve and spat, "Hook up tonight."

Oh, God.

Marc mentally smacked himself. He couldn't believe he'd just said that out loud.

"Hook up?" Allie asked with an arched brow.

"Sorry, hon. I'm an idiot. What I *meant* to say is that I really want to see you later." He was still cringing at his own words when he picked up Allie's suitcase. "Come on, let me walk you home."

She nodded and slipped on her backpack, but kept darting sideways glances at him that made it clear how badly he'd ruined the moment. She wouldn't let him hold her hand until they'd crossed the bow ramp into the dock parking lot, and even then, her fingers were stiff laced among his.

"Hey." Marc pulled her to a stop and brought their linked hands to his lips. "Did I mention that I'm an idiot?"

When her lips curved in a sweet smile, Marc knew he was forgiven. "Yes, but it bears repeating."

"I'm a complete moron. It's a miracle I can walk and chew gum at the same time."

"Then I'd better lead the way home."

She linked her arm through his, and they strolled through the French Quarter at a leisurely pace.

While they continued another two blocks, Marc mentally rehearsed the words he hadn't been able to say aboard the *Belle*. It seemed easy enough: *Allie, I know we haven't been together very long, but I think you should move in with me.* God help him, if he slipped and asked for another hook-up, she'd probably want to cut out his tongue.

And he had big plans for that tongue.

When they rounded the corner and caught sight of the Sweet Spot sign, Marc steeled his resolve and repeated the words in his head. *Move in with me.* He could do this. He *wanted* to do this.

But that didn't stop a sheen of perspiration from slicking his forehead.

Allie paused outside her shop and studied him. "Are you okay?" She pressed her fingers to his cheeks. "You're as white as a sheet."

"Fine," he lied, holding open the door for her. "It always takes a few days to get my land legs after a trip."

If she doubted his lame excuse, she didn't let it show. Instead, she hurried inside and waved at her sister, who squealed with delight while bolting toward Allie with her arms stretched wide. The two embraced each other, bouncing on their toes as if they'd been apart for a decade.

When they finally separated, Devyn raked a gaze over Marc and pointed toward the street. "If you're going to hurl, do it out there."

Marc started to say that he wasn't feeling sick, but the scent of freshly baked sugar cookies sent his stomach into a somersault. He set down the suitcase and swayed on his feet.

Allie checked him for a fever. "You're not warm," she said. "If anything, you're a little chilled."

Marc's lips began to tingle, and a cold warning crept up the base of his skull. Something was wrong. It felt like every cell in his body was rioting against him. He took Allie's hand and kissed it. He didn't want to leave her, but he had to get out, fast. "I'll call you later, okay?"

She watched him back toward the door, her expression unreadable. "Sure."

"We'll get together as soon as I tie up some loose ends on the *Belle*," he promised.

The last thing he saw was the nod of her curly head, and then he was gone—out the door and across the street as quick as his legs could carry him. It was the damnedest thing, but as soon as he filled his lungs with the humid, exhaust-tainted air, his pulse slowed and his skin quit crawling.

What had happened back there?

Marc shook his head, listening for the rattle of loose parts. Had he imagined the whole thing? Or had he worked himself up and brought on an anxiety attack? He'd never experienced anything like it.

The hair on the back of his neck stood on end, providing the answer before it registered inside his brain. He heard the echo of Beau's words inside his head: *It seemed like something was keeping me from getting too close, like an emotional fence.* As much as Marc wished he could deny it, there was only one logical reason for his reaction inside the Sweet Spot.

The curse was keeping him away from Allie.

Chapter 14

"What the hell?" Devyn peered out the front window. "That boy tore out of here so fast, I'm surprised he didn't leave burned rubber on the sidewalk." She spun to face Allie and shook her head in confusion. "I thought you said it was going great."

Allie shrugged off her backpack and let it thunk to the floor. "It was."

"Did you get in a fight?"

"No."

"Catch him with another woman?"

"No, nothing like that."

"Well, I can tell something's off between you two." Devyn picked up the neglected backpack and walked it behind the counter, where she stuffed it onto the shelf of voodoo supplies. "What's the deal?"

Shoulders slumped, Allie helped herself to a cereal treat. She bit off a chunk and spoke with her mouth full. "He's doing what all Dumonts do—pulling away before we get too heavy." Then she repeated everything she'd told Ella-Claire. "He's probably out there right now thinking he's cursed."

Devyn nodded. "It makes sense."

Allie rolled her eyes. She didn't have the energy for this. "For the hundredth time, there's no hex on his family."

"Of course there is." When Allie opened her mouth to argue, Dev cut her off with a lifted palm. "Open your eyes, sis. The women in Marc's family get married, but the men don't. That's more than a self-inflating prophecy—"

"Self-*fulfilling* prophecy."

"Whatever," Dev said. "Memère knew what she was doing. Neither of us is as strong as she was, but I hear there's a real mambo in the swamp. If we work together with his guidance, I think we can break the hex."

Allie shook the treat at her sister. "Do you hear the crazy coming out of you?"

"Who's crazy?" asked Dev. "Look, do you like this guy, or not?"

Allie resisted the urge to jut out her bottom lip. "I more than like him."

"Do you want to be with him?"

"So badly it hurts."

"Then let me help you reverse the spell." Devyn grabbed the suitcase and wheeled it toward the storage room. While towing the suitcase up the stairs to the apartment, she asked, "What's the worst that can happen?"

Allie threw her sister a sarcastic look. "Do you really want me to answer that?"

"No." Devyn opened the bedroom door and hauled the suitcase onto Allie's bed. "But think about it—Marc believes in the curse, right?"

"Like gospel," Allie said.

"So if he secretly believes the spell is real, to the point that he wouldn't walk on the same side of the street with you, then it stands to reason he thinks you have powers."

Allie nodded in agreement. "Most folks do."

Wagging her brows, Devyn added, "Maybe even the strength to break the hex . . ."

The message sank in slowly, until Allie gasped in realization. "I think I see where you're going with this."

"Make him admit that the curse is real; then we'll hold a cleansing ceremony to undo it. Even if the hex is fake—which it's *not*—going through the motions might change that self-fulfilling prophecy you were talking about."

It was an intriguing idea, one that Allie began to take seriously. Nobody understood the power of the human psyche better than she did. How many times had she bent the truth to help others—conveying false messages from "the spirits" to help her clients find a match or overcome their fears? Dozens, at least.

Why not offer herself the same service?

If she could convince Marc that she knew how to undo Memère's hex, it might free him from his psychological hang-ups and allow them to be happy together. Marc cared for her—she knew it. Only fear stood in his way.

"You can mess with his head while I work on breaking the curse," Devyn said. "One way or another, we'll fix him. What have you got to lose?"

Allie could think of one thing: her self-respect.

Even though she didn't believe in the otherworldly,

common sense told her it was bad juju to begin a relationship with lies. But then she remembered how Marc had treated her like a booty call, asking for a hook-up. If she didn't do something drastic, she'd suffer the same fate as every woman who'd come before her— another plaything to be discarded. This might be the only way to change him.

"I hate the thought of manipulating him," Allie said, "like he's just another teenager seeking a love charm."

Devyn plopped down on the bed. "Desperate times, desperate measures."

When Allie unzipped her suitcase one of Marc's T-shirts peeked at her from beneath a pile of dirty laundry. She must have accidentally scooped it up during her rush to get packed that morning. She lifted the shirt to her face and pulled in a deep breath. It still smelled like his aftershave, and her body heated at the sensation.

"Okay," she said, hugging the soft cotton to her chest. "Let's try it." She searched her luggage until she found Edward Dumont's letter and handed it to Devyn. "And if we want Marc to admit that he's cursed, this will do the trick in spades."

Marc stifled a yawn and poured himself another Folgers refill. He usually stopped after one mug, but that was pre-Allie, back when he'd been able to sleep at night. Now insomnia was his only bed partner. Each evening was the same: as soon as he'd doze off, Marc would awake shivering—never mind that his apartment was hot enough to fry okra—feeling lost and confused, like something was missing.

Or rather, *someone*.

Three days had passed since he'd seen the woman responsible for the bags under his eyes, though not for lack of trying on his part. Each of his phone calls to her had mysteriously dropped, even when he'd used a different line. Refusing to be deterred, he'd visited her shop a dozen times, only to be told that he'd "just missed her." During his last drop-in, the doorknob had shocked him—hard.

It was as if the universe wanted to keep them apart, which made no sense. Assuming the curse was to blame, why had the spirits allowed him to make love with Allie aboard the *Belle*, when all he'd wanted was dirty, no-strings-attached sex? To punish him now that his intentions were honorable seemed backward. But then again, so did hexing a whole lineage of men for a crime they didn't commit.

The doorbell chimed, drawing his eye to the stove's digital clock. Marc grunted. His friends knew better than to call on him at seven thirty in the morning. He was still in his underwear.

"Just a minute," he hollered while jogging to his bedroom to pull on yesterday's clothes. On his way to the foyer it occurred to him that Allie might have come to visit, and his heart leapt painfully in anticipation of glimpsing her face. He threw open the door with a smile already in place . . . which quickly drooped into a frown.

"Oh," he said. "It's you."

Ella-Claire thrust out her tongue. "Don't look so happy to see me."

"Sorry. I thought you were Allie." He stepped aside

to welcome his sister. "I haven't talked to her since the day we docked."

"Uh-oh, trouble in paradise already?" As she always did, Ella kicked off her shoes at the door. "That was fast, even for you." She slid him a sideways glance. "What did you do to her?"

Marc held both hands forward. "Nothing, I swear."

She answered by gripping one hip and giving him *the look*.

"Honest," he said. "I was going to take your advice on that whole 'grand gesture' thing, but the timing wasn't right. And I haven't been able to get ahold of her since."

"Huh," Ella said. "That's too bad. But on the bright side . . ." She raised a white paper bag. "I brought beignets."

"Thanks." He took her offering and peeked inside to find she'd already eaten one. "To what do I owe the doughnuts?"

Ella wandered a few steps, which brought her into his modest living room. She took a seat on the arm of his black leather sofa and scanned the bookshelves along the far wall, where his collection of Blu-rays vastly outnumbered books.

"I'm having a girls' weekend at my place," she said. "Mind if I borrow some movies?"

"Knock yourself out." Marc swept a hand toward the shelves while striding toward the kitchen. "I'm going to eat my beignets while they're still warm."

He'd just sat down at the table and lifted a fritter to his mouth when the doorbell rang again. He dropped his breakfast and rushed into the foyer, licking the powdered sugar from his fingers. This time, he opened the door to a much less friendly face.

"You," Devyn said accusingly.

Of course it was him. Who else was she expecting at his town house? He glanced behind her, expecting to find Beau or Allie. He couldn't imagine why she'd come here alone.

"What are you doing to my sister?" she asked.

Marc's hand tightened around the door. "What do you mean? Is something wrong with Allie?"

"You bet there's something wrong. Every time you call, she goes into a trance."

"A trance?"

"Yeah, you know . . ." Devyn made wide eyes while she staggered into his foyer like a zombie. "She blanks out."

"And you think I'm doing it to her?"

She propped a hand on her hip and stared him down. "Probably not on purpose, but it's still your fault."

The curse. Marc didn't need to say it aloud—he knew they were both thinking it.

"Well, maybe not *your* fault," Devyn clarified, pulling a slip of paper from her handbag. The note was dingy and creased with age. "Your great-great-granddaddy's fault."

Ella-Claire joined them near the front door and used a Blu-ray to point at the note. "Hey, is that the letter Allie and I found?"

Devyn nodded.

"Don't give it to him!"

Marc waved off his sister and took the note from

Devyn, then unfolded the paper, finding a solid block of meticulously penned text on the inside. He glanced at the loopy signature of *Silas P. Dumont*, then at the salutation, which read *Dear Edward*, dated 1915. It was to his great-great-granddaddy from the man's little brother.

At the same time, Devyn commanded, "Read it," and Ella-Claire begged, "Don't read it."

Curiosity piqued, Marc skimmed the note.

> *Dear Edward,*
>
> *I pray this letter finds you safe with our grand-parents, for I must confess, I have reason to fear for your well-being. I did as you requested of me, brother, and visited the St. Bartholomew Chapel this evening to convey your deepest regrets to your betrothed. I daresay Miss Mauvais was quite vexed at the news. She tore the veil from her head and rent it in two while chanting all manner of vile curses. . . .*

Marc's eyes met Devyn's, and he damn near dropped the note. "My great-great-grandfather was engaged to Juliette Mauvais?"

"*And* ditched her at the altar," she said, lifting a haughty brow.

Marc couldn't believe it. The man must have had oatmeal for brains to tangle with a woman like that—and then betray her.

"Keep going," Devyn said.

Marc read ahead.

When I followed Miss Mauvais to the chapel graveyard to intercede on your behalf, she procured soil from our father's grave. Raising her fist to the heavens, she vowed "Fickle love shall rot your family tree. None but purest faith will set you free." I believe she means to enspell you, Edward, and I beseech you—seek the guidance of a priest, or either endeavor to earn Miss Mauvais's forgiveness.

When he'd finished the letter, Marc glanced down and found his forearms prickled in goose bumps.

Devyn snatched the paper and shook it in his face. "Do you see what this means?"

"Yeah, I see." Marc wished he could travel back in time and smack some sense into Edward Dumont. "I'm cursed because that coward sent a teenager to dump his fiancée."

"Let's not jump to conclusions," Elle-Claire said. "The only curse is in your head—the limitations you've placed on yourself. If you want Allie, then go get her."

"Oh, he's hexed, all right," Devyn said. "And he's missing the big picture."

Marc turned up his palms. "What's to miss?"

"Think about it," Devyn said. "You and Allie are the direct descendants of Edward and Juliette—star-crossed lovers—and the hundredth anniversary of their ruined wedding day is approaching. . . ." She trailed off expectantly.

"And?"

Devyn huffed a sigh. "Do you love my sister?"

Marc stiffened at the abrupt personal question.

"Well?" she demanded when he didn't answer quickly enough.

"I think so."

"And I'm pretty sure she feels the same way," Devyn said. "I won't lie—you're not my favorite person in the world, but maybe you two are destined to break the spell."

"Destined?" he asked. "What, like a cosmic do-over?"

Devyn shrugged. "If you want to think of it that way."

It sounded like she'd been reading too many paranormal romance novels. "If it's our *destiny*," he said in a mocking tone, "to undo that old biddy's magic, then why can't I get within ten feet of Allie?"

Devyn tapped the letter against her chin and paced a circuit in the foyer. "Well, it's probably not supposed to be easy. Nothing worthwhile ever is. But the logical place to start is with me and Allie. Magic's in our blood—if anyone can break the hex, we can."

"Um," interjected Ella-Claire. "Or you could just tell Allie that you love her and commit . . . like a normal person."

He ignored his sister and spoke to Devyn. "You're forgetting that I can't get near her."

Reaching up, she lightly smacked him upside the head. "So try harder, Dumont! This is my sister we're talking about. She's worth it."

Marc rubbed his head and backed away from the shrew. But he couldn't deny she had a point. Allie was special, and he wouldn't let her get away—not without a fight.

"Fine," he said. "Tell me what to do."

*   *   *

At noon, Allie's cell phone rang. Before she could reach it, Devyn snatched the phone from the counter and checked the screen.

"It's Marc," Dev said with a wicked gleam in her eyes.

But instead of handing the phone back to Allie, she answered the call and crinkled a handful of cellophane near the mouthpiece, then disconnected.

"I'm still not allowed to talk to him?" Allie asked.

"Patience, Grasshopper. Now that he can't reach you by phone, he has to come over. He should be here in a few minutes."

Allie sighed while sliding a tray of fresh muffins into the display case. "I feel like I'm trapped inside an episode of *Scooby-Doo* and we're fixin' to set a trap for Old Man Jenkins."

"Just stick to the plan. Before long, the curse will be broken, and you can skip off into the sunset." Holding up a finger, Dev clarified, "After you take me to Vegas."

"Fine, but don't shock him again. That was unnecessary."

Dev giggle-snorted. "But fun."

"You're such a sadist."

"No worries, little sister. At this point, we want to encourage him, not drive him away."

Though Allie didn't say so, her faith in the plan was beginning to waver. She would continue to play along because it was her only hope, but she couldn't shake the feeling that deceiving Marc was the wrong way to change him.

"Get ready," Devyn said. "He's here!"

After avoiding Marc for so long, that first glimpse of him was like a taste of chocolate after Lent—so satisfying that Allie wanted to weep.

Sun-kissed golden brown waves brushed his broad shoulders, showcased beneath a faded blue T-shirt that was sexier on him than a tux on any Hollywood actor. A pair of worn jeans hung low on his hips, and when he removed his sunglasses and locked those dark eyes on her, she couldn't have held back her answering smile if she'd wanted to.

As he pushed open the door, Allie saw her excitement mirrored in his face in the way he gazed at her all soft and warm, with a grin that said she was the only woman in his world. Clearly, he'd missed her, and that validation lifted her spirits.

She only hated what she had to do next.

Shifting her focus to a point behind Marc's head, she wiped all traces of emotion from her face, relaxing her shoulders and dropping both arms to her sides.

Mingled pain and disappointment widened his eyes, but she maintained her vacant expression and refused to indulge in tears. This step was too important to the plan, and thus, their future.

This is for the best, she reminded herself. *Tough love, and all that.*

"Allie?" Swallowing hard, Marc approached the counter and peered at her from above the glass bakery display. "Are you with me, hon?"

She remained silent, and through her peripheral vision noticed Dev tipping her head to study her. Dev snapped her fingers in front of Allie's face.

"Hey," Devyn said. "Wake up." When her repeated

efforts failed, she gripped one hip and asked Marc, "See what I mean?"

Allie began chanting under her breath, and as intended, it didn't escape Marc's notice. "What's she saying?" he asked Devyn.

Dev bent an ear to Allie's mouth. "Sounds like *pickled dove*."

"Pickled dove?" he asked. "What's that supposed to mean?"

"No, wait." Dev pretended to listen again. "Scratch that. I think she's saying *fickle love*."

Marc huffed a breath and ran a shaky hand through his hair. "It's the same line from Juliette's curse."

"Makes sense," Dev said. "That old magic is keeping you away from Allie so you can't hurt her like your great-great-granddaddy did to Memère."

"But I don't want to hurt Allie." Marc's gaze traveled over the chalkboard of bakery specials while he scratched the back of his head in contemplation. "Don't you have some gris-gris lying around?" he asked. "Something we can tie around her neck to break the trance?"

"It's not that simple," Dev said. "Jinx removal isn't one-size-fits-all. I need a broken chain and ingredients specific to our memère, like—"

"Dirt from her tomb?" Marc interrupted. "Allie keeps some in her backpack."

Devyn spent the next several minutes assembling a gris-gris bag with Marc's help using, among other things, a broken silver anklet from Allie's jewelry box. When the bag was ready, Devyn tied it around Allie's neck and stuffed it down the front of her shirt so it lay directly against her skin.

"There." Dev patted the lump beneath Allie's shirt, then linked their hands and chanted a prayer in Creole. She stepped back and joined Marc in waiting for a reaction.

"Purest faith will set you free," was all Allie said. *Come on, Marc. Show some faith.*

He scrubbed his face with one hand and groaned in frustration. "What now?"

Devyn shrugged. "I'm not as talented as Memère was. Maybe we should wait and see what the mambo says."

Marc closed the distance and took Allie's cheeks between his palms, bringing with him the scents of sunshine and soap. She hoped he couldn't see the pulse pounding at the base of her throat.

"Allie," he murmured, gazing into her eyes.

When she didn't respond, he lowered his mouth to hers and nearly ruined everything. The soft brush of his lips made her breath hitch, a reaction he must have noticed, because he pulled back in surprise. Then he did something that caught Allie completely off guard.

Leaning into her midsection, he tossed her over one shoulder and pushed open the door to the storage room. Her eyes flew wide as her hair tumbled toward the floor and all the blood rushed to her head.

"Hey, what're you doing?" Devyn called.

"We tried it your way," Marc said as he hauled Allie into the back room. "Now it's my turn."

Chapter 15

Allie's head throbbed in the awkward upside-down position as Marc carried her past the storage room and up the stairs to her apartment. This wasn't the reaction she'd wanted from him.

She'd hoped Marc would demonstrate his faith by proclaiming his love, maybe asking for a long-term commitment or a weekend away, not by slinging her over his shoulder like an industrial-sized sack of flour. What was his strategy here? To lock her inside the bedroom until she snapped out of it?

As it turned out, she had the bedroom part right, but he had no intention of locking her inside without him.

He slammed the door behind them, and the next thing Allie knew, she was standing with her back to the wall, both wrists pinned above her head while Marc pressed his body against her. With his free hand he tipped her chin. Allie barely had time to gulp a breath before his mouth slanted hard against hers and turned her knees to pudding.

She kept her lips immobile, but Marc tasted of sweet cola and lust, his lithe hips pushing her into the wall and electrifying every cell in her body. Holding back was nearly more than she could bear.

"Come on, Allie," he whispered into her mouth. "Wake up for me."

She dug her thumbnails into her palms and gave him nothing.

He refused to accept defeat, taking her bottom lip and sucking it gently while stroking her cheek with his thumb. Lord help her, he felt so good—a cool drink of water after a week's drought. The blissful assault went on and on, weakening her defenses with each tender touch. She was only able to resist until their tongues met; then she folded like a cheap suit.

She'd missed him too much to pretend otherwise.

She closed her eyes and leaned into his kiss, opening to him with a sigh that betrayed the depth of her need. At her reaction, Marc made a male noise of contentment and lightened his touch, teased her with the tip of his tongue without allowing her to catch him. He brushed his lips back and forth against hers and whispered, "You're back."

Silently, she strained against the hold on her wrists so she could run her palms all over him, but instead of releasing her, he tightened his grip.

"I'm glad." He moved to her ear and took her lobe between his teeth, then kissed a trail down to the base of her shoulder. "I missed you."

While she struggled with whether or not to admit the same, Marc captured her breast in his palm and wiped her mind clean. He thumbed her nipple in lazy circles, bringing it to a hard point beneath her bra.

"Did you miss me, too?" he asked.

She answered with a gasp, and he bent low to gently bite her through the thin cotton shirt separating them.

"Did you?" he asked against her breast. When she didn't respond, he wedged a muscular thigh between her legs and pushed against her in just the right spot. A jolt of pleasure tore through her. "Answer me."

"Yes," she whispered, gazing at him from beneath heavy lids. "I missed you, Marc." *More than you can imagine.*

He pulled back his thigh and replaced it with his hand, then slipped it beneath the hem of her skirt. Without missing a beat, he cupped the dampened fabric of her panties and massaged her there.

"How much?" he asked.

It was all she could do to contain a moan. She arched against his palm for more pressure, but he halted his movements.

"I said *how much*?"

"A . . . a lot."

He chuckled quietly to himself while teasing her with a brush of his knuckles. "Did you mean that, or was it a confession under duress?"

"I meant every word," she said, tugging at her bound wrists. "Let go of me and I'll prove it."

"Uhn-uh." He pressed closer until she was trapped between two walls—one of plaster, the other of solid muscle. His thumb slipped beneath the bottom of her panties, and he started petting her, making her slick and swollen with desire. "Let me take the wheel."

Allie's legs trembled. She would have collapsed if Marc wasn't holding her in place. She quit struggling and surrendered to his control, allowed herself to savor the decadent play of his fingers, the graze of his teeth against her neck, the sinful whisper of breath in her ear. The minutes passed in delicious agony as he stroked her with masterful skill. Marc's dominance topped her most erotic fantasies, his devotion to her pleasure drawing a series of wild moans from her throat.

She closed her eyes and let him have his way with her, but just as her muscles coiled for release, a knock sounded on the bedroom door. Marc flinched and withdrew his hand, nearly sending Allie into hysterics.

"Allie?" Dev shouted from the hall. "Everything okay in there?"

God bless her, Devyn was a wonderful sister, but Allie needed her to go away—now. "I'm fine," she called, the desperation clear in her voice. "We'll be down in a few minutes."

"A few minutes?" Marc repeated and shook his head. "Not for what I have in mind."

"Make that an hour," Allie hollered.

From the other side of the door, Dev grumbled, "Pass the brain bleach," before her footsteps retreated briskly down the hall.

As if nothing had happened, Marc squeezed Allie's inner thigh and began kissing a trail along her jawline. "If you missed me so much," he said, "why didn't you call?"

Allie was pretty sure she'd prepared an answer for that, but all the blood had left her head and traveled south. After a moment's hesitation, she told him, "I wanted you to come to me."

Which was the truth, more or less.

"It worked, didn't it?" he said. "I couldn't stay away."

With a challenge in his eyes, he used the dull edge of his thumbnail to draw swirls along the inside seam of her panties. "So now that I'm here, what else do you want me to do?"

Heat crept into her face, but she was too far gone to stay quiet. "Touch me, like before."

He licked his lips and glanced down at the hand moving beneath her skirt. Again, he tucked his thumb beneath her panties and skimmed her with a whisper graze. "Like this?" he asked. "Or . . ." Gingerly, he pinched her slick bud between two fingers and slid them up and down, sparking to life a thousand nerve endings that lit her up like the Fourth of July. "Like this?"

Allie's eyes rolled back and her knees gave out. Marc reacted instantly; otherwise she would have collapsed to the floor.

Pride lifted the corners of his mouth. "I guess I have my answer." He stopped his erotic slide and speared her with a look so hot she nearly climaxed right there. "But I still want to hear you say it." He used one thumb in a taunting tickle. "How should I touch you, Allie?"

Her voice sounded foreign to her own ears when she told him, "The second way."

"Did you like that?"

"Yes."

"Ask me nicely."

She swallowed her pride and begged. "Please? Please touch me again."

After a lingering kiss, he resumed his massage, and for the next several minutes, they each watched Marc's wrist tendons flex as his gifted fingers rubbed sweet, mounting tension low into her belly. Both their breaths were deep and shuddering, Marc's control clearly slipping as he thrust his erection against her thigh. But every time she skated near the brink, he'd lighten the pressure to bring her back down, promising, "When you come, I'll be inside to feel it."

"Now," she said. "I want you, Marc."

"Not yet." He withdrew his hand and trailed a glistening index finger along her collarbone, then licked her skin clean. "I want to taste you first." Pulling back, he glanced at her wrists, still held high above her head. "But to do that, I'll have to let you go."

She bit her lip and nodded, both eager and disappointed to regain control of her hands.

Marc pointed at her wrists. "Keep them where they are. No matter what happens, you don't move. Understand?"

The dangerous timbre of his command sent a thrill through her. "Yes."

He released her, and she rotated both wrists to restore circulation while keeping them in place. Marc knelt on the floor and shoved her skirt around her waist, then shucked off her panties and tossed them aside. While guiding her heel atop his shoulder, he glanced up as if to make sure she'd obeyed him, and only then did he lift his mouth to the juncture of her thighs.

The first lick weakened her, arms slipping an inch. Marc used his mouth with just as much skill as his fingers, but that was the problem. With each decadent suckle and lap of his tongue, Allie found it harder to support her body, let alone her hands. Eventually, she couldn't stay vertical any longer.

"Please," she said. "I need you."

When Marc stood from the floor, she noted the change in him—the feral hunger in his gaze and the way he tore at the button of his jeans and jerked down his zipper. He took possession of her wrists with one hand while freeing his erection with the other. Allie widened her stance in anticipation of taking him inside her, smooth and hot and hard. In her impatience, she writhed against him, unable to wait a second longer.

Marc's desperation must have matched hers, because he didn't even bother to lower his pants before nudging his rounded tip inside her. At the contact, they shared a long groan, but he withdrew as abruptly as he'd entered.

"No," she pleaded. "Don't stop."

Marc tipped their foreheads together and reached into his back pocket for a condom. "This will just take a second."

"We don't need one," she said. More than anything, she longed to feel his warm, naked skin inside her, no barriers between them. "I've been on the Pill for years."

But a tear of plastic proved he was unwilling to take the risk.

He rolled the latex down the length of his shaft and wasted no time burying himself to the base in one powerful thrust that emptied Allie's lungs. Her disappointment vanished. All that existed was the rush of pleasure as he pinned her to the wall with his hips and slid in and out of her aching center in strokes so slow she wanted to scream.

Her breaths came in pants, her nerve endings glowing impossibly hotter while he ground a hard rotation against her, then another. Pleasure mounting, she whimpered and looked to him for release.

As always, he knew what she needed. Lazily, he traced her mouth with an index finger and stared at her in wide-eyed wonder. In that infinite moment, something beautiful passed between them. The last bit of Allie's heart melted in surrender, every piece of her now in Marc's possession.

He plunged deep, her lower back pounding the wall with each quick stroke. Marc never released her gaze, and as tension broke into ecstasy, her inner muscles shuddered in wild spasms that coaxed a cry from her lips. With another deep thrust, he held inside her, stiffening in his own climax. Connected as they were, both in flesh and soul, Allie didn't think it was possible to love him any more than she did right that second.

A few breaths later, Marc moved his hands to her face and kissed her, soft and slow—the kind of kiss that told her this was more than sex for him. Finally free, she twined her arms around his neck to extend the intimacy.

"I want to be with you, Allie," he said, still cradling her between his palms.

"I want that, too." She pictured their future together—a thousand exquisite moments just like this one—and she wanted it so badly it hurt. Any other outcome was unthinkable.

"But I need your help."

She listened as Marc recounted the previous days' events, down to reading his great-great-great-uncle's letter. She nodded and feigned surprise in all the right places, but her heart sank when he asked for assistance breaking Memère's hex. No matter how she justified the deception, she was still lying to the man she loved.

"We'll have to do some research," she said, unable to meet his gaze. "I've never tried anything this powerful."

He nuzzled the side of her neck. "Whatever it takes."

Those were the words she'd wanted to hear, but Allie had to force a smile. "Don't worry, baby. We got this."

She had to stay strong—she loved Marc too deeply to fail him.

Twenty minutes later, a very satisfied Marc took Allie by the hand and led her downstairs to the bakery shop, where her sister was leaning over the sales counter, using one of those handheld icing bags to draw cartoon dicks onto oblong sugar cookies.

Never a dull moment around these Mauvais women.

"Secret hobby?" he asked. Knowing Devyn, she'd probably take a rolling pin to all those innocent schlongs when she was finished. "Or wishful baking?"

She rolled her eyes while piping a pair of balls beneath a member that hooked a little too far to the left. "We got a last-minute order for a bachelorette party tonight." She slid a glare at Allie. "And since the owner was taking an extended break, I got stuck with this glamorous job."

"Oops," Allie said with an apologetic grin. "Thanks for being on top of it."

"While you were *under* it," Devyn muttered. "But no problem. It's my lifelong dream to sit around all day drawing dicks."

"Let me help." Allie filled another bag with white icing and began frosting the tip of each cookie.

Marc frowned at the implication. "That's disturbing."

"This is nothing," Allie said. "Once I had to bake a giant red velvet penis cake—with cream filling inside."

"Classy." Who knew women had such dirty minds? "Why don't you give me that voodoo book you were talking about so I can research spells while you two give those cookies their happy ending?"

Allie jerked her head toward the far end of the counter. "Second cabinet from the end. But be careful; it's older than mummy dust."

She was right. The volume of yellowed journal pages was hand-stitched together and bound in something that looked like aged burlap stretched over wood. A chill skittered down his spine when he rested it on the counter and opened the front cover.

"What am I looking for?" he asked.

Allie turned to her sister. "What do you think? *Lave tet*?"

"Nah, that takes three days." Devyn focused on her cookie art until she'd finished another wang, then turned a thoughtful gaze to the ceiling. "A smudge stick cleansing with extra gifts for Memère might be enough. We can always try the *lave tet* if that doesn't work."

It sounded like they knew what they were talking about, so why had Allie asked for his help? "You sure you need me?" he asked.

"Yes," Allie told him. "I've never tried this before. Look under *cleansing rituals* and make a list of supplies."

Marc turned each delicate page with caution while squinting at the inky calligraphy. He flipped past topics like *ge-rouge*, *mange loa*, *bokors*, and *zombis*. Halfway through the journal, he found an entry for spiritual cleansing, but Allie interrupted him before he had a chance to read it.

"First you have to do something special," she said. "Complete a task."

Marc tucked an old receipt between the pages to hold his place. "What kind of task?"

"You have to make things right with your pawpaw." Allie looked to her sister for affirmation. "We're basically healing an old family rift, so don't you think it makes sense to mend that relationship first?"

"Uh, yeah." Devyn pointed her icing bag at Marc. "Make nice with your pawpaw."

No way Marc would crawl on his knees to that meddling, crotchety old jerk—not after what he did to Allie. "When he's ready to apologize, he can come to me."

"We don't have time for that kind of stubbornness," Allie said. "Besides, this will show the spirits you're worth their help, so suck it up and be the bigger man."

Marc grumbled under his breath but didn't say no. Then, speaking of bigger men, the front door opened with a light *ding*, and Beau ducked his auburn head, barely clearing the frame as he pushed inside.

"Hey," he said to Marc before his gaze drifted to Devyn and caught there. His green eyes flew wide, his giant sneakers pausing midstride, causing him to stumble for balance. All the color drained from his face while he gaped like a suffocating catfish.

And he had the nerve to call Marc whipped. Beau probably couldn't talk over the hook in his mouth.

From farther down the counter, Allie drew a sharp breath, causing her sister to glance up from her tray of cookies. Devyn squeezed her bag so hard it sent spurts of icing clear across the counter. Her lips parted as widely as Beau's, but no sound escaped.

"Hey, Beau," Allie said nervously. "What're you doing here?"

Beau spoke to Allie, but never took his eyes off her sister. "Checking on my brother." Blindly, he pointed at Marc. "Ella-Claire said he seemed off, and when he wouldn't answer the phone, I figured he was with you."

Allie released a tight laugh. "Well, he's fine." Her stiff, folded arms added, *So you can go now*. Then she laid a steadying hand on Devyn, who appeared to have quit breathing.

Beau didn't move an inch. Finally, he whispered, "Hi, Dev."

She didn't answer.

"I didn't know you worked here," Beau went on. "Otherwise, I would have—"

"You would've what?" she snapped. "Stayed away?"

"No." Beau shook his head, then contradicted, "Yes."

"Which is it?"

"Neither," he said, beads of sweat beginning to collect on his forehead. "I wanted to call on you, but Allie made it sound like you might not want me coming around."

"Really?" You could cut a tin can on the razor-sharp edge of her voice. "I can't imagine why."

Marc and Allie shared the same uneasy glance. It was getting awkward in here.

"Look," Beau said, curling a muscled arm to scratch the back of his neck. "I'm awful sorry for . . ." He trailed off as his gaze fell on the tray of cookies; then he tilted his head and took a step closer. "Is that what I think it is?"

"That depends," Marc said to lighten the mood. "Do you think it's a left-leaning peen?"

"Yeah, and it's really happy to see me." Beau's upper lip hitched in disgust. "Do folks actually eat these?"

Devyn threw down her icing bag and shouted, "I don't work here! I'm just helping out!" then ran into the back room without another word. With a sigh, Allie handed her frosting bag to Marc and followed her sister, leaving him with a red-faced Beau and a tray full of half-decorated penis cookies.

"Real smooth," Marc said, tossing his brother the bag of white frosting while retrieving the flesh-colored one. "How could she possibly resist you now?" He bent over the counter and picked up where Devyn left off, outlining each member with a steady hand. The task was harder than it looked, no pun intended.

Beau used the other bag to frost the tips. "When I woke up this morning, I never guessed I'd be doing this."

"Or running into your ex, I take it."

"No, I definitely didn't see that coming." Beau glowered at the white buttercream trickling from the end of each cookie. "No pun intended."

Marc snickered. "I know, right?"

"I always wanted to tell her I was sorry," Beau said. "Had ten years to cook up a good apology. But my noodle went blank when I saw her."

Marc couldn't deny that his brother had botched it like a boss. "If she means that much to you, try again."

Beau made a noncommittal grunt. "Might do more harm than good."

"Wait a minute." Marc lifted his head and stared at his big brother—the same guy who'd flattened the senior fullback at fourteen. "Are you *scared*?"

"Psh," Beau scoffed and cocked his head. "Of Devyn? No."

"Liar."

"It's not that," Beau insisted. "She doesn't give two figs for me. Probably forgot I was even alive. What's the point?"

"I guess it depends on how long you're sticking around." As badly as Marc wanted to glance up to gauge his brother's reaction, he kept his eyes trained on the cookie. "You gonna settle here, or are you just passing through?"

Beau hesitated for a few beats. "I've got a few options. Sure do miss home, though."

"Me, too. I've got a place here in the city, but I'm thinking of giving it up and moving back to Cedar Bayou."

"Not a bad commute," Beau said. "And you can stay on the *Belle* during high season."

"That's what I figured." Marc faked a casual shrug. "You could do the same . . . if you wanted."

"You think?"

"Why not?"

"Can you use me on board?"

Marc knew what his brother was really asking: *Can we work side by side without tearing out each other's throats?* "It'd be nice to have you around, even if you are a pain in my ass."

Beau chuckled quietly. "The feeling's mutual, little brother."

"So you'll stay?"

After considering for a moment, Beau nodded. "Yeah, I think I will." His smile fell as he scrutinized his bag of icing. "But, damn. Did we just bond over penis cookies?"

Marc considered that for a moment. "Maybe. But no one needs to know."

Allie followed the sound of sniffles and hiccups until she found her sister in the storage room pretending to inspect a can of baking soda—in the dark. Allie flipped on the lights and approached Devyn, then rested a hand on her shoulder and gently turned her away from the shelf.

"You okay?" Allie said. "That must've been—"

Her words died when she saw the twin trails leaking down Dev's cheeks. In disbelief, Allie caught a teardrop on her finger and inspected it to ensure it was real. It was. She hadn't seen Devyn cry since their parents' funeral.

Devyn scrubbed away the tears. Her voice was scratchy when she asked, "You know what I've been fantasizing about for the last ten years?"

Allie wanted to say *Channing Tatum and a tub of pea-*

nut butter? but it seemed like the wrong time for a joke. So she simply shook her head.

Devyn jabbed a finger toward the front of the shop. "The day that asshole would come back to town, looking for me."

"But I thought—"

"Not because I wanted him back," Dev clarified. "To show him what he missed. I imagined I'd be gorgeous and successful with a hot stud on my arm. I'd rub it in Beau's face, and then he'd be sorry for what he did." Another tear slipped free as she gestured at her stained apron and her tangled ponytail. "But look at me—no makeup, no degree, lard in my hair, unemployed, and making pecker cookies!"

"Aw, honey." Allie tucked a stray curl behind Dev's ear. "I'm sure that's not what he's thinking." A hitched breath shook Devyn's chest, making her seem five years old. It broke Allie's heart.

"This isn't how I pictured my life," Dev whispered. "It's been ten years, and I'm no better off now than the day he left me."

"That's not true."

"Oh, yeah?" Dev challenged. "What have I accomplished?"

Allie opened her mouth but drew a blank.

Since Devyn had dropped out of college, she'd floated like cottonseed on the breeze from one dead-end job to the next—a summer traveling with the circus, three months as a dog walker, a week detailing hot rods, even a brief stint as a "virtual dominatrix." Allie wasn't sure what that entailed, and she didn't intend to ask.

"You helped me open the Sweet Spot," Allie said. "I couldn't have done it without you."

Dev waved her off. "That's your baby, not mine."

"Technically, it's *our* baby," Allie reminded her. "Silent partner, remember?"

A weak smile quirked Dev's lips. "I appreciate what you're trying to do, but we both know you're the real talent here."

"There's nothing wrong with trying new things," Allie said. "So what if you took some time off to experiment? Don't discount a whole decade of living because an old flame brought up bad feelings."

"It's more than that," Devyn insisted. "My high school reunion is in the fall, and I'm already inventing excuses not to go. All my friends have careers and kids and husbands . . . or at least ex-husbands. What am I supposed to say when they ask what I'm doing now?"

"Maybe don't mention the penis cookies."

That earned a small laugh. "I need to get my shit together—to buckle down and set goals."

"You can do it," Allie said with an encouraging smile. "And I'll help."

Dev took a deep breath as if to steel herself. Then she flashed a palm. "Maybe we should wait until after Vegas, though."

"Oh, totally. The road to hell is paved with tequila shots."

"And we're going to travel it well," Dev said. "But after our wild weekend of sin, I'm turning over a new leaf." She nodded firmly. "For real this time."

"I'll hold you to it."

"And even though you don't believe in the curse,"

Dev said, "I'm going to help you break it. It'll be the first useful thing I've done in years."

"Thanks, baby." Allie squeezed her sister's hand. "Everything's going to be all right."

For *both* of them—she had a good feeling.

Chapter 16

That good feeling was still lifting Allie's cheeks a few nights later when she passed the WELCOME TO CEDAR BAYOU sign and turned down the pockmarked road leading to the heart of her hometown. The setting sun sluiced through the windshield, blinding her to a new traffic light at the intersection of Fifth and Main that had just flashed from yellow to red.

How long had that been there?

She skidded to a halt halfway through the intersection, then backed up and hoped the deputy wasn't hiding in his usual spot behind the Frosty Queen drive-thru. Otherwise she'd get the wrong kind of welcome home. The eighty-five-dollar kind. Her voodoo heritage had kept half the town at bay, but it'd never saved her from a ticket.

Go figure.

Devyn reached over from the passenger seat and flipped down Allie's sun visor. "If you keep squinting like that, your crow's-feet will be as bad as mine."

"Only you," Allie said. "I almost ran a red light and you're lecturing me about wrinkles."

Dev swept a hand toward the adjacent street, populated by a handful of birds scavenging bits of discarded hot dog bun from the sidewalk. "Who would you hit?"

"With my luck?" Allie asked. "A troop of Girl Scouts. Walking puppies."

"Nah. We haven't had a Girl Scout troop since that unfortunate archery incident in the town square a few years ago." Devyn grimaced. "Now the mayor walks with a limp and I buy my Thin Mints in the next parish."

Allie stifled a laugh. "Poor Mayor Bisbee."

"He doesn't get much sympathy around here these days." Dev pointed at the traffic light, which had turned green. "Not since he put the kibosh on Tad Miller's shine operation."

"A lot's happened since I moved away."

Allie continued down Main Street, but nothing looked different since her visit at Christmas. The last freestanding video store in the known universe was still in business, a testament to the lack of technology in this tiny parish. Right on cue, Allie's cell phone beeped to announce an interruption in her signal.

"Scientists can clone mammals," she complained, "but they can't bring cell service to Cedar Bayou. How backward is that?"

"Preach it, sister."

But despite her complaints, Allie turned a loving eye to the honeysuckle bushes lining the St. Mary's churchyard. She rolled down her window and let the sweet breeze toss her curls as she pulled in a lungful of clean, bayou air—the kind you couldn't get in the city. She passed other childhood haunts, like the corner grocery, where fifty cents would buy a Drumstick ice-cream cone and two pieces of Dubble Bubble.

She drove onward, toward the edge of town where modest single-family starter homes replaced businesses. Overgrown lawns littered with bikes and plastic toys turned her thoughts to Marc, who'd said he wanted to move back here someday. Allie wasn't quite ready for a family, and neither was Marc, but she couldn't help feeling a rush of excitement when she imagined buying a little fixer-upper with him and filling it with memories of their own. And, someday, children.

If Devyn's plan worked, their future would begin tonight.

Candles, trinkets, and herb bottles clattered together in their box on the backseat—supplies for the mock cleansing ceremony she hoped would release Marc from his psychological barriers to intimacy.

Dev's thoughts must have traveled on the same wavelength. "You nervous?"

"Not really," Allie said, and meant it. "Marc's totally committed. He did everything we asked of him, and we ran that poor boy all over New Orleans." After he'd extended the olive branch to his pawpaw, she'd sent him hunting down gifts for Memère—everything from her favorite candy to the skin cream she'd used, which was only available in antique shops. "I even told him we needed eggs as a symbol of rebirth."

"Eggs?" Devyn asked. "Those aren't hard to find."

"*Snake* eggs."

Dev shook her head appreciatively. "Nice one. You're a harsh mistress, little sister."

Allie shrugged. "I'm not trying to be mean. The

harder he works, the more invested he'll be during the ceremony."

"Well, sounds like he bought in, so that's good," Devyn said. "It's the first step toward that 'purest faith' he's supposed to demonstrate."

"That's the key," Allie agreed. "He has to let go of everything he's lived since childhood and understand that we can be together." A shiver of unease trickled down her spine. Was she delusional to think his superstitious belief in the curse outweighed generations of poor role modeling?

No negativity, she chided herself. *Have a little faith of your own.*

Dev gave her a condescending pat on the shoulder. "Whatever you say. I'll be focused on the real issue keeping you two apart—dark magic."

Allie suppressed an eye roll.

They drove in silence until Allie spotted Marc's truck parked across the street from the St. Bartholomew Chapel. It was dusk now, the sun reduced to nothing more than a smear of pink against the sky, casting the cobbled stones of the church in a romantic glow.

But that gentle bathing of light was deceptive, much like the rite Allie was about to hold in the graveyard behind the chapel. There was nothing romantic about this crumbling ruin.

Centuries of floodwaters and neglect had eroded the house of worship, giving it an eerie, sagging appearance, like the face of a weeping crone. Allie wished the parish would demolish it. She usually loved visiting historical landmarks, but for some reason, St. Bart's had always made her skin prickle and her arm hair stand on end. When she stepped out of her car, she re-coiled at the heavy odor of mildew thickening the air.

She whispered to Devyn, "I can't believe I let you talk me into having the ceremony here. This place gives me the heebie-jeebies."

"Where else would Memère's spirit be strongest?" Dev asked. "Her tomb is here. And this is where she cursed old man Dumont."

"It's hard to believe they were supposed to get married that night," Allie said as she faced the chapel.

Two oak doors, splintered with age and hanging from their hinges at awkward angles, guarded the sanctuary entrance. How long had Memère stood in that doorway and watched for her lover before learning he wouldn't come? She must have been crushed—all her dreams severed in the blink of an eye, and in such a cowardly, public manner. Was it any wonder she'd lashed out the only way she knew how?

Allie shook off a chill and pulled the box of supplies from the backseat, then tucked it against her hip while she and Devyn strode toward the cemetery behind the church.

When the crooked iron gate groaned on its hinges, Marc caught Allie's eye and stood from the bench where he'd been waiting. He offered a grin and brushed off his backside, hoping he hadn't gotten too messy.

She'd asked him to wear white tonight to symbolize pureness of heart, and she matched him in an ivory cotton sundress that brushed her ankles. The sight of her took his breath away. Together, they almost resembled the ill-fated bride and groom who rested here among the dead, their stone tombs facing each other across a gravel path in an eternal standoff.

"Hey," he said, glancing up at the swollen moon. "Nice night for curse breaking." His words teased, but Marc's stomach was in knots. He needed this ceremony to work.

"The best," she agreed. She balanced a box of supplies on her hip, and Marc took it from her and asked where she wanted to set up. She scanned the dim graveyard, then pointed to a stone altar near the church's rear wall. "Over there."

"Wait," said Devyn, joining them from behind. She reached inside the box and pulled free a small crystal dish. "We need dirt from Edward and Memère's tombs," she said. "Blended in here to heal the rift between our families. I'll get it while you two dress the candles."

Marc wasn't sure what dressing candles entailed, so he tagged along with Allie and helped her clean off the limestone slab. They arranged an assortment of thick, white candles along the surface, and Allie dabbed them with scented oils that reminded him of medicated ointment—eucalyptus, maybe.

Next, she placed a framed photo of Juliette Mauvais in the center of the altar, adding to it a small statue of a dark, horned man.

"Who's that?" Marc asked.

"Legba," Allie explained. "He's an ancient spirit who's considered an intermediate to the world of the dead." She lit a single yellow candle and said it would help in seeking Legba's guidance. The candles illuminated Juliette's portrait, almost as if announcing her presence, too.

Despite the headdress concealing the woman's dark curls, the resemblance between Juliette and Allie was striking—right down to their mismatched eyes. But there was something else behind those eyes, a cold edge that raised Marc's hackles. She was a beautiful woman, but not someone he'd trust with his heart. He couldn't understand what his great-great-grandfather had ever seen in her.

It occurred to Marc that he probably shouldn't be thinking ill of Juliette during the ceremony—not if he wanted freedom from her spell. He crossed himself and apologized to her spirit . . . wherever she was.

Devyn returned with the bowl of dirt and set it atop the altar. "Ready?"

Marc glanced between the two sisters. "What am I supposed to do?"

"Did you bring gifts for the spirits?" Allie asked.

Marc jogged back to the bench to fetch his paper bag. "Got it right here. Even the snake eggs."

"Put the tokens on the altar." Allie said. When he'd finished, she indicated for him to kneel, then joined him on the soft grass and spoke directly to the statue of Legba. "Marc Dumont presents these favors and seeks your permission to commune with the spirit of Juliette Mauvais." She added a few coins to the altar. "As do I."

Devyn knelt beside Allie. "Now we'll join hands and pray."

Marc was surprised when Devyn recited the Our Father. He didn't know what kind of prayer he'd expected, but it wasn't that. After *amen*, Devyn lit a stick of incense, filling the humid evening air with a hint of exotic spice.

While Marc and Allie remained kneeling, hands joined, Devyn stood and told him she was going to invoke Legba. Then she began chanting in Creole, and Marc could swear he felt ice skitter down his back. He didn't know if that was a good thing or not.

"Now that we've asked his permission," Devyn explained, "I'll use a smudge stick to remove any negativity clinging to you."

A smudge what? Marc looked to Allie with a question in his eyes.

"Just be still," she whispered. "You don't have to do anything."

With a bundle of dried herbs in hand, Devyn ignited one end and gently blew on it until a billow of sage-scented smoke wafted up from the leaves. She circled Marc with the smudge stick, coating him in the smoke. After waving it above his heads a few more times, Devyn placed it on the altar and called to her great-great-grandmother.

"Juliette Mauvais," Devyn said, "we invoke your spirit and offer these tokens in hope that you will show mercy on Marc Dumont and break the hex upon his family." Devyn went on to recount the story of Juliette's betrothal to Edward, culminating in his abandonment on their wedding day. "Your vengeance was justified, but now we pray that you will show mercy on Marc. Unlike his fickle-hearted ancestor, he comes to you on bended knee seeking forgiveness and a bond with Allison Catrine, daughter of your own blood."

Marc's grip tightened around Allie's hand as they shared a hopeful glance.

"Let their love heal the ancient rift between our families," Devyn implored to the heavens. "Please accept his show of faith and free him from your wrath." Then she gave Marc an encouraging nod. "It's time."

From what Marc understood, he was supposed to prove his faith. But what did that mean, exactly? "What do I say?"

"Whatever's in your heart," Devyn told him. She nodded toward the street. "I'll give you two some privacy and wait by the car. When you're finished, someone needs to thank the spirits and release them, but Allie knows how to do that."

She kissed her sister on the head and gave Marc a *don't screw this up* glare, then strode out of view. The iron gate creaked and clicked shut, confirming her departure.

Marc's heart sprinted under the pressure. He didn't want to screw this up.

"It's okay." Allie cupped his face with one hand, her eyes brimming with patience. "I love you, Marc. Just tell me what you want."

That sounded easy enough.

Marc was crazy about Allie. He wanted her to move in with him, to share his bed and fill his arms like she'd done on board the *Belle*. Those short weeks with her were damned near perfect—*she* was damned near perfect—and he wouldn't make the same mistake twice by losing his nerve.

It was time to sac up.

He took a deep breath and began. "Allie, I want . . ."

Marc paused to catch another lungful of air. God bless, it was hotter than hellfire out here. How could anyone breathe this soup?

Allie stroked his cheek. "Go ahead, baby."

He swallowed hard while sweat broke out along his upper lip. He released her hand and blotted his face on his shirttails, but that didn't help. For every drop of sweat he wiped away, three more appeared to take its place. Before long, he was sweating like a sinner on judgment day.

He opened his mouth to try again. "I want . . ."

Damn it, he couldn't get enough oxygen.

Holding up one finger, he said, "Just give me a minute." His collar seemed to be choking him, so he undid the first three buttons. A glance down showed his chest rising and falling, so why did it feel like he couldn't breathe?

"Are you okay?" Allie asked, her whiskey-and-gray eyes widening in concern.

Marc's hands had turned to ice. He wiped them on his trousers and tried a third time. "I want you . . ." *to move in with me. Move in with me!* He screamed it internally, but the words turned to dust. Then a ball of fear rose in his throat and fanned out to squeeze his ribs as surely as any heart attack. His chest grew heavy and his vision blurred. If he didn't know better, he'd think he was dying.

There was only one explanation—the cleansing ceremony had failed.

He was still cursed.

"Marc?" Allie's voice was barely a whisper. "Talk to me."

Unable to bear the mingling of shock and fear in her gaze, he stared at the ground. "I want to keep seeing you."

"Seeing me?" she asked in disbelief. She seemed to chew on that for a while, the distant croak of cicadas filling the silence as seconds ticked by. "Seeing me," she repeated, "or sleeping with me?"

"Both." Shit, he was going down in flames, just like last time. He scrambled for control of his tongue. "But it's more than that," he quickly added. "I want to spend time with you, cook you dinner, and curl up on the sofa to watch old Westerns. And what I said before still stands: I won't cheat while we're together. I swear it."

"You won't cheat *while we're together*."

The flatness of her tone prompted him to peek up from beneath his lashes. When their gazes caught, he was shamed by the pain he saw there. The way she stared at him reminded Marc of the time his mother had caught him stealing baseball cards from the drugstore when he was six years old. More than angry, she looked disappointed, like he'd let her down.

"For however long that lasts, right?" Allie asked. "And when someone new catches your eye, you'll do me the courtesy of breaking up with me before you take her to bed. Is that what you're saying?"

Marc didn't know how to answer that without digging himself a deeper hole. In truth, Allie was the only woman he wanted, but according to statistics, they wouldn't last a lifetime. He'd promised to be faithful to her for as long as she kept him around—what more could he offer?

"Answer me," she demanded.

"I'm sorry," he said. "It's not you. It's the curse. We didn't break it."

Her eyes turned to slits as she released a humorless laugh. "The curse." She pushed to standing and brushed bits of dried grass from her dress. "What if I told you it's not real?"

Marc shook his head. "It is. I can feel it. But maybe if we try again—"

"There's no such thing as magic!" she shouted, shocking the cicadas into a beat of silence. Her eyes welled with tears as she snatched the wooden talisman from the altar. "See this? Legba is no more real than Zeus or Athena. He's just a legend." She tossed aside the statue and pointed to Juliette Mauvais's portrait. "And her? I don't know if Memère's spirit is in heaven or in hell, but I know this—she's not hovering around Cedar Bayou, meddling in your love life. She's gone! She has no power over you!"

Marc didn't understand. "Then why did we just go through all this?"

"Because I'm an idiot." Bending at the waist, she began blowing out the candles, one by one. "I thought the curse was causing you a mental block, and if I could convince you it was broken, you might actually commit to me."

Still on his knees, Marc drew back and turned a blank stare to the stone altar. It had taken days to find all those stupid tokens, especially the snake eggs. And what about the time Allie had gone catatonic? Was it an act?

"So none of this was real?"

"None of this was *ever* real," Allie said, exasperated.

Only one candle remained burning, but it was more than enough to illuminate the tears threatening to spill free from her lashes. A spark of anger ignited inside Marc's chest, but it died just as quickly. As much as he hated her deception, the sight of Allie's quivering chin hit him like a kick to the gut.

"There's no hex, Marc," she said. "It's all in your mind. The plain truth is that you don't love me enough to take the risk. You'll follow your daddy's path because it's safer and easier than forging your own trail and maybe getting hurt along the way."

"That's not true. I'm nothing like my father."

"You're exactly like him," she said. "Just without the children."

That stung, but when Marc geared up to defend himself, he couldn't summon a single argument to refute what she'd said. Still, he refused to dwell on the topic. Aside from genetics, he and the old man had nothing in common.

"I want more," Allie went on. "More than a physical relationship. I deserve your whole heart, and it looks like you can't give me that." A tear spilled down her cheek. "Or you won't. And there's no hex to blame for it."

Something broke behind Marc's breastbone. Hurting Allie was the last thing he'd wanted to do, and now he was losing her. He wanted to get back on track—to show how much she meant to him—but he didn't know how.

Her breath hitched, but instead of breaking into a sob, she locked her spine and peered down at him, square in the eyes. "So now that you know the truth, does it change anything?"

"Allie, please," he said, splaying his hands like a beggar. "I honestly do care about you. Let's slow down and talk this out. Maybe we should take a few days apart to—"

"I didn't think so." She licked her fingers and used them to extinguish the last candle. "Good-bye, Marc."

It took a moment for his eyes to adjust to the darkness, but he heard Allie turn and pick her way along the gravel path leading to the street, leaving him alone with nothing but the acrid burn of smoke in his nostrils to prove that this debacle had actually happened.

Glued to the ground, he knelt there and stretched an arm toward Allie's retreating shadow. "Come back," he called. "Please, Allie. If you'll just listen . . ."

But she continued on her way until she disappeared from view, and that fissure behind his breastbone widened into a virtual black hole.

The night's events seemed surreal. How had everything fallen apart so quickly?

A reflective glimmer of moonlight drew his attention to Juliette Mauvais's picture in its frame. The old biddy smiled down at him in sepia tones, her expression haughty, as if mocking his pain, and it occurred to Marc that on this centennial of the woman's botched wedding day, it was a *Dumont* who'd been dumped at the altar.

How fitting.

If that didn't prove the curse was real, nothing would.

Chapter 17

It rained for the next five days, which suited Allie just fine. She didn't have the will to leave her store anyway.

There was no place she wanted to go. Her body ached all over, and it took every ounce of strength to get dressed in the mornings. At first she'd thought she had the flu, but her thermometer had never registered a temperature above ninety-eight. Maybe it was broken, because her back muscles were throbbing and it was only noon. She leaned over the sales counter and rested on her elbows, sighing in temporary relief.

"Have you eaten anything today?" Devyn asked as she slid a tray of fresh cookies into the glass display case.

Allie stared out the front window, where rain fell in steady sheets against the glass. "I think so."

A skeptical grunt said Devyn wasn't convinced. "What did you have for breakfast?"

"I don't know." Allie retraced her steps from that morning, but her mind was foggy. "A ham biscuit from the corner store, I think."

"No, that was yesterday." Devyn reached into the

case and handed over a brown sugar pecan scone. "Eat this—every last crumb. That's an order."

"Yes, ma'am." Allie took a bite to appease her sister, but she noticed right away the flavor wasn't right. She forced down her mouthful and inspected the scone. "There's something wrong with this batch. It tastes like cardboard."

"Let me see." Devyn crammed half the scone into her mouth. Her eyes closed in rapture, a hand flying to her chest. "Oh, my God," she garbled, "that's better than sex."

A breath caught at the top of Allie's lungs. She'd once said the same thing, but that was before Marc had taken all her carnal expectations and turned them upside down. Now she was ruined—for men and desserts alike. She couldn't stop her eyes from flooding with tears.

"No, it's not," she choked out. "Believe me."

"Aw, sweetie." Devyn popped in the last bite and wrapped an arm around Allie's shoulders. She spoke around the chunk of scone. "There's nothing wrong with this batch. You can't taste it because that wanker killed your joy."

Allie tipped her head against Devyn's shoulder and let the tears fall. "I miss him so much."

"I know," Dev said, stroking Allie's curls. "The wound is still fresh. Give it time to scab over."

"Why hasn't he called?" Allie had hoped Marc would at least make an effort to win her back. She wouldn't have settled for anything less than happily-ever-after, but it would be nice to know he cared enough to try. "Why won't he fight for me?"

Devyn turned and gripped Allie's upper arms, then delivered a stern look. "Because he's a Dumont, that's why. It's not in his nature to fight for love. He's a runner."

"But last week—"

"Look," Dev interrupted, "I know you don't want to hear it, but maybe this is Memère's way of protecting you. As much as it hurts to let Marc go, better now than five years from now, when he's saddled you with a bunch of kids and ditched you for a cocktail waitress half your age."

Allie thought back to what Marc's own sister had said: *I'm not stupid enough to fall for a Dumont.* "I feel like such an idiot."

"Knock that off," Devyn ordered. "You're not the first woman to fall for the wrong guy, and you won't be the last. This won't kill you."

"Could've fooled me."

From atop the cash register, Allie's cell phone chimed to announce an incoming text message. Instantly, her stomach lurched, and she scrambled for the phone in hopes of hearing from Marc. But when she swiped the screen and saw a note from her fruit supplier, all that false hope settled inside her, heavy and cold.

"What if it *had* been him?" Dev asked. "You know he won't change. Why don't you block his number?"

Logically, Allie knew her sister was right, but try telling that to her bruised heart.

"You need an intervention," Devyn said. "No more schlumping around waiting for the phone to ring. Let's go to Vegas."

"But what about the store? It's not even the weekend yet."

"You won't go bankrupt if you close up shop for a few days," Dev told her. "Ask your staff to fill the standing orders and put a sign on the door that says you'll be back Monday."

"You make it sound so simple."

"Well, yeah. That's because it's vacation, not rocket science."

But Allie was so tired. She didn't want to go to Vegas, or anywhere else for that matter, except upstairs to her apartment, where she could crawl beneath her covers and sleep until the pain was gone.

"Let me think about it," she said.

Grumbling under her breath, Devyn let the subject drop and brought out another tray of fresh cookies.

A few minutes later, the front door opened and two women rushed inside, concealed by the red umbrella they shared. They shook off the rain and propped the umbrella in the corner to dry. Allie recognized one of them as Shannon Tucker, the woman who'd come to the Sweet Spot a few weeks ago for a love charm. Shannon's limp blond locks dripped a trail down the front of her T-shirt, her rubber flip-flops squeaking with each forward step. She offered a wide smile, bedraggled but clearly happy.

And very much in love.

A slow grin formed on Allie's lips. It seemed like forever since the last time she'd smiled, and it felt good. "I take it things went well with JP," she said.

The two rain-soaked customers shared a squeal of

delight as Shannon thrust out her left hand, displaying a sparkling diamond set in polished white gold.

"Engaged?" Allie asked, feeling a slight prickle of envy. "Wow, you two don't mess around."

A cherry blush stained Shannon's cheeks. "When you know it's right, why wait?"

Allie's grin faded. She understood. "You want to start your journey together as soon as you can." Unbidden, images of Marc appeared to her—the sinful smile that drew out the cleft in his chin, his chestnut waves tossing in the wind that rolled off the river. She could almost feel his fingers threaded through hers, but when she glanced down, all she saw was a lonely, naked hand.

"Exactly." Shannon and her friend admired the ring. "And it never would have happened without your help." She nodded at the other woman, a petite brunette with a pageboy haircut and bright blue eyes. "That's why I brought Kimmy. She's been with her boyfriend for five years, but he won't pop the question. And he forgot her last three birthdays. We're worried he's checked out of the relationship."

Allie glanced at Kim, who'd taken an abrupt interest in the floor tiles beneath her feet. "You want a love charm?"

"I guess," Kim said to the floor. "Or a potion. Grisgris, maybe. Whatever will make him stop taking me for granted."

Sympathy pains tingled in Allie's chest. *Oh, honey,* she thought. *If I had that kind of power, I'd use it for myself.* "Are you sure he's the right one for you?" she asked instead. "Because if he doesn't appreciate you while you're dating, you can bet he won't appreciate you once you're married. Then you'll have a whole new set of problems."

Shannon pointed at the oak shelf beneath the cash register where Allie kept her voodoo supplies. "Can you read the bones and find out if he's the one, like you did for me?"

Allie studied Kim's downcast eyes and rounded posture. She'd seemed chipper enough until the subject had turned to her life, which indicated the woman lacked confidence. What she probably needed was to ditch her boyfriend and focus on herself for a while. With some prompting, Allie could lead her in that direction . . .

But she didn't want to.

Allie had always taken pride in facilitating love matches or personal growth in others, but she couldn't seem to muster the enthusiasm for it today. She was so tired—of everything.

"It *would* be nice to know," Kim said, her gaze flickering up and down just as quickly.

What the heck. It wasn't like Allie had anything better to do. "Okay." She grabbed her Tupperware container of chicken bones and spread her mat on the counter, then launched into her usual spiel about the spirits rewarding true believers.

What a crock.

After the prayer, she scattered the bones across the mat and pretended to study the significance in their patterns while deciding how best to phrase her advice. Obviously Kim didn't want to end her relationship; otherwise she wouldn't have come here for a love charm, so the standard *Dump him and move on* wouldn't work. Perhaps she should say the spirits of Kim's ancestors considered her boyfriend unworthy, and that was why he hadn't proposed.

Yeah, right, quipped a sarcastic voice inside Allie's head. *Because lying worked so well with Marc. You're a regular miracle worker.*

Allie frowned at the bones and considered those words.

Her conscience had a point.

Using her perceived voodoo "powers" to manipulate Marc had blown up in her face. She could trick most people into following the path she thought was best for them, but was it really her place to try? Had she been an enabler all these years, fooling clients into thinking they had no control over their own destinies?

Maybe instead of blaming "the spirits" for everyone's poor life choices, she needed to butt out and let folks make their own mistakes—kind of like the parable of teaching a man to fish instead of giving him a trout for supper.

"I'm sorry." Allie grabbed a nearby wastebasket and swept the bones inside. "I can't do this."

Shannon blinked in surprise. "Should we come back tomorrow?"

"No," Allie said. "I'm done with all of it—charms, potions, gris-gris. You can come to me if you need a sugar fix or a shoulder to cry on, but that's all."

"But what should I do about my boyfriend?" Kim asked.

Allie gave it to her straight. "People rarely change. If your boyfriend's not giving you what you need now, I doubt he ever will. Ditch him and work on empowering yourself so next time, you won't settle for less than what you deserve."

Shannon and Kim wore similar masks of shock, their brows disappearing beneath dripping-wet bangs.

Devyn, who'd been silent this whole time, finally spoke up. "Want some gris-gris for clarity of mind and heart?" she asked. "I made a batch"—her gaze darted to Allie—"for a *friend* who's going through something similar."

Kim stammered, still caught off guard.

"Well?" Devyn snapped. "You want it or not?"

"Yes, please." Kim extended her hand, palm up, while keeping a wary distance.

Dev plucked a sachet from her pocket and gave it to the woman. "Keep this on you at all times, even when you're sleeping." When she noticed Kim reaching into her purse, Devyn barked, "And don't try to pay me. It's bad juju!"

"Sorry." Kim tensed and backed toward the door, her head bobbing like she didn't know whether to genuflect or run for cover. "Thank you." She and Shannon waved a stiff good-bye, and the two of them wasted no time in snatching their umbrella and hightailing it outside into the rain.

"Here's yours," Dev said, handing Allie a sachet of herbs. "I know you've lost faith, but do me a favor and stick it in your pocket."

"Thanks, baby." Allie was touched by her sister's concern. "That was sweet of—"

Her cell phone chimed, and Allie dropped the gris-gris bag in her haste to snatch the phone and swipe the screen. Her pulse raced, fingers trembled, but she was met with disappointment once again.

Hugs, Ella-Claire had texted. *I'm thinking of you. Call if you want to talk.*

The screen went blurry as tears welled in Allie's eyes. How long would she keep jumping at the sound of every text? If the hope inside her heart didn't fade soon, she'd lose her mind.

"Give me that." Devyn took the phone from her and began typing a response.

"Hey," Allie said, dabbing at her eyes. "What're you doing?" When her sister refused to surrender the phone, Allie peered at the screen to read the return text.

Thanks, but I'm fine, Devyn typed. *Going off the grid for a few days. We'll talk next week.*

Devyn hit the send button. "Go upstairs and pack a bag," she ordered. "We're leaving on the next flight to Vegas." She held up Allie's phone. "And this is staying here."

The storm broke the next day, but in his half-inebriated state, Marc barely noticed.

It wasn't until a beam of late-morning sunlight escaped the clouds and speared his throbbing eyeballs that it occurred to him the rain had stopped. He raised a hand to shield himself from the nuclear assault and stumbled onto the *Belle*'s bow ramp, thankful that he lived close enough to walk to the boat when he was still buzzed from the night before. Otherwise he'd be forced to give up his new girlfriend, Tequila Rose.

One kiss from the lip of that bottle could dull the pain from the ulcer that seemed to have developed on his heart. Relief only lasted a few moments at a time, but if he kept sipping long enough, eventually sleep would take him—which bought six more hours of anesthetized freedom. So what if he awoke with his brain on fire and his stomach turning flips?

It was a small price to pay.

His love affair with Rose explained the sudden influx of empty glass bottles in his recycling bin . . . not to mention the fumbling of his hands as he gripped the deck railing for balance. Whoa. Either the river was churning or Rose was having her way with him.

He pushed off the rail, propelling his leaden feet toward the stairwell, then pried open the door and made his way to the second-floor dining hall. A blast of cool air-conditioning sobered him up a fraction as he crossed to the executive bar. He noticed an odd smell in the room, sharp and chemical, but not altogether unpleasant. His instincts told him something was different, though he couldn't put his finger on what.

The dragging of his footsteps alerted the crew—his brothers, Ella-Claire, and Pawpaw. Five heads turned his way, five pairs of eyes displaying vastly different reactions to his presence: pity from Ella-Claire, concern from Pawpaw, twin looks of unease from Alex and Nick, and thinly veiled disgust from Beau.

"Nice of you to join us, Captain," Beau said while glancing at his watch. He raked a gaze over Marc's face. "Jesus, when was the last time you shaved?"

"Or showered?" added Alex, quirking a brow at the rumpled clothes Marc had slept in last night.

Suddenly itchy, Marc scratched the whiskers at his

jawline. He'd showered yesterday but hadn't used a razor since the evening of his so-called *cleansing ceremony* in Cedar Bayou—the one that hadn't worked because it wasn't even real.

Like shrapnel, a jolt of pain tore through his chest, so he pushed away the memory and locked it down tight, then took his seat at the head of the table. "I'll clean up fine by the next trip. Until then, worry about your own ugly mugs."

"You okay?" asked Ella-Claire from the other end of the table. "I tried calling you this morning, but it went straight to voice mail."

When Marc glanced at his sister, he noticed she sat so close to Alex that their legs were touching. For the love of God, she was practically in his lap. "I'm fine," he ground out, narrowing his eyes at Alex, who responded at once, scooting a few inches away from Ella and staring at his notepad.

Maybe it was time to have a chat with those two.

"Someone please pour me a drink," Marc said. "And fill me in on what I missed."

Ella stood and strode to the bar, then returned with a mug of black coffee. She placed it in front of him and offered a sympathetic pat on the shoulder. "I think you'd better have this instead."

He grumbled a reluctant thanks and took a sip.

"As for what you missed," she said, sweeping her hand toward the floor, "do you like it?"

"Like what?"

Her mouth dropped open. "The new carpet!"

That explained the unfamiliar smell he'd noticed earlier. The old red-patterned carpet that had always reminded him of *The Shining* had been replaced with a stylish Confederate gray Berber. "Yeah, looks nice."

"Looks *nice*?" she repeated. "That's it? You've been waiting years for the money to spiff up the dining room, and now it's like you don't care."

Shameful as it was, Marc couldn't deny the accusation. The *Belle* had finally turned a large enough profit to pay off his bank loans with plenty to spare for renovations and repairs. His maiden cruise as captain had been a smashing success, and they'd already sold out the next trip. A few weeks ago, reaching this point was his main goal in life, but now he couldn't bring himself to give half a damn.

He knew the reason.

During the voyage his goals had shifted, because the *Belle* was no longer his number-one girl. That role had been usurped by a curly-haired pastry chef with mismatched eyes and a penchant for bending the truth.

The worst part was that he didn't care about Allie's lies. If he thought she would have him, he'd throw himself at her feet for just one more day with her. But no matter how vehemently she denied the curse, it hung between them like a lead curtain, and he couldn't stand to see that look of disappointment on her face again.

"The boy needs a priest," Pawpaw said, studying Marc with a shrewd gaze. "He's still entranced." He jabbed a gnarled finger at Marc. "For years I've been warnin' you about them Mauvais women. Believe me now?"

Everyone else at the table avoided Marc's eyes.

"Don't start with me." Marc didn't try to conceal the

threat in his voice. He'd allowed his pawpaw onto the boat, but that didn't mean he'd tolerate the old man blackening Allie's name. "It's because of her that we're finally turning a profit. She's done nothing wrong."

Pawpaw scrunched up his mouth, clearly working on a counterargument. "Doesn't matter. You still can't meddle with her, or the hex—"

"Oh, come on." Ella threw her hands into the air. "Enough with the superstitious nonsense. There's no hex on your family. You make your own beds and lie in them, just like everyone else."

She was wrong—Marc knew firsthand. At the altar last week, he'd felt that dark magic pressing against his ribs, smothering him when he'd tried to ask Allie to move in with him. Something very real had kept his words from escaping, and it wasn't a mental block.

"Can we quit wasting time?" Beau checked his watch again. "I've got places to be, and we still need a status report on the train linkage."

Thankful for the change in subject, Marc asked, "What's wrong with it now?"

"Nothing." Ella reached for Alex's Coca-Cola and took a sip. Good Lord, why did she have to keep doing that? "It's purring like a kitten. Lutz said the hiccup we had in St. Louis must've been a fluke."

Marc shook his head. "It's just a matter of time before *Belle* gets the hiccups again. Call Lutz and have him take another look. I don't want any surprises on the next trip."

Then Ella said something that made him sit a few inches straighter. "You always assume the worst. O ye of little faith."

That was interesting. *Little faith*.

Marc couldn't discern why, but the phrase resonated with him and bounced against the inner walls of his mind, repeating over and over.

Little faith.

Voices from around the table faded into obscurity as Marc puzzled on the reason for his sudden curiosity. There was something significant to be learned here; he sensed it. He seemed on the verge of an epiphany, the answer barely beyond his reach.

Little faith.

Wrinkling his brow, he stared out the side window to the placid river as if the solution might appear to him on the water. Then he recalled the last line from Juliette Mauvais's hex, *none but purest faith will set you free*, and the jigsaw pieces clicked into place—complete and utterly clear for the first time.

"Holy shit," he muttered under his breath.

Now he knew why he'd failed to break the curse, and it had nothing to do with Allie's gravesite ritual being a fake. The fault was entirely his. Only one kind of ceremony would free him, and it wasn't a voodoo cleansing.

"Did you say something?" asked Ella-Claire.

Marc's mind reeled with the truth of his discovery. "I'm in love with Allie Mauvais," he said to no one in particular.

He was met with blank stares and silence.

"She's selfless and sweet," he continued. "I'm happy when I'm around her and miserable when I'm not. She even likes old Westerns." He locked eyes with his sister. "I've never met a woman who liked Westerns."

Ella gave him a sad smile. "She's special, for sure."

"She's more than special," Marc said. "She's my perfect match." And when a smart man found the love of his life, he didn't ask her to move in with him—he married her. "That's why I couldn't break the spell. I showed a *little* faith, and it wasn't enough." Marc stood from the table so quickly his chair fell over. "I have to find her and ask her to marry me." His chest went warm and tingly, a message that he finally had it right.

With that sole purpose in mind, he rushed toward the exit.

A scuffling noise sounded from behind, and a pair of arms tightened around Marc before he'd reached the door. Marc tried to squirm free, but the grip was too powerful.

"Hold up there, little brother," Beau said. "You look like a vagrant and you smell worse than a distillery. Let's not give Allie a reason to say no."

Marc quit struggling long enough to let Beau's advice sink in. He was right; Allie deserved the best, not some half-assed proposal from Marc with the kiss of Tequila Rose on his breath.

"Fine." Marc let his arms go slack. "Give me a lift home, will you?"

"You got it."

"No, to the jewelry store," Marc corrected. "No, wait. Not the jewelry store—to the pawn shop. I want to buy a ring that's completely nonrefundable." The more faith the better. "Take me to the bank!"

"Simmer down," Beau said with a good-natured laugh. "First let's pour you another cup of coffee. Then we'll go get your woman."

"My woman." Marc smiled. "I like the sound of that."

Once Marc was sufficiently caffeinated, Beau delivered him to Richman's Pawn & Loan, the swankiest resale shop in the city.

"Leave the car running," he said to Beau. "This won't take long."

Marc pushed open the front door and strode directly to the jewelry section near the back of the store. He waved to the owner, Mrs. Richman. The old woman was so shrewd, she'd charge you for breathing, but that didn't matter. He wasn't here looking for a bargain.

"I need an engagement ring, and fast," Marc said when Mrs. Richman made her way behind the counter. "Something huge. Sky's the limit."

The woman's eyes glazed over with delight. She indicated several cases, each teeming with glistening gems. "What style? Solitaire, three-stone, cathedral setting?"

Marc decided to go with his gut. "I'll know it when I see it."

"This one's nice." She pulled free an oval-shaped diamond set in platinum. "Two and a half carats, excellent cut, nearly colorless."

"Wow." She wasn't kidding—the thing was spectacular. Marc slipped the ring on his pinkie finger and admired the way it sparkled. Allie would love it. With any luck, he'd have this ring on her finger by noon. He was about to tell Mrs. Richman to wrap it up when a stone from the adjacent display caught his eye.

It was round, set low in a thin band of filigreed

gold, and about half the size of the diamond in Marc's hand. But despite that, the stone captured the overhead fluorescents and refracted the light in a spray of rainbows. It was like nothing he'd ever seen.

"Tell me about that one," he said.

"Ah." Mrs. Richman's voice flattened in disappointment, likely because the second ring was less expensive. "That's an estate piece, came in last week."

"It doesn't look like the others."

"That's because diamonds aren't faceted that way anymore," she explained. "It's an old European cut, popular in the early 1900s. The woman who sold it to me said her great-great-granddaddy bought it off Juliette Mauvais." She scoffed. "Can you believe that? Probably bad luck to have it in the store."

Marc's skin prickled. "You think it's really hers?"

She shrugged. "No way to tell, but it gives me the willies just looking at it."

That was good enough for Marc. His face broke into a grin so wide he nearly sprained his cheeks. "I'll take it."

Chapter 18

Two hours later, a freshly showered, clean-shaven Marc arrived at the Sweet Spot with a century-old solitaire in his shirt pocket and a single-minded determination to change Allie's last name from Mauvais to Dumont.

His blood rushed, but this time with excitement, not fear. He had faith—the purest kind—that he and Allie were meant to be, and he couldn't wait to begin their life together. If she wasn't ready to forgive him, then he'd return tomorrow. And the day after that. However long it took to win her back, he was in it for the long haul.

"Don't forget those," Beau said, thumbing at the bouquet of roses resting on the SUV's backseat. "Got the ring?"

Marc grabbed the flowers and patted his breast pocket. "Right here."

Thoughtfully, Beau glanced at the bakery window. "Mind if I come with you? I want to give it another shot with Dev when you take Allie upstairs to pop the question."

"Another shot?" Marc asked.

"At apologizing," Beau said. "I doubt she'll give me more than that."

"Maybe not, but forgiveness is the first step." Allie was always saying *You can't win if you don't play.* Marc shrugged and opened the passenger door. "Good luck."

They pulled open the bakery door, which *ding*ed to announce their arrival, and right away Marc noticed several things weren't right.

For starters, the heavy aroma of cupcakes and frosting was missing, replaced by vacant air-conditioning. Also, nobody was manning the cash register, and the glass display cases were empty. Marc glanced at the front door, wondering if Allie had taken the day off and forgotten to secure the dead bolt.

"Hello?" he called. "Allie?"

A college-aged brunette pushed open the swinging door leading to the back room. She smiled and greeted him with an apology in her voice. "Hey. We're actually closed today. I'm waiting for someone to pick up a wedding cake; then I'm locking up." She glanced between Marc and Beau. "You're not with the Jefferson party, are you?"

"No," Marc said. "I'm here to see Miss Mauvais. Is she upstairs?"

The girl shook her head. "She's on vacation with her sister."

Vacation?

Marc's stomach sank. The two hours that had passed since his realization aboard the *Belle* had crawled by slower than a millennium. He had to see Allie—now. Marc peered toward the rear of the store as if willing her to appear. When she didn't materialize, he asked, "When's she coming back?"

"Monday, I think."

"Is she staying somewhere local," Marc asked, "like the beach?"

The girl's face went blank while her eyes darted to the bouquet of roses in Marc's fist. She probably thought he was some kind of stalker. "Um," she told him, "I don't think it's my place to say."

Beau stepped up and gave Marc a friendly smack on the shoulder. "No problem," he said to the girl. "We'll get out of your hair."

"Just a second." Marc fished the phone from his back pocket. He dialed Allie's number, but as soon as it rang, the cell phone resting atop the cash register began vibrating. Squinting at the case, he recognized it as Allie's.

"Oh, yeah." The girl silenced the phone and tucked it inside a drawer. "She left her cell behind. She said she didn't want to be bothered."

Well, shit. How was Marc supposed to track her down? He could wait for her to return, but that was two more days. He'd barely survived two hours.

"Want to leave a message?" the girl asked. "She's been checking in, usually first thing in the morning. I can tell her you stopped by."

"That's all right." Marc's message was far too personal to be conveyed over the phone by a temp worker. "Thanks, though."

Defeated, he trudged outside and flung open the door to Beau's SUV, then tossed the flower bouquet onto the floorboard. If he hadn't thought it would spook the shop girl, he'd have given them to her. Seemed a shame to let a dozen perfectly good roses go to waste.

"Hey," Marc asked his brother as they fastened their seat belts. "Any chance you've got some supersecret government connections that can find Allie?"

Beau raised his chin in contemplation, his hand paused at the ignition. "Maybe, but only if she used a credit card to book her room."

"Which everyone does." Gradually, Marc's hopes lifted.

Beau started the car. "Let's head back to your place so I can make a few calls."

Two cans of Coke later, Marc had paced a matted trail into his living room carpet.

As it turned out, the government couldn't track citizens as easily as they did in the movies. Beau had phoned a buddy within the CIA, and when that didn't yield any results, he'd called in a favor from a friend in local law enforcement. Finally, he'd booted up Marc's laptop and contacted a Romanian hacker he'd met while serving overseas. *He's the best*, Beau had said. *If he can't help, nobody can.*

That was thirty minutes ago.

Just when Marc thought he couldn't take it anymore, Beau sauntered in from the kitchen, waving a yellow legal pad.

"I've got good news and bad news," Beau said.

"Give me the bad news."

"She's nowhere near here."

"And the good?"

"As cross-country travel goes, she's in the easiest place to fly to." Beau rotated his hips in an Elvis impersonation. "Vegas, baby."

A slow grin spread across Marc's face. His brother was right—on any given day, more than a dozen direct flights departed for Vegas from the nearest airport. The fares were cheap as dirt, and getting a room on the strip was a breeze. "I can be there by suppertime."

"Not that you asked," Beau said, "but she's staying at the Grand Palace Royale."

Marc tipped his head appreciatively. "High-dollar resort." It was fashioned after a medieval village, complete with a castle and moat, and the staff wore Renaissance period costumes. Not his first choice, but a nice place to romance Allie.

There was only one problem.

"It's bigger than some amusement parks," Marc said. "If I don't know which room she's in, I'd have better luck finding Jimmy Hoffa's body in the desert."

"I'm working on it." Beau lifted his phone. "My buddy's hacking the hotel computer to find Allie's room number. You get going. I'll text you when he's done."

Marc thanked his brother and rushed toward his bedroom to pack an overnight bag. In his haste to get on the road, he blindly shoved clothing into his duffel without a care for whether or not it matched, then carried his bag into the bathroom to scoop a handful of random toiletries inside. If he forgot something important, he could buy it at the hotel. Marc made a grab for the Trojans in the medicine cabinet, but he paused with his fingers curled around the box.

Each time they'd made love, Allie had insisted they didn't need protection beyond her birth control pills. In the logical part of his mind, Marc had known she was right, and yet he'd felt compelled to keep an extra barrier between them.

Not anymore.

Marc wasn't his father, and he refused to live in fear of repeating another man's mistakes. He shoved the box onto its shelf and shut the cabinet.

He was on his way toward the bedroom door when a flash of black and white caught his eye from inside the closet. It was his tuxedo, the one he'd worn at formal dinners on board the *Belle* before he was captain. He'd turned quite a few heads each time he'd put it on. If Allie had liked him in his captain's uniform, she'd love him in this. And nothing said *purest faith* like showing up in Vegas already dressed for a wedding.

What the hell—he dropped his bag and decided to change. It wasn't like another fifteen minutes would make or break his plans.

After three attempts, he finally got his bow tie straight, then pocketed the engagement ring, grabbed his duffel, and headed for the exit.

"Got the room number," Beau said while tapping his cell phone screen. "I'm texting it to you so you don't forget."

The phone in Marc's pocket buzzed in confirmation, and he gave it a quick glance. "Room 123," he said. "That's easy to remember."

"Godspeed, little brother." Beau folded his gargantuan arms and beamed. "Don't come home without her."

Marc thanked him. He liked this new and improved version of his brother. "You can count on it."

After leaving his truck in short-term parking—hourly rates be damned—Marc jogged into the terminal and took his place in line at the ticketing gate. He did his best not to glare at the passengers in front of him, but for the love of God, why didn't more people use the kiosk to check their luggage? Then it would free up a human employee and shorten his wait.

Finally, it was his turn. Marc approached the counter, staffed by a thirtysomething redhead with a flirty gleam in her eyes. Her lips slid into a wide smile while her gaze roamed over his torso.

"We don't see many tuxes in here," she said with a wink. "Are you one of Marty's limo drivers? If so, you must be new, because I would've noticed you before."

Marc didn't have time for this. He forced a grin and resisted the urge to snap at her. "I need the next plane to Vegas, doesn't matter which airline. I saw there was a nonstop flight leaving in forty-five minutes. Any chance there's a seat left?"

"Oooh." She grimaced and drew a sharp breath. "Afraid not. If you'd gotten here fifteen minutes ago, I might have been able to get you on board. But two of the inbound planes for Vegas were just grounded for technical issues, and we had to reroute the displaced passengers onto existing flights." She gave him a pity-ing look. "I can put you on the standby list, but it's al-ready thirty passengers long."

Marc huffed a sigh. Of course the Vegas-bound planes

were busted. Just his luck. "When's the next available flight?"

Her red-tipped fingers few across the computer keys for a few interminable seconds. "Looks like . . ."—just when he thought she might answer, she began typing again—"I can get you a seat tomorrow afternoon at three."

"*Tomorrow?*" And not even a red-eye flight. This would set him back another twenty-four hours, meaning he might as well wait for Allie to come home. "That won't work. I have to get there today."

The woman turned up her hands, her expression hardening in a way that said he'd tried her patience. "Well, I can't wave a wand and make that happen."

Marc folded his arms against the counter and made his best puppy dog face, then tapped his tuxedo lapel and told a little white lie. "You don't understand. If I don't get to Vegas tonight, I'll miss my own wedding."

She softened at that, lips parting in an oval while her hand flew to her breast. "Oh, bless your heart." Head tipped to the side, she blinked at Marc like he was a kindergartner with a skinned knee. "I wish there was something I could do. Have you looked into hiring a charter?"

Marc stood a bit straighter. "A charter plane?"

"Mmm-hmm." She rooted around beneath the counter until she found a business card and slid it across the laminate surface. A toothy cartoon nutria waved at Marc above simple black font advertising *River Rat Charters.* "Rick's your best bet for a last-minute booking. He's a real sweetie."

Marc didn't care if the guy was a sweetie. He wanted

someone to fly him safely to Vegas, not pinch his cheeks and tuck him into bed. "That's nice, but can he fly?"

"Oh, sure." The woman waved off his concern. "He's been doing this forever." She pointed at the phone number listed on the card while her gaze darted to the line of customers forming behind Marc. "Give him a call and see if he can help you. And congrats on the wedding, by the way." Then she motioned for the next passenger to come forward.

Marc took the hint and carried his overnight bag to a quiet corner to contact the pilot. When he dialed the number, a woman with a two-pack-a-day voice answered, "Y'ello."

"Hi," Marc said. "I'm looking to charter a plane to Vegas."

"When you wanna leave?"

"Preferably now."

"Just a sec." She didn't bother covering the mouthpiece when she hollered, "Hey, Ricky! You wanna fly to Vegas today?"

A distant male voice shouted, "Mm-kay," and the old woman gave Marc directions to the landing strip, which she said was in a field behind her house.

The exchange didn't exactly fill Marc with confidence, but he wasted no time in jogging back to his truck and following the woman's instructions. The sun hung a little too low in the sky for his liking, proof that the clock was ticking.

Twenty minutes later, he turned down a dirt road toward a small brick ranch in the distance. For a moment, he worried he'd arrived at the wrong address, but when he pulled onto the gravel driveway, he noticed a cartoon nutria painted on the side of an aluminum garage resting beside the house.

Must be the right place.

Marc strode to the front stoop, punched the doorbell, and a middle-aged man with a *Duck Dynasty* beard answered. He wore a Parrot Head T-shirt, cargo shorts, and a grin that said he'd spent some recent time in Margaritaville.

"Are you Vegas?" the man asked, chuckling at Marc's tuxedo. He extended a palm. "I'm Ricky."

"Yes, sir." Marc shook his hand. "Marc Dumont."

"Dumont?" Rick's bushy brows drew together over narrowed blue eyes. "You're not Jack's boy, are you?"

"One of them," Marc said. "I've got four brothers— five if you count the baby on the way."

"Mmm." This revelation didn't seem to please Rick. Knowing Daddy, he'd probably seduced the man's sister. "Well, I won't hold that against you."

With that roadblock settled, Marc peered at the adjacent field. "I don't see your plane. Do you keep it parked at the airfield?"

"Nah." Rick removed his ball cap and pointed it toward the aluminum garage. "The old girl's in the hangar."

Marc stopped breathing. That oversized shed was a hangar? He had a bad feeling about this.

"C'mon," Rick said as he stepped out of the house and led the way. "You can help me pull her out."

"We're going to haul it out of the hangar, just the two of us?" Mercy, how small was this plane?

"Don't worry," Rick assured him. "You won't break a sweat and ruin your penguin suit."

Once the hangar's aluminum doors parted, Marc nearly swallowed his tongue. When he'd heard the words *private charter,* his imagination had conjured images of sleek ten-passenger jets—the kind celebrities and professional athletes hired to whisk them away to secluded islands. The aircraft that faced Marc from the shed looked more like a tin coffee can with wings, smaller than Beau's SUV. Wasn't this the kind of plane that had killed John Denver? And a couple of the Kennedys?

All the blood must have drained from Marc's face, because Rick studied him and took a defensive tone. "I know what you're thinking."

I'm going to fall to my death, screaming like a schoolgirl at a Bieber concert. That's what Marc was thinking.

Rick smacked the side of his plane. "That it's going to take forever to get there, considering how many times we'll have to stop and refuel."

"Nope, that's the last thing on my mind."

"Good, because my girl's quicker than she looks. Not as fast as a jetliner, but I can have you in Sin City tonight if you don't mind the close quarters."

At that point, Marc had two choices: turn around and go home, or climb inside Rick's paper airplane and risk death for a chance at knocking on door 123 and seeing Allie's sweet face.

Marc extended his hand to shake. "You've got a deal."

Allie was fairly certain she had glitter stuck to her tongue. She picked off a fleck and frowned at the offending sparkle. Unlike Devyn, she hadn't licked any naked chests tonight, so how had it wound up inside her mouth? And more importantly, from which sweaty body in the club had it originated?

Never mind. She didn't want to know the answer to either of those questions.

"Gross." She wiped her finger on her jeans and took another swig of merlot in hopes that the alcohol would act as a sterilizing agent.

The other women experiencing the *Bare Booty Beef-cake Review* whooped and hollered, waving dollar bills in the air in hopes of luring a young muscled dancer in their direction for a few minutes of awkward simulated sex.

But not Allie.

She didn't appreciate half-naked men thrusting their junk in her face, no matter how toned and gorgeous the owners of that junk happened to be.

Sinking back into her chair, she avoided eye contact as a nearby "soldier" peeled off his shirt and flung it into the crowd. Experience had taught Allie the best way to go unnoticed in here was to stare into her lap. The one time she'd made the mistake of watching the show, a dancer had dropped to his knees in front of her chair and buried his face between her legs.

That just wasn't right.

She snuck a peek at her watch to check the time, which seemed to be going backward. But as much as she longed to return to the hotel, she'd booked this trip as a reward for Devyn, who was currently onstage with both legs wrapped around a bouncing cowboy's waist, screaming, "Yee-haw! Giddyup, stallion!" A second wrangler galloped up from behind and put Dev in the middle of a stripper sandwich, not that she seemed to mind. Reaching behind her, she snatched off the second man's Stetson and placed it atop her head.

If the hickeys on Devyn's neck were any indication, she was having the time of her life, and Allie wouldn't be the wet blanket.

"Hey, pretty lady." The soldier—or "Private Privates" according to the embroidery on his red, white, and blue thong—tugged on Allie's wrist. He flashed his teeth and nodded toward the stage. "Consider yourself drafted"—his voice dripped with sexual innuendo—"for *service*."

Oh, no. Allie wanted no part of this. She reclaimed her hand and massaged both temples. "Sorry. I've got a headache. Maybe next time."

With a shrug, the private extended his hand to a willing volunteer at the next table, and Allie exhaled a sigh of relief. While the music blasted and women cheered, she sipped her wine, trying to make herself invisible. Finally the song ended and a flush-faced Devyn returned to the table.

Dev used an index finger to tip back her pilfered Stetson. "Okay, party pooper. Let's go back to the hotel."

"No," Allie objected. "We can stay as long as you want. The firemen are up next. You haven't ridden any of them yet."

Devyn took a sip of her martini and glared at Allie. "I can't have fun when you're sitting down here looking like you'd rather get a colonoscopy than dance with a hot guy."

"There's dancing," Allie pointed out, "and then

there's dry humping to loud music. The two are not mutually inclusive."

"You say dry humping like it's a bad thing." Dev lifted her martini toward Private Privates. "He's been checking you out all night. A rebound fling is just what you need."

Allie wrinkled her nose. "Even if I were into him—which I'm not—I'll bet he's with a different woman every day of the week. Not everything that happens in Vegas stays in Vegas . . . like gonorrhea."

What she didn't say was that no man could replace Marc, and she wasn't ready to try.

"You're hopeless." Dev grabbed her handbag and threw back the rest of her drink. "Let's go. Maybe there's a good chick flick on pay-per-view."

"Now you're speaking my language." Maybe Allie would take a bubble bath, too. "And room service. I'm craving a cheeseburger."

Dev wrapped an arm around Allie's shoulders. "Anything for my favorite sister. I've even got a surprise for you."

"What is it?"

"Duh, if I told you, then it wouldn't be a surprise."

After a brief cab ride back to the Grand Palace Royale, Allie slipped her key card into the slot and walked inside their medieval-themed room, scanning it for a basket of chocolate or a tray of cupcakes. But nothing looked different aside from the beds being turned down.

Allie gave her sister a questioning glance.

"Pack your things," Devyn said with a smile. "Because I called the front desk this morning and got us upgraded to a deluxe suite—two bedrooms, a free minibar, and a hot tub so big we can swim in it. Surprise!"

"No way."

"Way. There's even a TV attached to the hot tub, so we can watch chick flicks in our bikinis while we sip champagne and soak away our cares."

Squealing, Allie threw both arms around her sister. "This is just what I needed. You're the best!"

"Damn right, I am," Dev agreed. "If we're going to act like homebodies, we might as well do it in style. Seventeenth floor, here we come!"

By the time Marc's plane landed in Nevada, he didn't want to simply kiss the ground—he wanted to give it Allie's ring and make passionate love to it.

He unclenched ten white-knuckled fingers from his knees and drew a deep breath to loosen the vise around his chest, but he couldn't quite manage to unclench his jaw. Lord, if he never flew in a froghopper again, it would be too damned soon.

Rick slapped him on the back. "Told you I'd have you in Sin City tonight."

With twelve o'clock rapidly approaching, *tonight* was a stretch. By the time Marc called a taxi and drove to the hotel, it would be morning, but not morning enough to knock on Allie's door. He would've been better off getting a decent night's sleep and flying out at dawn.

"Want to share a cab into town?" Rick asked. "I need to rest up before I head back. Maybe I'll catch a show and hit the craps tables, too."

Marc agreed, and after helping Rick stow the plane in a rented hangar, the two men rode together to the city. They chatted the whole way, and Marc shared the reason for his visit.

"A Dumont getting hitched?" Rick asked, smoothing his beard. "There's something you don't see every day."

"I'll leave here a married man or die trying," Marc promised.

"Good luck to you, son." When they reached the Grand Palace Royale, Rick wrote his cell phone number on the back of a business card and handed it over. "I imagine you'll want to fly back with your bride on a commercial jet, but call me if you change your mind."

Marc pocketed the business card, but knew he wouldn't need it. Then he thanked Rick and waved good-bye as the cab shuttled the man to a less extravagant destination.

At the front desk, Marc's credit card took a beating, but he gladly plunked down the money for a deluxe suite with the honeymoon package, then hurried to his room on the seventeenth floor to freshen up. He didn't care if it was two in the morning. If he waited any longer to apologize to Allie, his head might explode.

Looking as dapper as possible in his sleep-deprived, travel-weary state, he took the elevator to the first floor and approached room 123. Then he knocked on the door, arming himself with a repentant grin and a single rose he'd borrowed from a floral arrangement in the lobby.

When the door swung open, Marc's smile fell.

"Yeah?" A chiseled young man stood there, looking

like he'd stepped off a J.Crew billboard. He was naked with nothing but a sheet wrapped around his waist. He rubbed his eyes and scanned Marc's tuxedo. "We didn't order anything."

Marc's face heated while raw jealousy surged through his veins. In the span of two seconds, he couldn't hear his own thoughts over the pounding pulse in his ears. "Who the hell are you?" he demanded.

The man drew back. "Who the hell are *you*?"

"Where's Allie?"

"Who?"

"My fiancée, that's who!"

A classic *oh, shit!* expression passed over the guy's features as he darted a glance into the room. "She told me her name was Mandy. And she didn't say anything about having a fiancé."

Marc pointed into the darkness. "Just put on your clothes and get lost. I'll take it from here."

The guy propped one hand on the doorframe, blocking the way. "Listen, buddy, I can sympathize, but it's obvious she doesn't want to be with you. Why don't you quit embarrassing yourself and go drink it off or something?"

Drink it off? Who did this punk think he was?

"Drink *this* off, you son of a bitch!" Marc dropped his rose and pushed up both jacket sleeves, gearing up to knock this cocky bastard into next week.

Too bad sheer exhaustion had slowed his reflexes. The last thing Marc saw before losing consciousness was a ham-sized fist connecting with his face.

Chapter 19

When Marc came to, he was flat on his back in the hallway with a curly-haired blonde kneeling over him. She wore a fluffy white bathrobe and a worried expression.

"I don't know this guy," the woman said to someone standing behind her.

"Well, he said you're his fiancée," came a man's response.

"I don't care what he said." The woman tightened her robe's belt tie and frowned at the man. "I've never seen him before in my life."

Marc pushed to his elbows, groaning when the slight change in altitude made his head throb. One of his eyelids had begun to swell shut, so he turned the good one toward the couple staring at him.

They were strangers.

Understanding dawned, bringing with it sweet relief. Allie hadn't moved on with another man. Marc sniffed a dry laugh at his own stupidity—and that of Beau's hacker.

"Sorry," he said in a voice roughened by the fall. "I had the wrong room."

The woman smiled triumphantly at her partner. "See? Told you."

Cringing, the man inspected his knuckles. "Guess I should have just closed the door and called security instead of whaling on you like that. Sorry, man."

"No hard feelings." Marc wasn't a stranger to black eyes and busted lips. "I'm glad you didn't call security. I can't afford to get kicked out of here." At least not until he found Allie and won her forgiveness; then the hotel staff was free to toss him into the street. He pushed himself up to a sitting position while the hallway spun around him.

"Whoa, there." The man steadied Marc's shoulder. "Take it easy before you pass out again."

"How long was I unconscious?"

"Not long—a few seconds, tops. I think you hit your head when you fell."

That explained the pounding at the back of his skull. Marc closed his eyes, but that made the spinning worse. "I'm fine. I need to get back to my room."

"Let me get dressed and I'll help you," the man said. "It's the least I can do, since I kicked your ass, and all."

Laughing, Marc agreed, and they slogged arm in arm to the seventeenth floor. Once inside his suite, the guy helped Marc to the king-sized bed before returning downstairs.

While Marc iced the back of his head, he considered his next move.

He could call Beau and ask his hacker friend to give it another whirl, but that didn't seem worth the effort since the original information had been wrong anyway. At this hour, it didn't seem wise to walk through the bars or casinos looking for Allie. She'd almost certainly be asleep, especially considering the schedule she kept at the bakery—early to bed, early to rise.

His gaze darted to the bedside phone. Maybe he should try calling the front desk. Could the solution be that easy?

Marc dialed the check-in station and waited for an answer before asking, "Can you connect me with Allie Mauvais's room?"

"Just one moment," came the reply. "I'm sorry. That room has issued a DND request."

"DND?"

"Do not disturb."

Marc uttered a curse under his breath. Of course it wouldn't be that easy. He decided not to leave a message. Allie wouldn't return his call, not after the way he'd behaved at the cemetery.

Back to the drawing board.

After a few minutes of brainstorming, he decided to wait until six in the morning, then grab some coffee and sit in the lobby to watch for her. All the elevators in the complex emptied into the lobby, so sooner or later she'd have to cross his path. It wasn't the best idea, but he couldn't come up with anything better. Tossing his impromptu cold pack into the ice bucket, he reclined on the bed to rest his eyes for a few moments.

When Marc opened his eyes again, sunlight streamed through his windows so brightly he cringed and raised a hand to block the assault. The thick haze of slumber began to clear, and he bolted upright in panic.

Oh, shit! How long had he slept?

His head ratcheted toward the alarm clock, where a red digital display told him it was almost noon—a full six hours later than he'd planned to camp out in the lobby.

"Son of a bitch."

Marc sank against his pillow while mentally smacking himself. He should have played it safe and set the alarm. Allie could be anywhere by now, maybe even off the resort.

So much for that idea.

Still cursing his own name, he sprung out of bed. Marc didn't have a plan, but since he wouldn't find Allie in his suite, he freshened up and headed downstairs to explore the resort. His head didn't hurt anymore, so at least one thing had worked in his favor today.

He began his search at the indoor restaurants and gift shops, then scoped out the casinos and swimming pools. He struck out everywhere. By the time he reached the athletic complex, he began to lose hope of ever tracking her down in this mini-metropolis. What if she'd taken a tour of the Hoover Dam? Or gone shopping on the strip? The possibilities were endless.

Marc plopped down on a lobby sofa and cradled his head in both hands. Why was the universe making this so difficult? Hadn't he demonstrated enough faith to prove that he deserved another chance with Allie? He expelled a frustrated breath and glance down at his feet.

That's when he noticed that Rick's business card had fallen from his pocket. There on the pristine marble tile, a cartoon nutria grinned up at Marc and gave him an idea.

A crazy idea. An utterly ridiculous idea.

But the more he thought about it, the more he found himself smiling. If *this* didn't get Allie back in his arms before her vacation ended, nothing would.

Allie yawned and stretched, blinking awake gradually to the hum of an air conditioner instead of the screeching of an alarm clock. It was a nice change. The sun was visible as a faint halo of light along the edges of her room-darkening shades. She lifted her head only enough to check the clock, then lay down again, smiling. The last time she'd slept until noon was the summer vacation before senior year.

I could get used to this, she thought. *Wonder if Devyn's up.*

She sniffed the air and noticed a light aroma of roasted coffee beans mingled with something sweet—pancakes or waffles. Allie rolled out of bed, tugged down her polka-dot nightgown, and shuffled into the living area, where last night's room service tray had been replaced by a cart bearing fresh fruit, whipped cream, and a stack of Belgian waffles.

"Nice spread," Allie said to her sister, who lounged by the window, sipping coffee.

Devyn lifted her mug. "Good afternoon, Sleeping Beauty. It's about time you graced the world with your presence."

"Don't blame me," Allie said. "Someone kept me up until the wee hours of the morning watching *Under the Tuscan Sun*."

Dev sighed dreamily and pressed a hand to her chest. "I love that movie. I think our next vacation should be to Italy."

"Then start saving your pennies." Allie snuck a peek

at the room service invoice. Ouch. "For as much as they cost, these waffles had better make me see God."

Dev pointed at the cart. "Use an extra dollop of that sweet cream and you'll hear angels, too."

While Allie scarfed down a plate of fruit-topped waffles—which really were worth every penny—Devyn fanned out an assortment of tourist pamphlets.

"It's our last full day of vacation," Devyn said. "What should we do?"

Scanning the brochures, it became clear their options were infinite. They could go horseback riding, catch an auto race, visit the aquarium, take a helicopter tour of the Grand Canyon, sign up for a rock 'n' roll fantasy camp, or even go skydiving.

"It's overwhelming," Allie said around a bite of waffle. "Just looking at all this makes me want to go back to bed. I'm too tired for an adventure."

"Then I take it 'pole-dancing lessons' are out of the question." Dev tossed aside that particular pamphlet. After inspecting the options again, she asked, "Want to take it easy today? Maybe hang out by the pool and order froufrou drinks that come with tiny umbrellas?"

The suggestion appealed to Allie. Vacations were supposed to be relaxing, weren't they? She didn't want to spend her last day in Vegas working a pole or tumbling from an airplane. "I like it. Besides, I'll bet time passes slower at the pool."

"Then the pool it is," Devyn declared. "Let's get our bikinis on before we miss all the best rays."

After donning their bathing suits, they bypassed the family pool—bursting at the seams with shrieking children and bouncing beach balls—and continued to the adults-only area, the one surrounded by tall, noise-canceling shrubs and offering a fully stocked bar. This was the best spot at the resort, and it showed. There were only two reclining lounge chairs left, which they quickly claimed.

Allie and her sister had barely finished spreading their towels onto the chairs when a waitress arrived to take their drink orders.

Devyn pointed to Allie. "Like Garth Brooks said, bring her two piña coladas—one for each hand. I'll have a Tom Collins."

The waitress hurried back toward the bar before Allie could correct her sister. "I don't need two," she chided. "You'll have me soused by lunchtime."

"It already *is* lunchtime, so consider yourself behind schedule."

Allie slathered on some SPF fifteen and lay back on the cushioned chair, sighing at the delicious warmth of the sun caressing every inch of her exposed skin. Before long, she had two slushy piña coladas in hand, and she couldn't deny that this was as close to paradise as she was ever going to get.

"We chose well," Dev said, turning onto her belly and unfastening her bikini strap to avoid the dreaded tan line. "This is way better than pole-dancing lessons."

"I'll drink to that." And Allie did.

But as the tranquil minutes passed with nothing to distract her, Allie's thoughts crept dangerously toward Marc and what he might be doing right now. Did he miss her? Had he tried calling, and if so, did he wonder where she'd gone?

She doubted it. He probably didn't even know she'd left town.

Her heart grew heavy as she peered around the pool at the happy, hand-holding couples, some of them leaning in for occasional kisses. She wanted that same contentment for herself, and she had a feeling all the fruity alcohol in the world wouldn't dull the ache building inside her.

What was she going to do when vacation ended and she returned to New Orleans? If she saw Marc with another woman it would kill her. And eventually it had to happen.

The devil on Allie's shoulder whispered that she could go to Marc and take whatever he was willing to give, but she shook her head and cast out the tempting idea. Yes, she missed Marc, but the pain would deepen the longer she stayed with him. If he wasn't willing to share his whole heart, she had to stay away.

She took a long sip of her drink and tried to exorcise Marc's image from her mind. When that didn't work, she kept slurping on her straw until a brain freeze shut down all her synapses. She set down her piña coladas, donned her sunglasses, and closed her eyes to focus on the scents of chlorine and tanning lotion and the gentle brush of the desert breeze.

A distant airplane droned, its buzz an oddly soothing sound when combined with the sloshing of water. But as it approached, the noise became grating and tinny, unlike any plane she'd ever heard. It seemed to circle the area, and Allie wished it would move on.

"Allie Mauvais," someone muttered from across the pool.

Eyes flying open, she propped on her elbows and scanned the rows of lounge chairs for the person who'd called her name, but everyone was peering at the clouds. She glanced up and her lips parted in shock.

An airplane that looked more like a flying go-kart towed a sloppy spray-painted banner that read, ALLIE MAUVAIS TO THE FRONT DESK!

She peeked down at her piña coladas, wondering how much she'd had to drink. Not enough to induce hallucinations.

"Hey, Dev," she said. "Tell me you see this, too." When her sister lifted her head, Allie pointed at the sky.

Squinting, Devyn craned her neck at the plane. "Holy shit. Do you think they mean you?"

"What are the odds that two women named Allie Mauvais are staying here?" Slim to none. "I'm going to check."

"I'll come with you."

In flip-flops and with towels wrapped around their waists, Allie and Devyn followed the winding sidewalk that led to the main lobby. Allie tried to speculate on the reason behind the bizarre summons, and for a moment, she worried there might be an emergency back home. But surely the hotel would have used their intercom system for that, not a miniature airplane.

When they reached the lobby, Allie pushed her sunglasses atop her head and approached the front desk. She still didn't know what to expect, but in her wildest dreams she hadn't anticipated that Marc would be waiting there for her.

In a tuxedo.

With a black eye and a bruised cheek.

Allie's feet quit moving, such was her confusion. Maybe she *had* tangled too much with Captain Morgan today. She blinked at Marc twice, but he was still there each time she opened her eyes.

His polished wingtip shoes clicked against the tile as he crossed to the middle of the lobby to meet her. Visitors and employees strode to and fro, but their presence barely registered. Allie stood there transfixed by the gorgeous man who'd broken her heart.

It seemed there was no escaping him.

"Hi, Allie." Marc had the decency to keep twelve inches of space between them, but he was close enough for her to notice his wrinkled clothes and crooked bow tie. It looked like someone had stuffed him inside a burlap sack and dragged him behind a pickup truck. "Thanks for coming."

Devyn wrapped a protective arm around Allie's shoulders. "She came here to get away from you, asshole. Get a clue."

Marc held up both hands. "I'll be on my best behavior."

"It's okay," Allie told her. "Just give us a minute."

Devyn's fists were still clenched, but she reluctantly nodded toward the lobby coffeemaker. "I'll be right over there"—she jabbed a finger at Marc—"watching you."

Once her sister had moved out of earshot, Allie tried to form a coherent sentence, but shock had tied her tongue. What was Marc doing here? Why was he dressed for prom? Who'd socked him in the eye this time, and what had he done to deserve it?

After a moment's hesitation, she pointed at the ceiling. "So, the plane, that was you?"

He nodded and eased forward another inch. "It was my last hope. I've been tearing this place apart looking for you since yesterday."

Allie's brows shot up. "You've been here for two days?"

"Almost."

"Why?"

Then he let loose the *real* shocker. "I came to get you back."

Allie's wounded heart leapt with hope, the sensation making her dizzy. Or maybe it was the booze. She touched her temple. "I need to sit down."

"Of course." Marc ushered her to a grouping of sofas in the center of the thoroughfare, then took a seat beside her. "I meant what I said," Marc told her. "I'm here to make things right, if you'll let me."

Cautiously, she nodded for him to go on. "I'm listening."

"I figured out why the cleansing ceremony failed."

"Oh, no." Not this again. Allie rose from the sofa while her spirits sank. Damn her for getting her hopes up again. "Enough with the curse. Go back home, Marc."

"Please!" he begged, falling to his knees. "Give me one minute. That's all. And if you still want me to go, I promise I will."

He looked so pitiful kneeling at her feet, his hair loose and one eye half-swollen shut. She couldn't say no. She took her seat and folded her arms. "Talk fast."

"We couldn't break the curse, because I failed you." That got her attention. For once, he put the blame where it belonged instead of on some supernatural force of nature. "I had a chance to show faith in us, but instead I panicked. I offered a small piece of my heart instead of giving you everything—which is what you deserve." He extricated one of her hands and held it firmly between both of his. "It's what we both deserve."

His confession made Allie's throat grow thick while hot tears pressed against her eyes. "You hurt me, Marc," she whispered. "I told you I loved you and then—"

He pressed a gentle finger to her lips. "I'm sorry, Allie. I was a coward."

She nodded in agreement.

"But not anymore." He jutted his chin toward the roof. "Remember that pea-sized plane you saw up there? I rode in that thing all the way from New Orleans because I couldn't wait another second to be with you."

Allie drew a breath. No wonder his tux was crumpled; he'd probably hugged his knees the whole way.

"And when I got here," Marc continued, "I went to the wrong room and got my ass beat. But that didn't stop me. I refused to quit." He placed a kiss inside her palm. "And I mean to go on living that way—never, ever quitting on you—because I love you too much to give you anything less than forever."

Marc's stunning face was visible only as a wet blur, but the sincerity shone in his eyes. Allie told him, "Say that again."

He didn't hesitate. "I love you. I've never loved any woman but you, and I swear I never will." He reached into his breast pocket and pulled out a gleaming diamond ring. "This is what I should have done last week. This is how much faith I have in us."

A gasp parted Allie's lips.

"There's a chapel down the hall," he said. "Let's get married right now. I'm asking you to be my wife. Take this leap of faith with me."

She couldn't believe it. Five minutes ago, she was missing him so much it hurt and now he wanted to marry her. It was too much. She couldn't think straight.

Excited whispers sounded from nearby, and she noticed a crowd of gawkers had formed around them, including Devyn, whose pale cheeks said she was surprised, too. And old woman gave Allie the thumbs-up sign and mouthed *Say yes!* But it wasn't that simple. Did Marc truly mean what he'd said?

"It's so sudden . . ."

"Allie, please marry me." Pure emotion choked him, blocking his words for a moment while melting all her doubts. "I can't stand the thought of spending another night without you. I'm already yours. You own me, body and soul, and I want the whole world to know it. Please say yes."

She glanced down at her bikini, which didn't do much to cover her breasts. "But I'm not dressed. I can't get married like this. What if we wait until we get back home, then—"

"I already checked," he said. "If we get married in Cedar Bayou, there's a three-day waiting period." He presented the ring, dazzling her with a grin that drew out the cleft in his chin. Lord, how she'd missed that smile. "This ring belonged to Juliette Mauvais. I think I was meant to find it, because it belongs on your finger.

This wedding is a hundred years overdue. Please don't make me wait another minute."

With tears spilling down her cheeks, she extended her left hand. "Yes. I'll marry you."

The lobby erupted in cheers and wild applause with shouts of "Congratulations!" and "Kiss her!" rising above the din.

Marc slipped the ring on her finger and drew her in for a soft kiss. The touch of his mouth sent a wave of comfort washing over her. She locked both hands behind his neck and took more of his warmth. The brief taste wasn't enough to sate the hunger rising low in her belly, but Allie reminded herself that they had the rest of their lives to make up for lost time. It seemed too good to be true.

When they parted, Devyn jogged forward and took Allie's hand. She studied the ring for a long time and asked, "Was this really Memère's?"

"Yep," Marc said. "It just turned up last week."

Dev turned and assessed Marc, staring him down for several silent beats. "And you love my sister?"

"More than anything," he said.

"You'll be good to her?"

"I swear it."

Devyn gave a slow nod. "Then I guess the spirits have spoken." When she reached out her arms to hug Allie, tears shone in her icy blue eyes. "Let's have a wedding!"

Chapter 20

There were no supernatural forces standing in Marc and Allie's way when they linked hands in the resort chapel and prepared to recite their vows. If anything, the stars aligned to give Allie the wedding of her dreams . . . even if it was a tad unconventional.

A stately gentleman dressed like King Arthur cleared his throat and announced, "Hark, all ye fair maidens and knights, for we come together on this hallowed eve to bind together Marc and Allison in sacred matrimony."

Allie bit her lip to contain a giggle. The folks at the Grand Palace Royale really took their work seriously.

The chapel walls were lined with a gray stone façade that mimicked the interior of a castle, complete with richly embroidered red tapestries. Clusters of wick-shaped bulbs flickered from a wrought-iron candelabra hanging from the ceiling, casting the wedding party in a soft glow. The experience reminded her of the Renaissance fair, minus the jousting horses and the oversized roasted turkey legs.

"Who giveth this maid to be joined in marriage?" the king asked.

Devyn stepped forward wearing a leopard-print sarong around her waist and a medieval-inspired circlet of daisies on her head. "I do, my liege."

"And do ye know of any cause that might impede this solemnization?"

Devyn shook her head. "No, I do not." She grinned at Allie and placed a kiss on her cheek before resuming her place beside Lady Guinevere.

"Then let us begin," declared the king. "Marc Gerard Dumont, wilt thou take Allison Catrine to be thy lawfully wedded wife? Wilt thou love and honor her in sickness and in health, keeping only to her for as long as ye both shall live?"

Marc took her free hand and gazed at her with so much love, it brought a fresh set of tears to her eyes. In that breath, Allie knew he was right when he'd said this wedding was a hundred years overdue. It felt like every step she'd ever taken had led her to this moment.

"I will."

The king nodded sagely and turned to her. "Allison Catrine, wilt thou have Marc to be thy lawfully wedded husband? Wilt thou serve and obey him in all—"

"Excuse me?" Allie asked over Marc's snickering. *Serve and obey?* They were taking this "Middle Ages" thing a little too far.

"Ah," King Arthur said. "I see thou art a modern wench, Allison Catrine. I shall adjust thy vows accordingly."

"Thank you, your grace," she said with a bow of her head.

"In times of feast and famine, wilt thou love, honor, and cleave to him for as long as ye both shall live?"

Now *that* she could do. "I will."

Lady Guinevere handed the king the simple gold bands Marc and Allie had purchased from the adjoining shop just minutes ago. Arthur explained the symbolism of the rings and handed the smallest one to Marc, with instructions to place it on Allie's finger.

"With this ring," Marc said, sliding on the band with a sure and steady hand, "I thee wed, and pledge to thee my troth."

Next it was Allie's turn. "With this ring I thee wed. And with my body and soul, I honor thee, for all the days of my life." The sight of the polished band standing in contrast against Marc's tanned skin filled Allie with so much joy she feared she might burst. He squeezed her fingers and gave her a smile that reflected all the love in her heart. There, wearing her bikini and tacky borrowed veil, she'd never felt more like a princess.

King Arthur took their joined hands between both of his and raised them high in the air. "What God and the great state of Nevada hath joined together, let no man put asunder. I now proclaim that Marc and Allison are husband and wife. May their union be long, fruitful, and filled with merriment!"

The wedding party's applause was followed by the recorded music of lutes and tambourines playing through speakers in the ceiling. As soon as the king released their hands, Marc took Allie's face between his palms and kissed her, slow and sweet.

"I love you, Mrs. Dumont," he whispered against her lips.

"I love you, too." She held him close and tried to

make room inside her for this newfound happiness. "I can't believe we're really married."

"Me neither." Marc admired his ring and then hers. "I think we should lock ourselves inside our suite until it starts to feel real—even if it takes all month."

"Let's get a picture first," she said. "Then I'm yours."

They posed for the digital camera, and minutes later, Guinevere brought their souvenir photo tucked inside a cardboard sleeve titled YE OLDE WEDDING MEMORIES.

Together, they laughed at their portrait—Allie's wild curls barely contained by the sunglasses pushed atop her head, her nose sunburned, a line of deep cleavage spilling from her bikini top. Marc's eye was swollen and blackened to a sickly shade of purple, his bow tie askew, and his shirt rumpled. But they were smiling like they'd won the lottery.

And in a way, they had.

"Not the most traditional wedding," Marc said, "but I've never seen a happier groom."

"Or a more dashing one." Gently, she touched the edge of his swollen eye. "There's nothing sexier than a man willing to fight for his fair maiden. Does it hurt?"

A soft grin lifted one corner of his lips as he took her hand and kissed it. "Sugar, a grand piano could fall on me right now and I wouldn't notice a thing."

For Allie it was the opposite—she was so filled with joy that it almost hurt to breathe. Every cell in her body called out to Marc in need for closeness, to feel him inside and above and all around her. She rose onto her tiptoes and whispered in his ear, "Take your new wife upstairs. This honeymoon's a hundred years overdue, remember?"

She didn't need to ask him twice. After a round of

quick good-byes to the wedding party and a hug for Devyn, Marc scooped Allie into his arms and carried her over every threshold all the way to his suite on the seventeenth floor—which turned out to be right across the hall from hers.

What were the odds of that?

Allie pulled the key card from his jacket pocket and unlocked the door, smiling when she spotted a bottle of champagne chilling on ice and enough red roses to fill the room with a rich floral scent. Someone had even folded a set of towels on the bed into the shape of swans and arranged their necks to form a heart.

"When did you plan all this?" she asked.

"Yesterday, when I checked in." Marc shrugged. "I had faith in this honeymoon."

With the greatest care, he placed Allie on the king-sized bed, then swept aside those adorable swans and kicked off his shoes. After shucking his tuxedo jacket to the floor and tugging off his bow tie, he knelt above Allie and took a moment to study her, shaking his head in reverence.

"Have I told you how much I love you?" he asked.

"I can stand to hear it again."

So he murmured it in a litany as he lowered himself onto her body and wrapped her in his warmth. Gradually, his gentle kisses grew possessive, and Allie's fingers worked the buttons on his shirt in desperation to get closer. Their mouths never parted as they clumsily peeled off tops and pants, socks and flip-flops. They'd made love before, but this was different—each caress and nibble lingered as if they had all the time in the world.

Because they did.

Finally skin to skin, they moved beneath the covers, where Marc slipped inside her, hot and hard and completely bare. They gasped at the brand-new sensation of smooth flesh gliding against wet heat. Just when Allie thought making love with Marc couldn't feel any better, he surprised her with something as simple as bare contact.

Her pleasure heightened by unencumbered friction, she fought to last longer than a few moments, but it was no use. He was too good. She came for him quickly, then again with him while he clasped their left hands together, their gold bands clinking against each other as their gazes held and made them one soul.

Allie had never cried during sex, but this was so much more than the joining of two bodies. Marc had taken everything from her while giving all of himself, and the experience overwhelmed her. Their connection was so primal and beautiful that she couldn't contain her emotions—they leaked from the corners of her eyes and dripped onto the pillow. Marc held her face between his palms and brushed away each droplet, replacing it with a kiss.

When the tears stopped, Marc rolled to the side and pulled her firmly against the safety of his chest, wrapping an arm around her while using his free hand to stroke her curls. She traced circles against his skin, smiling when her touch raised chills to the surface of his flesh.

"Love you," he said for what seemed like the hundredth time, not that Allie was complaining.

"Love you more."

His chest shook with quiet laughter. "Give me a minute to recover and I'll prove you wrong."

She used her fingertips to graze his nipple, then moved lower to brush his lower belly. "Challenge accepted." Through the sheet, she could see him hardening again, and it brought a grin to her lips.

She filled her lungs with the masculine scent of her husband and lifted her left hand to admire the rings that proved they were married. She had a feeling she'd have to keep gazing at them to reassure herself this wasn't a dream.

He must have felt the same, because Marc glanced at his own ring. Then he said something that caught her off guard. "I wonder if the curse is broken for my whole family, or just for me."

Allie pushed up on one elbow and peered down at him to gauge his expression. He wasn't kidding. "You're serious?"

"Of course I am."

"Marc," she said with a smile in her voice, "you're not hexed. You never were." She'd explained that to him at the cemetery. "It's psychology that kept the men in your family from getting married, not voodoo."

He lifted one shoulder. "Believe what you want, but I know what really happened."

Just as she geared up to argue with him, she noticed something amiss. Marc's fleur-de-lis tattoo stood in dark contrast to the skin on his muscled arm, but the wine-colored splash above his heart was gone—the mark all the men in his family had carried since birth.

She leaned in to get a closer look and scrubbed a

hand over his chest. "Your birthmark," she said, still scanning his torso. "Did you have it lasered off or something?"

"What?" He glanced down and examined the smooth patch of skin where the blotch used to be. "No, I haven't messed with it."

"Are you sure?"

"Honey, I think I'd remember if someone sand-blasted off my birthmark."

"Then where'd it go? It was there a couple of weeks ago."

"Exactly." He smiled smugly. "Before we broke the curse."

"Oh, come on." But even as she needled him, she couldn't help wondering if the two were somehow related. It *was* a bit coincidental. She bit her lip and stared at his chest, wondering if his brothers still bore the mark above their hearts. "It's probably a temporary fluke."

Chuckling, Marc rolled her onto her back and pressed her into the mattress with his solid weight. "Married less than an hour, and we're already having our first argument." When she began to object, he silenced her with a kiss and used a knee to part her thighs. "Does it really matter?" he asked. "Hex or no hex, we get to do *this* for the rest of our lives."

"Mmm." He had a point—and *this* felt awfully good. Allie tugged on his shoulders while wrapping a leg around his hips. "Who spends their honeymoon talking, anyway?"

"Sad, misguided fools, that's who."

She gave him a sly smile. "So why are we still talking?"

"Beats the hell out of me." He buried his face at the crook of her neck and nibbled her speechless. One final thought drifted through Allie's mind before she sank into oblivion. . . .

Voodoo or not, we'll make our own magic.

Epilogue

"Hey, Cap'n?" Alex and Nicky set down the keg they were hauling, narrowly avoiding the tips of their bare toes, the idiots. Everyone knew you didn't wear flip-flops for heavy lifting. Simultaneously, they asked, "Where do you want this?"

Marc nodded toward the side deck rail. "Over there, next to the rocking chairs. Make sure you keep it in the shade this time. Warm beer's a crime against nature."

"You got it, boss."

Boss.

He used to like the sound of that, but the responsibilities of managing the *Belle* had kept him from fully enjoying his first few weeks as a newlywed. The twins had given him nothing but hell since he'd returned from Vegas. They'd lost another jazz singer, thanks to Nicky, and this morning Alex had been too busy trailing after Ella-Claire to run payroll on time. Now the checks would be a day late, which meant fielding interference for a pissed-off staff. Additionally, there were repairs to schedule and kinks to work out before the next trip. He just wanted to spend some time with his wife.

Wife.

Marc smiled. He definitely liked the sound of that.

He needed a managing partner to share the workload, and he half wondered if Beau was the man for the job. They butted heads once in a while, but Beau knew how to run a tight ship. Marc covertly watched his big brother as he supervised the workers setting up for Allie's surprise wedding reception.

Beau pointed to the banner hanging from the mid-level deck. "Straighten that sign," he hollered. "The end is wrinkled, so it looks like *Congratulations, Marc and Al.* I don't want to give folks the wrong idea about my little brother's sexual orientation."

From the other side of the deck, Marc laughed appreciatively. Good to know someone was looking out for him.

After Beau checked the buffet warmers, he joined Marc and clapped him on the back. "How long until crunch time?"

Marc checked his watch, noting he had thirty minutes before Devyn lured Allie to the boat under the pretense of taking inventory in the galley. "Not long enough."

"What can I do?"

Marc nodded at the buffet table. "What you do best—get the burgers on the line." He delivered a good-natured smack to his brother's shoulder. "Thanks, man. I owe you."

"It's the least I can do," Beau said. "Hell, for the first time in a hundred years, one of us finally tied the knot. If that's not a damned fine reason to tap a few kegs and fire up the grill, I don't know what is."

Marc couldn't agree more. His new bride had insisted she didn't need a party, but he wanted her to have a proper reception. He'd even hired a photographer and ordered a wedding cake that Devyn and the Sweet Spot crew had baked on the sly. Now he had to help the deejay set up and see to the decorations, which still weren't finished.

He needed Ella-Claire, his Chief Party Planner. Where was that girl?

It didn't take long to spot her—all he had to do was find Alex, who'd already abandoned his keg duties. Like two halves of a peanut butter and honey sandwich, Marc could always find the duo stuck together. Arms linked, the pair leaned against the side wall, smiling while scrolling through pictures on Ella's phone. Their bodies pressed a little too close; their gazes held a little too long to fool him into believing it was platonic.

Best friends, his ass.

Marc took a calming breath while stalking toward the two, determined not to blow a fuse and ruin his mood for Allie's big day. "Hey," he called, making them jump. He crooked a finger at Alex. "Come help the deejay while Ella tends to the decorations."

Alex must have sensed he was in trouble, because he kept a safe distance while they made their way to the dance floor. Before they got there, Marc spun on his little brother and brought him to a clumsy halt.

"I don't know what's up with you and Ella-Claire," Mark said. "But if you want to keep your walnuts, you'd better back off."

Alex's blond brows shot up while his eyes widened in denial. "It's noth—"

"Don't tell me it's nothing," Marc interrupted. "Just

steer clear of my sister." He shot Alex a pointed look. "We clear?"

Alex's fair cheeks began to redden. "Crystal." He crouched down, turning his attention to the tangle of cords and wires at their feet, before flagrantly changing the subject. "Did you talk Pawpaw into coming?"

Right on cue, the old man shuffled up the bow ramp, holding a tattered paper bag, which he deposited onto the gift table with a clatter. Probably his usual wedding present: a bottle of homebrewed shine, "guaranteed to make any marriage bearable," as he'd often said.

Pawpaw wore a scowl, but at least he'd dragged his crotchety ass down here to support his new granddaughter-in-law. A few minutes later, Worm loped aboard right ahead of Daddy and his flavor of the month, a thirtysomething brunette whose belly was round with the sixth Dumont brother.

The gang was all here—one big, dysfunctional family.

When Devyn brought Allie to the dock, Marc met her on the bow ramp and carried her aboard. She laughed and gave him a questioning glance that turned to shock when everyone shouted, "Congratulations!"

"What did you do?" she asked.

"What any decent husband would do," he told her. "Made sure we get our first dance." He led her to the center deck and held her close while the deejay played Bonnie Tyler's cover of "I Put a Spell on You." When the music ended, Marc whispered, "There. Now we have a song."

Allie's adoring smile sent a wave of pleasure washing over him, worth every second of effort he'd invested. "You're too good to me."

"Don't speak so soon," he teased. "It's time to meet the rest of my family."

After introducing his wife to every Dumont in Louisiana, Marc stole her away to the side deck rocking chairs and pulled her into his lap, where she curled up and rested her pretty head on his shoulder. Marc figured life didn't get any better than this.

Their location didn't remain private for long, probably because they'd settled too near the kegs. Beau lumbered forward, red Solo cup in hand. "Congrats, brother," he said. "Never thought I'd say this, but marriage suits you."

"Thanks." Marc nodded at the keg in a silent request. "Never thought I'd agree with you, but you're right. Allie's made me a lucky man."

She kissed his neck. "You're welcome."

"Let me get you a beer," Beau said. "Want one, Allie?"

"I'll just share his."

Beau cocked an eyebrow. He must have recalled that Marc never shared his drinks. "She gets a pass," Marc said.

With a shrug, Beau leaned down to reach the keg and began filling a cup. The foam quickly rose to the surface, then spilled over the top, pooling onto the deck.

"Dude," Marc called. "That cup's not getting any fuller."

Beau glanced at his hand to find it covered in suds.

He swore under his breath and passed the drink to Marc while wiping his fingers on his T-shirt, then went back to staring at something in the distance.

Marc followed his brother's gaze to figure out what had distracted him. Not surprisingly, he spotted Devyn Mauvais bent over the gift table, her rear end showcased in a tight black miniskirt. Marc bit back a chuckle. He had a feeling which Dumont man would be the next to fall.

"Hey," Marc asked his brother. "Do you still have that birthmark over your heart?"

Beau eventually took his eyes off Devyn long enough to ask Marc, "What?"

"The red splotch," Marc said, tapping his own chest. "Is it still there?"

"Of course."

"You sure?"

With one hand, Beau tugged the hem of his shirt all the way to his neck. The birthmark was there, just as he'd said.

Too bad. Looked like each Dumont man would have to break the curse for himself.

A loud *thunk* sounded from nearby, and Marc turned just in time to see Devyn walk into the railing, her gaze still fixed on Beau's exposed chest. The act didn't escape Beau's notice. A shit-eating grin curved his mouth while Devyn's frosty blue eyes narrowed in contempt.

"Real classy," she spat at him. "You can't even keep your clothes on at my sister's wedding reception."

Beau held his shirt in place and gestured at his stomach. "Did you get an eyeful, or do you want some more? Maybe take a picture for later?"

She flashed him the bird and addressed Allie. "Got anything to drink besides beer?"

"You bet," Allie said. "Beau's our designated bartender."

Devyn didn't seem to like that.

"Name your poison," Beau said, finally lowering his shirt. "If we don't have it on board, it doesn't exist."

"Can you make a lemon drop?"

"In my sleep."

Devyn leaned back against the rail. "All right, then."

Beau hurried inside to the executive bar and returned five minutes later with a sugar-rimmed martini glass. He handed it to Devyn, who scrutinized it from every angle before taking a sip and glancing at the deck ceiling in consideration.

"Well?" Beau asked. "What's the verdict?"

"Not bad."

"Coming from you, I'll take that as a rave."

"Don't jizz in your pants, Dumont," she said dryly. "I've had better."

Smiling, he leaned far enough into her personal space to make her freeze. "Are we still talking about martinis?"

Devyn's mouth pressed into a hard line, but she couldn't conceal the pink flush creeping into her cheeks. "Yes, but even if we weren't, my statement stands. I've had *all kinds* of better than you."

Beau clutched his heart in mock agony. "Darlin', you know how to cut a man to the core."

"Please." She handed back her martini and pushed off the rail. "You're indestructible, and I'm done here."

He lifted the martini glass toward her. "At least take your drink."

"Keep it." She took another step back. "I meant it when I said I've had better."

Her words were foam bullets, softened by the tremor in her voice. Clearly, Beau wasn't the only one with unresolved feelings.

Beau toasted her with the martini and took a sip. "It's too tart. But I'll get it right next time." Marc had a feeling his brother was talking about more than the drink, and judging by the redness spreading across her face, Devyn knew it, too.

"I can make my own martinis." She left him with one shaky command before charging toward the buffet. "So do us both a favor and disappear again."

Beau grinned as he eagle-eyed the sway of her hips. "Disappear again?" he muttered to himself. "Not a chance."

Marc gathered Allie into his arms, feeling her breathy laughter against his throat. He was pretty sure they were sharing the same thought—that Beau would have a fight on his hands if he wanted a second chance with his ex.

But if Devyn was anything like her sister, the fight would be worth it.

A thousand times over.

Acknowledgments

Publishing a novel is a group effort, and I've been blessed with a fantastic team, who works hard behind the scenes to bring each of my stories to fruition.

Many thanks to my editor, Laura Fazio, whose suggestions and guidance made this book so much stronger than when I first placed it in her capable hands. I'm grateful beyond words that she "inherited" me.

Much gratitude to my literary agent, Nicole Resciniti, for her unyielding enthusiasm for my projects. She's my biggest fan . . . or at least tied with my mother.

Big hugs to my critique partners, Lorie Langdon and Carey Corp, for their edits—and especially for their friendship. This journey wouldn't be the same without them.

Finally, infinite thanks to my friends and family, who continue to amaze me with their depth of support. I'm a lucky lady.

Read on for a preview of Macy Beckett's
next novel in the Dumont Bachelors series,

MAKE YOU REMEMBER

Available in November 2014 from
Signet Eclipse anywhere books
and e-books are sold.

Devyn Mauvais looked at the gratitude in her client's rheumy eyes and said the most expensive words in recent history. "Now, don't you worry about my fee, hon. Your happiness is payment enough." Then she helped the old woman tuck a folded twenty back into the pocket of her tattered housedress, along with the talisman she'd just "bought."

"Thank you, child." The woman wrapped her bony arms around Devyn's waist, bringing with her the scent of arthritis cream. "You do your mama proud, God rest her."

No, not really. Mama would have spun in her grave if she'd known her oldest daughter was peddling sacred oils and ritual kits out of her living room. The first rule she'd taught Devyn was that it's bad juju to profit from helping others. Out of habit, Devyn crossed herself while patting her client's back.

After walking the woman to her car, Devyn returned to her sagging front porch, where her gaze landed on the brand-new sign affixed near the screen door. In odd contrast to the faded aluminum siding, the sign announced: EFFECTIVE IMMEDIATELY, A FEE OF $20 PER HOUR WILL BE CHARGED FOR ALL SPIRITUAL CONSULTATIONS. POTION, SPELLS, AND CANDLE PRICES ARE AVAILABLE UPON REQUEST. INQUIRE WITHIN OR BOOK AN APPOINTMENT AT MAUVAISVOODOO.COM.

God, she had a Web site. Could she possibly sink any lower?

She threw open the front door and tried to ignore the prickle of shame tugging at her stomach. A month ago, she never would have accepted a cent for reading bones. Funny how quickly life could spiral out of control when you lived paycheck to paycheck. Since she'd lost her temp job at the Lord of the Springs mattress store, bad juju was the least of Devyn's worries.

The rent was overdue, her cupboards were bare, and for the past week, she'd parked her Honda behind a Dumpster a few blocks away in a game of hide-and-seek with the repo man. She'd even resorted to "borrowing" wireless Internet from the trailer park across the street, something no twenty-seven-year-old woman should ever have to do.

But not even *she* was desperate enough to take grocery money from little old ladies.

"Yet," she muttered.

Checking her cell phone, Devyn noted she had five minutes before her last appointment of the day, some out-of-towner named Warren Larabee who'd prepaid online via credit card. In preparation, she lit a stick of incense, then mixed a satchel of herbs, coins, and ancestral soil from Memère's tomb for a Good Fortune charm. Nine times out of ten, that was what men wanted. The other was "natural male enhancement," which she couldn't provide. If the flag wouldn't fly, there was something wrong with the pole, and that was a job for the doctor.

She was a Mauvais, not a magician.

At six o'clock on the button, a gentle rapping sounded at her door, and she ushered a middle-aged man with a thick salt-and-pepper crew cut into her living room. He wore a business suit and an easy smile that told Devyn he wasn't a true believer in voodoo. With his relaxed posture, both hands tucked loosely inside his pockets, it looked like he'd come here to bring the word of the Lord. Not that she needed it. A devout Catholic, she'd chaired the Saint Mary's fish fry six years running.

In any case, it was obvious that Warren Larabee hadn't come here for a reading. Devyn's eyes found the Louisville Slugger she kept propped in the corner. The man seemed harmless, but creepers came in all sorts of packaging.

"Mr. Larabee?" She swept a hand toward the sofa while taking the opposite chair. "What brings you in?"

He ignored her question and smiled while assessing her strapless red mini dress and black stiletto pumps. "You're not what I expected."

Devyn laughed when she imagined what he must be thinking: that for an extra fee, she would offer spiritual *and* sexual healing. "Trust me, I don't usually wear this to meet clients. My ten-year high school reunion is tonight." And if she wanted to make it in time for the complimentary open bar—which she did—she'd have to rush out the door as soon as this appointment ended.

"Well, you look lovely," Warren said. "I'm sure you'll make your classmates green with envy."

"Isn't that what we all want?" Joking aside, she folded both hands in her lap and got down to business. "You're not here for a charm, are you?"

"Very perceptive." He nodded his approval like a proud parent. "No. I'm here to offer you an opportunity."

Visions of sales pitches danced in Devyn's head, but she suppressed an eye roll. "You paid for an hour. How you use it is your prerogative."

"I own Larabee Amusements," he said. "Maybe you've heard of it?"

Devyn shook her head.

"We sell sightseeing packages in cities all over the country." He shifted forward to rest both elbows on his knees. "Celebrity mansion tours in Hollywood, honky-tonk pub crawls in Nashville, boat trips in the Everglades—that sort of thing."

"And let me guess," Devyn said. "You're branching out in New Orleans."

"No—that market's already saturated. We're opening a franchise right here in Cedar Bayou." He lifted a shoulder. "It's only twenty minutes away, and the town has a rich history. I can't believe nobody's capitalized on it yet."

"If you're looking for investors, I can't help you." Devyn had already depleted her nest egg by helping her sister get the Sweet Spot bakery off the ground. Several years later, they were finally breaking even, but not doing well enough to keep Devyn from assembling lunches from free samples at the grocery store.

"That's not why I'm here," he assured her with a lifted palm. "I'd like to hire you."

She perked up. Now he had her attention. "To do what?"

"You're Devyn Mauvais," he said as if that fact had slipped her mind. "Direct descendant of Juliette Mauvais, the most-feared voodoo queen in Louisiana history. From what I hear, the locals are still afraid to speak her name." Warren pointed to Memère's portrait on the wall, where Juliette looked down her nose at them, her full lips curved in a smirk. With her smooth olive skin and exotic eyes, she'd been the most beautiful woman in the bayou, but anyone who trifled with her did so at their own peril. There was a local family—the Dumonts— who knew it firsthand, even after a hundred years.

"You look like her," Warren said.

Devyn gave a dismissive laugh. "Not as much as my sister. Those two are the living spit."

"But enough that you could pass for Juliette if you wore traditional period clothing and a headdress." Warren paused as if for dramatic effect, then made jazz hands. "Just imagine how chilling a haunted cemetery tour would be if you were the one leading it."

Devyn's stomach sank. This wasn't the kind of opportunity she'd hoped for. She would rather spend all day asking, *You want fries with that?* than lead gawking tourists to her great-great-grandmother's resting place so they could pose for cheesy pictures in front of her tomb.

"There's more," Warren added when she didn't respond. "I'll set you up in a shop near the cemetery so you can sell"—he thumbed at the rows of dressed candles on display—"your little trinkets when the tour is over."

"Wait just a minute." She held up an index finger. "Little *trinkets*? This is my heritage you're talking about, not some Tupperware party."

Warren's eyes flew wide. "Of course. I didn't mean to offend."

"Well, you did."

"But in addition to a generous salary, you'd make tips from the—"

"No, thank you." Devyn reminded herself that she'd earned twenty dollars listening to this drivel, which would make a small dent in the electric bill. But that was a bargain for this man, and she'd had enough. "Not even for tips."

Warren fell silent, taking in the peeling paint on the walls as if to ask, *Seriously, lady? Don't you need the cash?* "If the salary is an issue, we can negotiate."

"Do you need spiritual guidance, Mr. Larabee?" When he lowered his brows in confusion and shook his head, she added, "Then I'm afraid our appointment is over."

To his credit, Warren didn't push. He fished a business card from his shirt pocket and set it on the coffee table, then stood up and offered his palm. "I'll be in town until Halloween, so take a few weeks to think about it. I hope you'll change your mind."

Devyn shook his hand and walked him to the door, but that was as far as her courtesy extended. Warren gave a final wave, then strode to the sleek Mercedes parked at the curb. Seconds later, he was gone, taking his job offer with him.

Devyn blew out a breath and told herself she'd made the right choice. Selling a few gris-gris satchels during a time of need was one thing, but cashing in on her heritage was another. No amount of money was worth her dignity.

So why was she still on the porch, watching his Mercedes fade into the distance?

She shook her head to clear it and went back into the house for a quick lipstick touch-up. There was free booze awaiting her in the Cedar Bayou High gymnasium, and she was overdue for a good time.

Devyn parked her Honda behind a Salvation Army clothing receptacle at the rear of the school, then locked the doors and paused to admire her reflection in the driver's-side window.

She had originally planned to skip the reunion, but that was before she'd found this amazeballs Gucci dress for thirty dollars at a thrift store in New Orleans. Fire-engine red and so short it barely covered her butt, it hugged her curves like it was hand-stitched for her—by angels. The only thing wrong with it was a tiny spot of ink on the side hem, but who cared? It was Gucci!

This dress almost made her forget how far she'd fallen. Maybe she didn't have a job or a family of her own, but her body was still bitchin'—if she did say so herself—and one out of three wasn't bad.

Devyn clicked across the parking lot and through the school's back door, her peep-toe stilettos echoing in the narrow hallway. She had a sway in her hips tonight, the kind only a custom-fitted designer dress could inspire. Even Jenny Hore—appropriately pronounced *whore*—would eat her heart out. The one girl in school unfazed by the last name Mauvais, Jenny had made it her unholy mission to steal everything that mattered to Devyn: her lunch money, her project ideas, her spot on the varsity cheer squad, even her junior year boyfriend, Slade Summers—may they both rot in hell.

With any luck, Jenny and Slade had aged horribly and had grown miserable in each other's company. The prospect put extra pep in Devyn's step as she approached the sign-in station.

The table was unmanned, so she scanned the rows of name tag stickers for her own. When she didn't find it, she picked up the attendance clipboard and ran her fingernail down the class roster.

"Excuse me, miss," said a familiar baritone voice before its owner plucked the clipboard from Devyn's hands. "That's mine."

Instantly, her jaw clenched. She slid a glare toward the voice, which brought her eye level to a gray polo stretched tight over the broadest chest in Cedar Bayou. She would know. From there, she craned her neck toward the ceiling and met a pair of arrogant green eyes smiling beneath a thatch of auburn hair. Mirrored sunglasses were pushed atop his head, despite the fact that the sun had set an hour ago. His name tag said HELLO, MY NAME IS INIGO MONTOYA, but she knew better. This overgrown muscle head was Beau Dumont: high school football star, ex-marine, class demigod, and a constant pain in her ass since the day he'd returned to town a few months ago.

"I was hoping you'd stay home," she said. "But then who would the idiot masses have to worship?"

His gaze took a leisurely stroll up and down her body. "With you in that dress, nobody's going to notice little ol' me."

The compliment didn't touch her. She'd learned a long time ago that Beau's pretty words carried no weight. She sneered at his clipboard. "Who put you in charge?"

"Why wouldn't I be in charge? I was voted Most Likely to Succeed."

"What's that?" She leaned in, cupping an ear. "Most Likely a Sleaze? I'd say that sounds about right."

Beau chuckled low and deep, then lifted a dark curl from her shoulder. He rubbed it between his thumb and index finger before using the end to tickle her cheek. "You didn't always think I was sleazy, Dev."

Devyn's knees softened, and she discreetly grasped the folding table for support. "That was before you—" *said you loved me and disappeared for almost a decade.* "Left me on the hook for what we did after graduation."

His lips slid into a crooked grin that used to make her panties fall off, back when she'd naively thought she could break the curse that had turned all Dumont men into liars, cheats, and runners. Now that cocky grin made her palm itch to smack him upside the head.

"Best night of my life," he said.

She narrowed her eyes. "That's because you weren't the one who got arrested."

"Aw, now. I said I was sorry for that." He pulled her name tag from his pocket and began scanning her dress for a place to stick it. "Besides, I heard the charges were dropped."

Devyn snatched the name tag from him. "Bite me."

"Anytime you want." Beau tipped her chin, leaning close enough to fill the space between them with the scents of shaving cream and male body heat. "I still remember all the delicious places you like to be nibbled, Kitten."

Kitten.

The casual use of her old nickname sent fire rushing through Devyn's veins. She batted away his hand. "In your dreams. The only thing giving you a good time tonight is your hand. It's a match made in heaven. Not even *you* can ruin that relationship." She whirled toward the gymnasium and strutted away, shaking her moneymaker to give him a sweet view of what he was missing—what he had abandoned ten years ago.

Screw Beau Dumont and his big, gorgeous chest. She was *so* over him.

She reminded herself of that as she strode into the gym, where the bleachers were folded against the walls and the basketball hoops were cranked toward the ceiling. The decorating committee had covered several rows of cafeteria lunch tables with white linen and a scattering of balloon clusters, transporting her back to a time when her greatest worry was which outfit would make a boy's jaw drop.

Aside from her financial woes, it would seem she'd come full circle.

Streamers crisscrossed the dimly lit room, and Snoop Dogg's "Drop It Like It's Hot" played from someone's iPod docking station in the corner. It was like prom night all over again, except for the standing bar erected near the floor mats. She made a beeline for the booze, and once she had a lemon drop martini in hand, she scanned the room for a familiar face.

"Dev!"

A woman's shout drew Devyn's attention to a small group gathered on the opposite side of the gym. She squinted in the dim lighting and recognized Margo and some of the other cheerleaders who'd moved away from the bayou after graduation. When Devyn waved, Margo bounced with excitement, then cringed and cradled her pregnant belly between both hands.

"Hey," Devyn said, joining Margo with outstretched arms.

After a long hug, Margo pulled back to look at Devyn. "You're stunning. I hate you." But her warm smile promised the opposite.

"Oh, please." Devyn flapped a hand and patted her friend's swollen tummy. "You're absolutely glowing. Congratulations! Is this your first?"

"Our third," Margo said and introduced her husband. One by one, each woman in the group did the same until they glanced at Devyn and paused expectantly.

She held up her naked left hand. "Still single." The girls followed with a chorus of *Good for you*, and *Nothing wrong with that*, but a shadow of pity softened their tones. "My sister, Allie, got married, though," Devyn said, shamelessly deflecting. "Just a couple of months ago, to Marc Dumont."

That made eyebrows rise. Until recently, no Dumont man had made it to the altar since the day Memère jinxed their line. Few people believed in the curse, but firsthand experience had shown Devyn it was like thunder—impossible to see, but very real. She still didn't know how Marc had broken the hex, but for her sister's sake, she was glad that he had. Allie's feet hadn't touched the ground since their Vegas wedding.

"Maybe Beau's next," said Margo with a teasing elbow nudge. She nodded toward the gym doors. "He's been watching you since you walked into the room."

Devyn glanced over her shoulder and saw him standing there, the top of his head barely clearing the doorway as he leaned against the jamb and folded his muscled arms. He winked at her, and she turned back to Margo with an eye roll. "Don't hold your breath."

From there, the discussion turned to careers. Devyn learned that her old cheer squad had gone on to become Web designers, freelance writers, and stay-at-home moms. When her turn came to share, Devyn played it off with a carefree shrug. "I haven't quite decided what I want to be when I grow up."

Everyone laughed and Devyn was able to unclench her shoulders. Margo had just pulled out her iPhone to show everyone pictures of her children when she glanced across the room and squealed in delight. "Jenny's here! And Slade!"

Devyn smoothed the front of her dress, sucked in her tummy, and turned slowly toward the gym entrance to catch a glimpse of her nemesis. Would Jenny's eyes have grown dull, darkened by circles of exhaustion? Had her golden hair faded with time and too much chemical processing? Would Slade have lost half his hair and gained a hundred pounds?

As it turned out, no.

The pair strutted into view looking better than ever, damn it.

Jenny tossed a curtain of glossy blond hair over one shoulder, rocking a designer halter dress paired with knee-high stiletto boots. Even in the dim lighting, a set of obscenely large diamond studs winked from her earlobes, and she made sure everyone spotted the quilted Chanel bag on her shoulder. Slade was dressed more like a Greek billionaire than the soccer stud that Devyn remembered. Whatever the pair had been up to these past ten years, they had clearly made more money than the Rockefellers.

The bastards.

After a round of hugs and hellos, Jenny pinned Devyn with a critical gaze. "Well, if it isn't Devyn Mauvais. Bless your little heart."

Whatever. Every Southern girl knew that was code for *go die in a fire.*

Devyn smiled sweetly. "Well, if it isn't my favorite *Hore.*"

"Actually, it's Summers now." Jenny thrust forward her left hand to display a diamond approximately the size of the moon.

Devyn quietly sipped her martini, but her lack of enthusiasm didn't stop Jenny from launching into a story about her sunset-wedding ceremony on a private beach just outside Cabo San Lucas. For the next ten minutes, she spun a tale of nauseating excess that had the whole group transfixed. Even Beau Dumont had ambled over to hear the details.

Devyn had long since tuned out the prattle, so she was caught off guard when Jenny abruptly stopped and pointed at her.

"What?" Devyn asked.

Jenny covered her mouth to stifle a giggle. "Nice dress, Dev."

Devyn stood a bit straighter and smiled. "Thanks. I picked it up for a steal."

"I know," Jenny said. "From the Tulane Avenue Goodwill, right? That's where I donated it." She leaned down to inspect the side hem. "Yep. There's the stain I never could get out."

Devyn stopped breathing.

"It looks cute on you, though," Jenny added with a shrug that said, *But not as good as it looked on me.* "One girl's trash is another girl's treasure, right?"

At once, Devyn felt the weight of two dozen gazes shifting in her direction. Her upper body went numb, as if she had slept with both arms tucked beneath her pillow and cut off her circulation. Several charged beats passed in silence before she forced a wide grin and toasted her enemy. "Are you calling a Gucci design trash? I do believe that's blasphemy."

A few people chuckled, but it was a *this-is-getting-awkward* kind of laugh.

Jenny smoothed her fingers possessively through Slade's hair. "You crack me up, Dev. Always have."

Maybe it was the public humiliation, or maybe it was the martini, but something hijacked Devyn's vocal cords and forced her to blurt out, "That's what my boy-friend says."

Oh, shit. What had she just done?

"Hey." Margo delivered a good-natured shove. "You didn't say anything about a boyfriend. Spill! I want to hear all about him."

"Yes," Jenny said as if sniffing blood in the water. "Spill."

It took a moment for Devyn to find her voice. "He's . . . great. Big and gorgeous and super sweet. We're crazy about each other."

"Is he local?" asked Margo.

"Uh . . . kind of."

"Kind of?" Jenny asked with an arched brow. "What's his name?"

Yeah, you idiot, Devyn chided herself. *What's his name?* "I can't say. We're keeping things on the down low." Double shit! Who actually said *on the down low* anymore?

"What does he do for a living?" asked Margo.

Devyn said the first thing that came to mind. "He owns a business." When that didn't seem to satisfy anyone, she fumbled, "I can't say anything more, or you'll know who he is."

The triumphant smile that curled Jenny's lips said she knew it was a lie. And clearly she would take great pleasure in raking Devyn over the coals. "Oh, come on," Jenny crooned. "Give us a hint. We won't tell." She glanced around at her friends. "Will we?"

Everyone shook their heads and peered at Devyn, waiting for her to speak. Her eyes locked with Beau's for one interminable moment, the intensity behind his gaze hot enough to tighten her stomach. Why did he have to be here to witness this? She had always hoped to make him sorry one day, but he probably thought he'd dodged a bullet when he ditched her all those years ago.

"Go on," Jenny prodded. "Tell us who he is."

Devyn's palms began to sweat. This was like a nightmare, only worse. Because she would rather deliver a naked speech in front of the whole school than admit she'd invented a fictitious boyfriend. Just when she opened her mouth to dig herself a deeper hole, Beau crossed through the center of the group and stood by her side.

Slipping an arm around her waist, Beau pulled her hard against him and announced, "It's me. I'm Dev's boyfriend—*and* her boss."